WOLF WORM

BY T. KINGFISHER

Nine Goblins
Swordheart
The Twisted Ones
The Hollow Places
Nettle & Bone
A House With Good Bones
Thornhedge
A Sorceress Comes to Call
Hemlock & Silver
Wolf Worm

THE SWORN SOLDIER SERIES
What Moves the Dead
What Feasts at Night
What Stalks the Deep

WOLF WORM

T. KINGFISHER

NIGHTFIRE

First published 2026 by Tom Doherty Associates / Tor Publishing Group

First published in the UK 2026 by Tor Nightfire
an imprint of Pan Macmillan
The Smithson, 6 Briset Street, London EC1M 5NR
EU representative: Macmillan Publishers Ireland Ltd, 1st Floor,
The Liffey Trust Centre, 117–126 Sheriff Street Upper,
Dublin 1 D01 YC43
Associated companies throughout the world

ISBN 978-1-0350-5272-1 HB
ISBN 978-1-0350-5273-8 TPB

Copyright © Ursula Vernon 2026

The right of Ursula Vernon to be identified as the
author of this work has been asserted in accordance
with the Copyright, Designs and Patents Act 1988.

All rights reserved. No part of this publication may be reproduced,
stored in a retrieval system, or transmitted, in any form, or by any means
(including, without limitation, electronic, mechanical, photocopying, recording
or otherwise) without the prior written permission of the publisher.

Pan Macmillan does not have any control over, or any responsibility for,
any author or third-party websites (including, without limitation, URLs,
emails and QR codes) referred to in or on this book.

1 3 5 7 9 8 6 4 2

A CIP catalogue record for this book is available from the British Library.

Printed and bound in the UK using 100% Renewable Electricity by CPI Group (UK) Ltd

This book is sold subject to the condition that it shall not, by way of
trade or otherwise, be lent, hired out, or otherwise circulated without
the publisher's prior consent in any form of binding or cover other than
that in which it is published and without a similar condition including this
condition being imposed on the subsequent purchaser. The publisher does not
authorize the use or reproduction of any part of this book in any manner
for the purpose of training artificial intelligence technologies or systems.
The publisher expressly reserves this book from the Text and Data Mining
exception in accordance with Article 4(3) of the European Union
Digital Single Market Directive 2019/790.

Visit **www.panmacmillan.com** to read more about all our books
and to buy them.

For the crew in Secret Artist Room

AUTHOR'S NOTE

In 1899, the state of North Carolina referred to the Lumbee people as "Croatan." In 1952, the tribe voted to adopt the name Lumbee. Although it is anachronistic, I have chosen to use the name that they took for themselves, rather than the one provided by the state.

WOLF WORM

CHAPTER 1

The rail station was very new, the paint still bright on the lettering that read SILER STATION. An enormous cloth banner proclaimed that it was HOME OF THE WORLD-FAMOUS CHATHAM RABBIT. I stepped off the train, clutching the cardboard suitcase that held all my worldly possessions, and wondered what, exactly, was special about the rabbit.

Unusually colored fur? Immense size? Third eye in the middle of the forehead?

Activity swirled around me as men hastily unloaded freight from the train cars. There was only one small passenger car, and I had been the only person to disembark, so I moved to one side, looking for the person who had come to meet me. My employer had sent the train ticket, and while I did not expect him to come himself, presumably he would have sent someone to collect me.

I craned my neck, but did not see any likely candidates. The anxiety that I had kept at bay threatened to rise up into my throat and I told it sternly to get back down where it belonged. *There is nowhere here to wait. Perhaps they have only just seen the train arrive, and are coming now.*

You have been here for less than five minutes. There is no reason to assume that anything has gone wrong.

The sky overhead was a blue watercolor wash, the clouds picked out in white gouache against it. Some skies look hard, but a Southern sky is usually soft, almost thready. If you pressed against it, you'd expect it to yield like cloth, or a soft network of roots. The upper edge was just starting to darken a little, a second wash of color to indicate that the afternoon was growing late.

From the station platform, I could see a warehouse and what looked like a general store. A mill poked up from the surrounding countryside, but once the town proper ended, there was nothing but a sea of thick trees in every direction.

A half dozen small boys came pelting up the station steps and rushed the passenger car's windows. They were all brandishing furry objects, which were . . . yes, those were indeed dead rabbits. From what I could tell, they were the usual color and had the usual number of eyes. "Chatham rabbit!" a small boy shouted into the passenger car, waving a limp body in the air. "World-famous! Only three cents!"

My fellow passengers on the train from Wilmington had all been reasonably polite, and the worst of them—a middle-aged man passionately in love with both President Cleveland and the sound of his own voice—still didn't deserve having rabbit carcasses waved at him. I wondered if I should intervene.

One of the boys glanced over at me, sized me up as unlikely to be prosperous enough for a dead rabbit, and turned back to the windows. While I'd had students that age, they had all been girls, and I wasn't entirely certain of my ability to enforce discipline on strange boys. I abandoned the passengers to their long-eared fate and looked around again for my employer's representative.

It's been almost ten minutes now. Has something gone wrong?
(he thought better of hiring you and didn't bother to send a letter)
(he died and nobody knows you're coming and you'll have to turn around and go back)

Stop that, I ordered myself. *You're catastrophizing again. They've just been delayed. Or possibly the doctor lives right by the station and if you ask for directions, it's a five-minute walk.*

This seemed possible. I shifted my handbag on my shoulder

and approached the small station office, where an exasperated-looking man with a pocket watch was muttering to himself, or perhaps to the watch.

"Pardon me," I said. "Can you direct me to the home of Dr. Halder?"

He blinked at me. Apparently, whatever he'd expected me to say, it wasn't that. "Halder?"

"Dr. Matthias Halder, yes."

The stationmaster rubbed his hand through his thinning hair. If I were painting him, I would use layered washes of red across his face, and a few thin lines of umber for his hair. "Halder lives south of here. About ten miles, give or take. Outside of Goldston."

Ten miles! My heart sank. Surely Dr. Halder didn't expect me to walk there? But there was no sign of anyone coming to greet me either.

(he doesn't expect you because he decided not to hire you, you came all this way for nothing)

"What do you want with Halder, anyway?" I felt the stationmaster's eyes flick over me curiously. At thirty-three years old, I made an unlikely chambermaid, and no one would expect a doctor to have a female colleague. *What does that leave? Distant relative? Mail-order bride?*

"He's hired me as an assistant," I said. "I thought he'd send someone to meet me, but perhaps I was wrong."

"Doubt he even thought of it," said the stationmaster bluntly. "Old Halder's not one for practical details."

I sighed. Naturalists, in my experience, tended to be that way. My father would have stopped in the middle of a burning forest if he happened to spot a rare orchid, and if he was ever on time for a meeting, it was purely by accident.

Well. It was substantially after noon already. If I started walking now, assuming I didn't get lost, it would still be dark by the time I got to Dr. Halder's. And I'd be footsore and sweaty and covered in road dust, which was not the impression I wanted to make on my new employer.

Still, there was no help for it. I had less than a dollar wrapped in my handkerchief, which were all my funds in the world, and even if I was willing to squander money hiring a coach, Siler Station did not look like the sort of town that had coaches simply lined up and waiting.

I hefted my suitcase. It was extremely heavy, although most of that weight was my sketchbooks and paints. I had only a single change of clothes and an extra pair of shoes. I would rather have my arms give out than abandon my sketchbooks, and it seemed unwise to leave my shoes. *Footsore, sweaty, covered in road dust, and listing to one side because my back has given out from lugging my suitcase. Also late. This impression gets better and better.*

"Could you give me specific directions?" I asked. "It appears I have a walk ahead of me."

"No!" said the stationmaster, almost yelping. "You can't— I mean— It's a long walk, particularly in the dark. Let me see if I can find someone going that direction."

"That really isn't necessary."

"Believe me," he said, "it is."

Torn between gratitude and embarrassment, I sat down on the single bench outside the office while he hurried down the platform to the men unloading. I smoothed down my skirt. It was late April, and not as punishingly hot as it might be later in the year, but I already missed the sea breezes of Wilmington.

A few minutes later, the stationmaster returned and beckoned to me. "Phelps will take you," he said. "He's going more or less that way."

"More or less?" I asked wryly.

"More or less." And then, dropping his voice, "Phelps won't give you any trouble either."

"Thank you," I said gravely. My face and figure were not the sort generally held to incite lust—a scarecrow was among the kinder comparisons I'd heard—but a certain type of man requires only that a woman be in their power. It was kind of the stationmaster to be concerned, since the only weapons I possessed were a hatpin and a palette knife, and I would have had to dig through my suitcase for the palette knife.

The man I was to ride with was tall, gaunt, and looked as if he had last smiled sometime before the war. If I had known then what kind of role he would play in my life, wild horses could not have dragged me onto that wagon, but I suppose that's hindsight for you. At the time, I was simply grateful that I wouldn't have to drag a suitcase ten miles in the dark.

Possibly there's a moral here somewhere, but if so, it's buried deep.

The man nodded to me as I climbed up beside him on his wagon, introduced himself as Asa Phelps, then clucked his tongue at the horses and proceeded to say nothing at all for the next few miles.

The road was rough, and as far as the wagon was concerned, most expense had been spared. It was probably just as well that my backside was already numb from the long train ride, because otherwise rattling on the wooden seat would have been agonizing instead of merely horrific. We passed several fields where tobacco was just beginning to come up, then entered the woods I had seen from the station platform. Pine, sweetgum, and hickory dominated the edges, but as we went deeper in, oak and stately chestnut began to spread their branches overhead.

When the silence had grown so excruciating that I had to break it, I said, "I appreciate you giving me a ride. I know this is somewhat out of your way."

"It is my Christian duty," he said.

It is extremely difficult to make conversation with someone who uses the phrase "Christian duty" with utter sincerity. I lapsed back into silence, watching the trees on either side of the road. The leaves were the hot green of new growth and the redbuds were blazing pink, even in the fading light.

Hooker's green, I thought, studying the trees. *Sap green too. Flicks of gamboge yellow for the light, and a wash of Prussian blue through the shadows. But mostly green, in all the shades that I can mix. Though I'd have to do something to keep the pink for the redbuds from mixing in with the rest.* The usual way to separate a color out that sharply is to use frisket on the paper to cover all the spots you want to keep unpainted, but that requires a great many extra steps and the watercolor must be absolutely bone-dry before you try to peel up the frisket. It's much easier to ruin a painting than to save one with the stuff.

Dr. Halder probably wouldn't have me painting redbuds. He studied insects. I'd painted insects before, usually in proximity to the flowers they haunted, but I couldn't say that I had a great deal of experience with them.

(he'll see your work and turn you off immediately you'll have to go back to the school with your tail between your legs it was foolish to think you could ever do this)

Stop that.

"The woods are beautiful this time of year," I offered, trying to drown out the voice of my anxiety.

"Do not be fooled," Phelps said, to my surprise.

"Beg pardon?"

He glanced over at me, his jaw working like a horse with a bit in its mouth. "The Devil walks these woods, Miss Wilson."

My eyebrows shot up. Well, really, what are you supposed to say to a thing like that? I wracked my brain for anything that might live in the woods that would merit such a description. There were no longer any pumas in this part of the state, and indeed, there were those who said they had been wiped out completely. The Klan had similarly been stamped out a decade prior, though God knows hatred is more resilient than wildlife. "Are you . . . ah . . . speaking metaphorically, sir?"

"I am not." Phelps worked his jaw again, then lifted an arm and pointed past me. The shadow of his beard made a Payne's gray wash across his cheeks. "We're only a mile or two from the Devil's Tramping Ground. Are you familiar with it?"

I shook my head.

"It's a bare circle of ground on which no grass will grow. It's said that the Devil walks there at night, plotting wickedness. Do you believe in the Devil, Miss Wilson?"

This was a difficult question to answer, since the truth might get me thrown off the wagon, and I wasn't certain how much farther we had to go to Halder's. "I don't *dis*believe," I said cautiously. "Though most wickedness I have seen has come from men."

"Mmm." Thankfully Phelps showed no sign of stopping the wagon to make me walk.

Emboldened, I added, "I don't know that I believe that the Devil has a physical body, or that that body is in North Carolina though."

"Might have answered the same, once." Phelps clucked his tongue again and slapped the reins, urging the horses on a little faster. "But then I saw her. I saw the Devil in these woods, Miss Wilson. And that is why I cannot let a woman walk these woods at night, regardless of how far out of my way it may take me."

CHAPTER 2

It was full dark when we arrived at my employer's house. Conversation had faltered after Phelps's revelation. It may be difficult to follow up the phrase "Christian duty," but that's nothing compared to a claim of having seen the Devil in person. *And calling it a her?* I desperately wanted to ask what she had looked like, if she had two legs or four, hooves or hands, and if there had been any other witnesses, but these all seemed likely to end up with me walking the rest of the way to Halder's. Small talk was entirely out of the question.

I didn't know what Phelps had seen, but I definitely didn't believe it was the Devil. Father had been raised Quaker but had acquired Unitarianism in his boyhood in Boston, which he passed down to me, mixed with occasional bouts of transcendentalist philosophy. He'd then compounded the issue by sending me to a Methodist school. My faith was perhaps best described as "vague idiosyncratic Christianity," but it definitely did not allow for Satan to be wandering North Carolina in the flesh.

Our pace slowed as it grew darker, as Phelps let the horses pick their way along the road. *Is he not worried that the Devil will get us if we go too slowly? Does Satan not bother wagons? Or is she simply not very fast? Then again, if she isn't that fast, it probably isn't dangerous to walk in the woods. Unless the Devil is an ambush predator?*

It occurred to me then that the station master had been unexpectedly alarmed about the prospect of me walking through the woods. At the time I'd put it up to chivalry, but what if it had been something else?

Perhaps he and Phelps go to the same church.

I could hear frogs calling around us, the finger-on-a-comb call of chorus frogs and the shriller notes of tree frogs. They, at least, were not concerned about the Devil. A lone whippoorwill repeated his name off in the distance. My father always said that whippoorwills were polite birds, because they told you exactly who was calling.

If my father had still been alive, he would have been proud of me for finding work as a scientific illustrator. *Of course, if he were still alive, I wouldn't have needed to go looking for work in the first place, so there's no point in getting maudlin about it.*

Eventually the wagon turned onto a long drive that looked as if it had once been very wide. Greenery had begun to creep in around the edges though, until it narrowed into a gloomy tunnel. Brick pillars flanked the entryway, both with lamps, but they were unlit.

Did they not expect me this evening?

Apparently they did not. As the wagon rolled up the drive, wheels crunching loudly, I saw the house in the dim moonlight, a grand confection of windows and pillars, but with only a single small lamp lit in a room on the second story. I swallowed hard.

(they didn't expect you. you clearly aren't wanted. you're in the wrong place)

A side door opened, spilling light onto the ground, and a woman emerged, carrying a lamp. She turned toward us, lifting the lamp high. "Now who's coming around at this hour?"

I slid down from the wagon, anxiety curdling in my stomach. "My name's Sonia Wilson. I . . . err . . . I was hired as an illustrator? By Dr. Halder?"

"Lord help us," the woman said, coming closer. I could hear her feet crunching on the gravel. "He said something about hiring one, but he never said any more than that. If I'd known, I'd have made up a room." She frowned, though I don't think it was at me.

In the glow of the lamp, I could see that she was Black, tall and lean, her hair braided tightly back from her face. She wore a shirtwaist dress with an apron over it.

I thrust out my hand, hoping to overcome the terrible impression I'd made by arriving so late. "Sonia Wilson." *No, you said that already. Say something else, quick.* "Err . . . it's nice to meet you."

She took my hand, bemused. "Mrs. Kent. I'm Dr. Halder's housekeeper." Her grip was firm, but she dropped my hand quickly and looked past me to the wagon. "Mr. Phelps? Is that you?"

"Ma'am," said Phelps. His voice was as emotionless as mud.

"He was kind enough to give me a ride from Siler Station," I said, sensing tension between them. Mrs. Kent nodded, but didn't say anything.

I went back to the wagon to retrieve my suitcase. Now that I was actually at my destination, I was curiously reluctant to see Phelps go. He had been an uncomfortable companion, but his Christian duty had gotten me here. If I had been on my own, I would still be walking and probably ready to weep from exhaustion.

Or maybe I'd have encountered the Devil by now. I bit down my desire to laugh and nodded to Phelps. "Thank you," I said, stepping back with my suitcase in my arms.

He tipped his hat. "Miss Wilson. Remember what I said. I will look for you in church on Sunday." Then he turned the wagon and it rattled off down the drive, into the dark.

I turned back to Mrs. Kent, still clutching my suitcase against my chest. "I'm sorry to make so much trouble," I said. "Dr. Halder sent me the ticket, so I assumed . . ."

"Oh, I don't doubt it," she said, sighing. "Come inside. You must be fair famished. I can probably rustle something up for you to eat before I go to bed."

"I'm sorry to keep you up," I said, feeling even more guilty. At the school, we got so little sleep that I begrudged every minute someone kept me awake. Was the life of a housekeeper like a teacher in that regard?

"No need to keep apologizing," she said, gesturing me toward the door. "I know who's to blame, and it isn't you."

The door led through a small scullery into the kitchen. The walls needed whitewash and the stove was a monstrous iron beast the size of a coffin, but it was warm and smelled like baking bread. My shoulders, which had been inching up around my ears, relaxed a little. Such is the power of bread.

"Sit," Mrs. Kent said, waving to the table. There were four chairs, but one held a washtub full of potatoes. I set down my suitcase and collapsed into one of the non-potato chairs. Either it was extremely comfortable or any seat that wasn't moving had become a hedonistic delight. I smothered a groan.

"Here," said Mrs. Kent. "They're this morning's, so they ain't rocks yet." She slid a plate of biscuits across the table. "There's honey in the jar there."

"*Thank you.*"

"Mmm. Ain't nothing."

It was a good deal more than nothing. The biscuits were huge and delicious, even if they'd started to go hard. I found the jar of honey, spooned some out onto one of the biscuits, and attacked it. Crumbs went everywhere, but at the moment, I didn't care. It had been so long since breakfast that even the Chatham rabbits were starting to sound good.

I studied Mrs. Kent out of the corner of my eye while I ate. She had a young face and old hands. I wondered which one was closer to her actual age.

She left the room for a moment, then returned with a tin cup and a pitcher of water. I washed down the biscuits and mumbled my gratitude, hoping that I wasn't making too terrible an impression with my lack of table manners. If I was, she didn't show it.

A large orange cat leapt up onto the table, startling me. The housekeeper sighed. "Smiley, get your tail down off that." The cat ignored her completely, gazing intently at the biscuits. I put my hand up to shield them.

"Smiley . . ." She swooped in and picked him up, dropping him unceremoniously on the floor. He stalked away, tail held high, very fluffy and completely unrepentant.

"He won't marry you," said Mrs. Kent abruptly.

I blinked at her, the last of the honey congealing on my tongue. For a confused instant, all I could think of was the cat, and why she thought I'd want to marry outside my species. "Beg pardon?"

The housekeeper shook her head. "The doctor. If you took the position thinking he'd marry you at the end of it, put that thought out of your head."

It seemed that I still had energy enough to bristle. "I assure you," I said, "that I had *no* such thoughts. I am an illustrator and—and a naturalist, not a—a—" I couldn't even think of the right words, probably because of all the other words playing through my head.

(scarecrow, hatchet-faced, bag of bones)

Mrs. Kent's lips twitched. "All right," she said. "Didn't mean to get your back up. I figured it was better to have that out in the open, that's all. Some women would be thinking this was a stepping stone to the other." She wiped her hands on her apron. "And you wouldn't want it anyway. He's mean as an old snake, that one."

"Then why do you work for him?"

Probably I wouldn't have been so bold if I wasn't tired and cross and resentful of having been forgotten at the station. Fortunately, Mrs. Kent did not seem to take offense. She snorted, removing her apron and hanging it on a peg. "Because he's mean to everyone the same way. Doesn't matter what color you are or if you're a woman or a hundred years old. The doctor's got no use for anybody." She smiled ruefully. "There's worse people to work for, here in the South."

I sighed, my irritation ebbing away. I was so tired. I'd been tired for years, ever since my father died. But Mrs. Kent was old enough to have seen the War Between the States, and probably she was even more tired than I was. "You'd think we could do better," I said glumly.

"You'd think." She picked up the lamp. "I'll show you to your room. Well, *a* room. It'll do for tonight, and we'll find you something better tomorrow."

I nodded and stood up, brushing the biscuit crumbs off my skirt. "Thank you," I said. "For the food and the room. And staying up."

"Mmm. Well. Nobody starves in my kitchen, no matter what hour they come in." I followed her out of the kitchen and down a hallway, then through two doors and up a staircase. I couldn't follow the twists and turns very well, and was thoroughly lost by the time we reached a door. "Here you go. It's clean." She pushed the door open. "And there's water in the cistern, so if you turn the tap, you'll get something. Don't know if I'd drink it, but it's good enough for washing up."

"Thank you," I said, lugging my suitcase into the small room. It was plain but serviceable, with an iron bedstead, a clothes press, and a stand with a basin and a tap. Cistern-fed water on demand seemed absurdly luxurious. At the school, we'd only had a hand pump. "Err . . . why wouldn't you drink it?"

Mrs. Kent paused with her hand on the doorknob. "Bugs," she said. "They get into everything." And then she closed the door behind her and was gone.

———

There was a swarm of white dragonflies on the ceiling. I stared up at them, profoundly confused. Why was that there? *How* was that there? Had one of the girls done something to my ceiling as a prank?

The dragonflies were larger than my head, which meant that they were not native to North America, and they were evenly spaced and all facing in the same direction, which meant that they were . . . pressed tin tiles? Yes. Painted white.

This did not explain why they were on my ceiling. I sat up, wondering how to even begin explaining this to the headmistress, and caught a glimpse of my suitcase sitting on the floor next to the clothes press. Memory pushed back my disorientation and I rubbed my forehead. *Right. I'm at Dr. Halder's residence. I've arrived. I'm going to work as a scientific illustrator again. And apparently his ceilings have tin tiles with dragonflies on them.*

I felt a stab of panic that I had overslept, but a glance out the window showed that it was still quite early. I was still on school time. The headmistress had no use for sluggards, and her definition of "sluggard" began at 6:00 AM. Given how tired I was, I could easily have gone back to sleep until noon, but that seemed like a poor way to start my employment.

I had been too tired to wash up the night before. Now I ran water into the basin and learned what Mrs. Kent had meant about the bugs. A dead June bug floated on the surface of the water, green and shiny against the white porcelain. I had no particular fear of insects, but I never liked June bugs, because of the way they fly in your face if you're standing anywhere near a light source. This one wasn't going to be flying anywhere, but I still didn't want to share the water with it. I fished it out, sighed, and used twice as much soap as normal.

I put on one of my two good sets of clothes, then made my way downstairs, wondering what to do next. *Do I go and present myself to him? Is he even awake?* My experiences with naturalists warred with my experiences teaching. Would Dr. Halder be pleased with my punctuality, or appalled to be bothered before breakfast?

For want of any better ideas, I made my way to the kitchen. Perhaps Mrs. Kent could advise me. She'd been kind enough last night, even if her suggestion about marriage had bordered on offensive. I had no plans to marry anyone. At thirty, I was officially a spinster, and it wasn't as if one met many eligible bachelors at a girls' school.

As a girl, I'd always assumed I would marry a naturalist and collaborate with him on scientific works. It was almost a cliché in my father's circles that one eventually married one's illustrator. Indeed, I'd met a number of wives who were clearly doing the lion's share of the research, no matter whose name appeared on the frontispiece. My lack of physical charms had never seemed important, because my future husband would be marrying me for my ability to properly render leaf venation.

But somehow it had never quite happened, and then Father had died and the scientific world began to drift out of reach. I don't think it was ever malicious. It was simply that we had come as a set, Dr. Wilson and his daughter. If any of his old friends ever thought about me, it was probably with general goodwill. "Oh yes, Wilson had a daughter, didn't he? Bit dowdy, but by god could she paint a terrestrial orchid!" And they'd make a mental note to see what I was doing these days and then they'd see an interesting lichen and then it would be five years later.

I couldn't even be angry. It was hard to compete with a good lichen.

I got lost twice looking for the kitchen, but eventually found the dining room. It had high ceilings and elegant moldings. The table that ran the length of it had no tablecloth, though the wood had been polished until it nearly glowed, even under a thin film of dust. There were silver candlesticks on the mantle, but they were beginning to tarnish. The whole room had an air of disuse about it and the fireplace did not look as if it had been lit in months. It reminded me uncomfortably of our home during Father's illness, as I closed off the rooms one by one to save money. The rooms, when I walked through them, had the same oddly hollow feel, as if the echoes took a little longer to return than they should.

Just beyond the dining room, I found a narrow door painted the same color as the walls. I pushed it open and found, unsurprisingly, the servant's stair. The sound of clattering crockery grew louder as I descended.

"Now I know those dishes aren't done," Mrs. Kent said as I stepped into the kitchen. Her back was to me, sleeves shoved to her elbows. "You can't even have done the silver yet."

"Um," I said. "No?"

The housekeeper twisted around, blinked at me, then laughed. "Miss Wilson! Goodness, I thought you were young Sally. Never mind the silver."

I smiled. "Quite all right. Err—I was hoping to ask you when I should call on Dr. Halder?"

"Lord, I don't even send his breakfast tray up until ten. He keeps late hours, unless he's getting up early to chase bugs around." She glanced my way. "You'll probably be wanting breakfast though."

"I don't want to be a bother—"

Mrs. Kent snorted. "Feeding people's no bother. Do you want to eat in the dining room, or here in the kitchen?"

Remembering the air of disuse in the dining room, I suspected that really *would* be a bother. And the notion of sitting all alone in that quiet room, while Mrs. Kent ferried food up the stairs—God, no. "I'd rather eat down here, if I won't be in your way?"

"Not at all." Her smile seemed a trifle more genuine, and I wondered if I'd passed a test of some sort. She pulled a cast-iron pan from a back burner of the stove and cracked a pair of eggs into it. "You always up this early?"

"Force of habit," I admitted. "But I don't actually need anything but coffee at this hour, if you'd rather I ate when you're preparing the tray for Dr. Halder."

"Pfff. Makes no never mind to me. I keep the coffee on for myself and Mr. Kent." She poured out a mug and handed it to me. I slid into a chair and spooned a little sugar into it. Smiley appeared to see if he could leave some cat hair in the sugar bowl, and seemed vaguely annoyed that I wouldn't let him.

The mug was halfway to my lips when it occurred to me that it might have worse things in it than cat hair. Where had the water come from? Would there be mosquito larvae mixed in with the coffee grounds?

It's coffee, I told myself sternly. *The water was boiled to make it. Even if there's mosquito larvae, they'll be . . . er . . . pasteurized.* I took a sip. It tasted like coffee. Nothing wriggled against my tongue.

"Anything you particularly like for breakfast?"

I blinked at Mrs. Kent. At the school, the teachers ate the same things as the students. (At least the junior teachers did. I had my suspicions about the headmistress.) Breakfast was oatmeal and an apple. Sometimes there was toast, and at Christmas there were often hotcakes, but the oatmeal was eternal. I had almost forgotten that there were other breakfast foods in existence.

"Um," I said. "I . . . err . . . hotcakes? If you ever feel like making them?"

"I make 'em twice a week regular anyway," Mrs. Kent told me. "Mr. Kent's partial to them. Just eggs today though."

"Eggs would be wonderful," I assured her. "I love eggs."

"Good." She turned and slid two freshly cooked eggs onto my plate. "Bacon in a minute."

"Bacon?"

She raised an eyebrow at me. "You don't eat bacon?"

"Oh, I *would*! I do, I mean. It's just . . . it's been a long time." Truth be told, if not for tiny, mushy bits of pink that occasionally turned up in the school supper, I would have had no proof that bacon was not a hallucination of my youth.

Mrs. Kent didn't pry. I heard a sizzle and the smell of bacon drifted through the kitchen. My stomach growled loudly and I applied myself to my eggs.

"And Dr. Halder doesn't mind?" I asked when two thick slices of bacon landed in front of me.

"Mind?"

"That we're eating this well." The headmistress would have fallen into strong hysterics at the notion of the junior teachers having bacon and eggs for breakfast. Even the coffee had been more than half chicory, and the milk so watered you could read through it.

"Why should he care? He eats the same thing every day regardless." She counted it off on her fingers. "One poached egg, two pieces of toast, one slice of bacon, black coffee with one sugar, served at exactly ten o'clock. He may be a tightfisted, mean-spirited old cuss, but I'll give him this, he isn't stingy about food."

I considered this while demolishing the bacon. "Mean-spirited" didn't bode well. Was he mean-spirited enough to dismiss me immediately upon meeting, if I said something wrong?

When you want to know something, consult an expert. I washed the bacon down with a slug of coffee and said, hesitantly, "Mrs. Kent? Can I ask you something?"

"Ask away."

"Is there anything . . . err . . ." I paused, not sure how to continue. "That is, if I want to make a good impression on Dr. Halder, is there anything I should or shouldn't do?"

"Mmmmm." A thoughtful sound, not a negative one. "Not sure if there's such a thing as a *good* impression, mind you. Don't act scared, I'd say. I don't say argue with him, but don't cower. He'll likely insult you. If you get mad, he'll think it's funny, and he'll keep poking that spot for the next twenty years."

"Charming," I muttered.

"You know it."

I took my empty plate and mug to the scullery and checked the clock in the hall. Barely eight. Assuming that I didn't want to beard the lion in his den before he'd had his breakfast, I had at least three hours to kill.

"Will anyone mind if I look around the grounds?" I asked.

Mrs. Kent snorted. "Nobody around *to* mind. Mr. Kent's the only one you'll run into, unless you go across the road and start walking. And if you see Mr. Kent, tell 'im I need a chicken killed for dinner."

I agreed to carry this message if I saw Mr. Kent, collected my sketchbook, and went outside.

The house was different in daylight. My impression in the dark had been an impressive construction of pillars and windows, a veritable mansion. By day, gazing up at it, it seemed somehow less than the sum of its parts.

Great columns rose for two stories, holding up a roof that extended outward, providing a broad shaded porch all the way around the building. Massive windows lined both lower floors. The third floor, under the eaves, was probably servant quarters, although I had not as yet seen anyone beyond Mrs. Kent.

And yet, despite the size and grandeur, Dr. Halder's house had clearly seen better days. Algae had powdered the white wood with flecks of green, and here and there, I saw the telltale signs of paint that had peeled and been repaired.

A house like this would normally be surrounded by formal gardens, but these had long ago left formality behind. The paths were paved with red brick and kept neat enough, but where one might expect to see clipped topiaries and trimmed boxwood hedges, there were instead thick perennial borders. Even these had gone to seed, though they held up better than the house. I saw weeds lurking in corners and morning glory throwing narrow green ropes up through the shrubs, making a solid slope of leaves. The headmistress would have been appalled. The insects clearly were not. Bees and slender-waisted wasps formed a living cloud around the flowers. I watched a tiger swallowtail . . . *Papilio something or other* . . . stab its delicate proboscis into the tiny cups of a clary sage, and had a sudden suspicion why Dr. Halder did not care that his garden had gone to seed in such a fashion.

I circled the house by way of the garden. In the back, a pair of long balconies flanked the two wings of the second floor. On one side, the flower garden gave way to a practical-looking vegetable garden. The trees grew closer to the house on the other side, leaning out over the cleared ground. This was the side with the kitchen door. A patio had been picked out in red brick, running almost up to the edge of the woods. I could see at a glance which places got sun during the day and which lay in shade. The shady areas were carpeted with dry pine needles and softly moldering leaves. The sunny patches grew thick and lush, tangled up with greenbrier and Virginia creeper. Someone was obviously cutting it back occasionally, but there is only so much that one can do in the South. My father used to say that the vegetation down here wanted very badly to be a jungle.

Perhaps the lushness of the woods was the problem with the house, now that I looked at it from this side. The building didn't *fit*. It made the whole scene feel unfinished, like a square of paper left blank and white in the middle of a painting of carefully detailed green leaves.

And that is a botanist thought if there ever was one. Enough of that. You're here as an illustrator, not an architectural consultant. I looked up to the second story, where Halder's office lay, according to Mrs. Kent.

Had it been three hours? *My kingdom for a pocket watch.* Father had had a lovely one, etched with silver, but it had eventually been sold along with everything else. I went back inside and checked the clock. Ten thirty. Surely that was close enough. I paused long enough to tell Mrs. Kent that I had not encountered Mr. Kent and ask directions to Dr. Halder's office.

He kept his quarters on the second floor, and Mrs. Kent had pointed me toward the main entrance, which boasted a grand central staircase. Light streamed in through the windows that flanked the door, waking deep red undertones in the polished wood. It looked oddly unreal, as if it hadn't actually been made to walk on. I looked around nervously, as if someone might disapprove of the hired help using it, but there was no one there, and no other, more inviting staircase. I put my hand on the banister, which felt smooth and tepid as a beetle's shell.

Halder's house was strangely empty. Since I arrived, I had only seen Mrs. Kent, who had mentioned her husband and someone named Sally, but a house this size should have a small army of servants scrubbing and polishing, shouldn't it?

Then again, remembering the empty dining room, perhaps Halder didn't feel he needed any more. But why build such an immense house and then let it sit empty?

I shook myself. It was none of my business how my employer spent his money, so long as he spent some of it on me. I reached the second floor, the boards creaking under my feet. The creaks seemed to echo much longer than they should have before dying away.

Stop it. It's just nerves.

Halder's door loomed in front of me. I wiped suddenly clammy hands on my skirt. *This is it, you'll walk in, he'll take one look at you and tell you there's been a mistake and turn you off...*

Stop.

I knocked.

"Eh? What is it?"

That wasn't exactly an invitation, but I pushed the door open anyway and beheld my employer.

Dr. Halder sat at a desk surrounded by papers and books, with a tray of half-eaten breakfast at his elbow. I had often seen my father in a similar pose, but there the resemblance ended. Dr. Halder looked rather like an insect himself. A weevil, specifically.

He had enormous spectacles and a thin, drooping nose, and no eyebrows to speak of. His hair was thinning and almost the same color as his skin anyway, which made it look even thinner. Everything about him was faded and oddly colorless, clothes, skin, hair, even the spectacles. If I were painting him, I would lay down washes of sepia and then probably blot most of them right back up again, leaving mere suggestions of color on the page.

Halder blinked at me behind his glasses and said, "You're the girl I sent for. The one who can paint."

Don't act scared, I thought, and did not curtsey. Instead I gave a little half bow of acknowledgment. "I am Miss Wilson."

He sucked on his front teeth. "I thought your ticket was for yesterday."

"It was. It is a long way from the train station, however, and there are no coaches at Siler Station."

If I had expected an apology, I would have been disappointed. (I hadn't really expected it. Between the stationmaster and Mrs. Kent, I already had a fair idea that I wasn't getting one.) He grunted instead, and gestured to the chair in front of his desk. "So you're the illustrator." He frowned. "I expected an older woman."

"I am thirty," I said, sitting. "But I began assisting my father as an illustrator when I was fifteen."

"Hmm. My great interest, Miss Wilson, is in in parasitic and necrophagic species." He looked over his glasses at me.

"Carrion eaters," I said, wondering if this was a test of my vocabulary.

"Precisely. I do not expect that you will have read any of my papers, but my reputation in the field is unmatched."

As is your humility, clearly. Aloud, I said only, "I look forward to learning from a master of the field."

Either my flattery did not move him, or I hadn't been able to keep a trace of irony out of my voice. He studied me silently over his glasses again. I had been subjected to such scrutiny by far better people—Headmistress Silverton had a glare that would send a charging rhinoceros tiptoeing apologetically from the room—and so remained seated calmly with my hands folded in my lap.

There was a gallon jar on the desk in front of me, full of clear liquid and some strange object resembling an exotic fruit, shaped rather like an artichoke, but with hundreds of small, pale lobes. I wondered where it had come from.

Perhaps realizing that I wasn't going to speak first, Halder harrumphed and looked down at his papers. "I have devoted much of my life to a work that will revolutionize our understanding of the life cycle of insects that live on flesh. I trust that you are not squeamish, Miss Wilson?"

My father drowned in his own lungs, and when he coughed so hard it made him vomit, I cleaned it up. When he pissed and shat himself in his final delirium, I changed the sheets. And you think your insects will trouble me? "Not at all, Dr. Halder," I said, in my most pleasant tone.

"I ask because your prior work appears to have mostly been *botanical*." He pronounced the word with obvious disdain.

One advantage of having worked as a teacher for so long was that I could seethe internally while keeping an expression of polite interest on my face. *My father's work cataloguing plants was groundbreaking, you pompous old bastard.* "I assure you, I have painted many animal specimens as well."

"That is good to hear." He started to say something more, but the large orange cat that I had seen in the kitchen suddenly leapt up onto his desk. Halder sighed and made a shooing gesture, which the cat ignored utterly. One tawny paw snaked out to bat at a paper on the desk.

"This wretched beast is named Smilodon," Halder said. "After—"

"*Smilodon populator*," I said. "The saber-toothed cat."

I had surprised the doctor this time, I could tell. He took his glasses off and polished them on his shirt. "Very good, Miss Wilson."

Smilodon stopped attacking the papers when I spoke, apparently noticing another person in the vicinity. I offered my fingers and he rubbed his cheek along them, showing oversized canines that stuck out just slightly. No question what had inspired the name, then.

"Precision is key when studying insects," Halder said. I had an odd feeling that he was reciting a predetermined speech. "There is no room within my work for flights of fancy. This is a work of science, not an illustrated storybook for children."

"I have little interest in flights of fancy, Doctor." I withdrew my hand from Smilodon—or Smiley, as Mrs. Kent had called him—and he stalked off toward a bottle of ink. Halder rescued it, glaring at the cat but making no attempt to remove him.

"I am glad to hear it." Halder opened a desk drawer and withdrew a sheaf of papers, keeping them well away from the cat. "This is a list of the insects which I will require illustrated at each point in their life cycles. The library contains specimens of each of them. Under no circumstances are you to remove the specimens from the library, do you understand?"

I dipped my head in acknowledgment. "Certainly, Doctor."

He passed over the papers. I read down a list of Latin names, most of which I did not recognize. Some had notes beside them—*show life cycle* or *larval form only*. One was tagged *note markings on metathorax!*

I swallowed. What the devil was a metathorax? I had a vague notion that a thorax was part of insect anatomy, but did a metathorax go under it or over it . . . ? Or was it like metamorphosis, and it was a thorax that had changed? Was it something that happened when an insect changed from one form to another?

It doesn't matter. You'll figure it out. So long as there were specimens, I could work it out as I went. Surely there were books somewhere with diagrams that I could consult. He'd mentioned a library. Libraries had books. *It will be fine.*

"This does not seem like so many," I said, paging through. It looked like the work of a season or two at most. My stomach knotted at the thought that I had left the school for a job that would not last out the year. Possibly less, if I admitted my ignorance of metathoraxes.

"That is only the first two chapters," said Halder. "When I have seen your work, then I shall prepare the rest." He pushed his glasses up again.

I relaxed slightly. "Certainly, Doctor. Is there a particular visual layout you would prefer?" When he frowned at the question, I added, "In my experience, many scientists have a very specific format in mind, and I do not wish to waste your time or my labor by producing something unsuitable."

Halder looked past me. I thought he seemed almost indecisive about something, which seemed at odds with what little I'd seen of him so far. "No," he said at last. "No, the time should not be wasted."

I did not have time to wonder at his phrasing. He rose to his feet and made his way slowly to a tall wooden cabinet on the far side of the room. He withdrew a key from his pocket and unlocked the doors.

I started to rise and he snapped, "Stay where you are!" over his shoulder.

What, does he have live wasps in there or something? Admittedly, that seemed unlikely, but some of my father's naturalist friends had kept stranger things in the house. *Say what you like about Father, at least plants are easier to deal with than live rattlesnakes . . . or that one fellow with the fox.* Opening the front door to his house had produced an eye-watering blast of ammonia, and a weeklong stay during trillium season had cured me of any childhood desire for a pet fox. Between the urine and the screaming, they did not have a great deal to recommend them. (Granted, I feel much the same way about babies, but they at least grow out of it.)

Halder stood in front of the cabinet for some time. I could hear papers being shuffled about. Rather than twist about and stare at him, I studied his desk, and the mysterious object in the gallon jar.

After a moment, I realized that it wasn't an object, but *objects*. The jar was full of grubs preserved in liquid, probably alcohol. Hundreds of them, stuffed in like candy in a jar, their bodies pale and wrinkled from the solution. Despite my brave thoughts earlier, I felt a twinge of nausea. I stamped it down and forced myself to stare at the pickled larvae. *You are a naturalist. These are creatures of nature. How would you paint them?*

Raw sienna greatly thinned and mixed with white gouache. Raw umber for the shadows of organs inside. A touch of blue for shading, applied very thin, so that it does not turn the yellows to green.

The queasiness subsided. (My nerves remained, but you can't have everything.)

Eventually I heard the cabinet doors close and Halder returned to his seat, then slid a thin folder across the desk.

"These are some of the completed illustrations," he said. "I'll expect you to match them."

I opened the folder and felt my heart stutter in my chest.

The top sheet contained a series of illustrations of the American burying beetle, and they were *magnificent*. Black and orange carapace, tiny segmented antenna leading to a vivid orange comb, delicate spines on the back set of legs—it was a work of art as well as science. The uppermost illustration showed the beetle with spread wings, which the artist had rendered with veins so fine that they must have been painted with a brush the size of a hair. The pattern on the shell was not merely a flat wash of color but had richness and depth. Even the beetle grub elsewhere on the page seemed to glow from within.

"These are . . ." *Beautiful. Elegant. Gorgeous.* ". . . exquisitely done." I suspected that Halder, with his scoffing at flights of fancy, would not appreciate admiration of their beauty. "Who was the artist?"

"That need not concern you," said Halder. "Your job is simply to finish the illustrations."

I swallowed and lifted the page. The second sheet was just as glorious. An American carrion beetle, from egg to adulthood. The heavily armored larva was black, yes, but the artist had layered the shell with subtle washes of indigo and Tuscan red, making the black richer and more complex. Had the great Hans Simon Holtzbecker been obsessed with flesh-eating beetles instead of flowers, he might have produced something like this.

I am a good illustrator. I am inspired some of the time and competent all of the time. For all my gnawing fears, I had never truly worried about the technical aspects of this job.

But *this* . . . he wanted me to produce work to match this? I felt as if I had fallen into a fairy tale where a wicked fairy demanded that I spin watercolor into gold.

My mask of calm must have slipped, because Halder's eyebrows slammed together over his nose. "Is there a problem, Miss Wilson? Can't you do it?"

If I were as good a person as I was an illustrator, perhaps I would have told him the truth. But I needed the job too badly. I composed my face despite the sudden knot in my gut and set the folio back on the desk. "I do not have the pigments to match these," I said calmly. "The artist appears to have used both watercolor and gouache, which I am proficient in, but I will require additional paints and finer brushes."

The doctor scowled. The knot in my gut drew even tighter. *Don't think like that. He hired you, he's seen your work in the* Botanica, *he knows what you're capable of. He knew what he was getting.*

Smiley leapt back onto the desk between us and broke the tension. I snatched the folder out of the way while Halder pushed the cat aside. "Very well," he said, no longer scowling.

"Tell Mrs. Kent I said to put you in the studio suite. There should be plenty of brushes and paints in there, and you are welcome to them."

This sounded like a dismissal. I picked up the list of Latin names and rose to my feet. "I shall deliver the completed illustrations to you as I finish them." Inspiration struck. "Would you prefer that I come to you when I have questions, or are there texts you would like me to consult first?"

Please, God, let there be texts. I could all too easily picture Halder shouting at me about metathoraxes and then perhaps throwing something. I desperately needed a reference book.

"I do not want my time taken up with foolish questions. But it is the specimens that are definitive, not the books." He pointed a finger at me, eyes narrowing. "I have no desire to see my work as error-riddled as that fool Fitch's, Miss Wilson. Consult whatever books you like, but do not repeat their mistakes. Do you understand me?"

"Certainly," I lied. *Who on earth is Fitch?* And then, because I was already lying, I added, "I look forward to working with you, Dr. Halder."

He grunted and turned away. I let myself out of the room and leaned against the wall, my knees shaking.

I had survived the first face-to-face meeting. Halder hadn't thought better of hiring me or thrown me out on my ear. Now I just had to figure out how to match some of the most spectacular illustrations I'd ever seen, in a field that I knew virtually nothing about, without repeating the mistakes of books I'd never heard of.

No problem at all, I thought, and didn't know whether to laugh or burst into tears.

CHAPTER 3

"The studio suite?" Mrs. Kent frowned at me, not a negative frown but a puzzled one. "Huh."

"Is there something wrong?" I asked timidly. "He said I should use the paints there."

"No. Just surprised, that's all." She squared her shoulders. "I haven't done more than dust it for the last year. I'll have Sally bring fresh sheets."

"I'm sorry to keep making more work for you," I murmured.

"No, it's fine. I . . ." She stopped, clearly thinking better of what she was about to say. "It's a very fine room."

She led me up to the second story, on the far side of the house from Halder's study, and pushed open a door. I stepped inside and felt my eyes go wide.

Glass doors on the far side of the room opened onto a narrow widow's walk, flanked by floor-to-ceiling windows that left the room filled with light. The walls were painted white and had no wallpaper, and the polished wooden boards gleamed. *Yellow ochre and burnt umber for the wood, gamboge for the squares of light across them* . . . It was a beautiful, airy space, and it was clear that I wasn't the first person to think so, because the room was strewn with books and brushes, pencils and palettes, even a silk dressing gown tossed carelessly over the back of a chair. It looked as if the owner had simply stepped out a moment earlier.

A doorway on my left led to a bedroom. The bed had been stripped, but that was the only sign that it was unoccupied. One door of a wooden wardrobe stood ajar. It still had clothes in it.

"Are you sure . . ." I began, and stopped. *Are you sure no one is using this?* I wanted to ask, but that was a ridiculous question. Obviously Mrs. Kent would know.

"I'll just get these out of here," the housekeeper said, following my gaze to the wardrobe. "They should be packed in a chest anyway."

"But who was using it before—"

"If you want to fetch your suitcase," Mrs. Kent interrupted, "I'll send Sally up with the sheets."

"Oh! Yes, of course." By the time I had returned with my suitcase, the wardrobe was empty and Mrs. Kent had gone. I unpacked my clothes again, then stood in the center of the studio, looking around helplessly. Even though Halder had said that I was to use this suite, I felt as if I was intruding.

I drifted to the worktable near one of the windows. Tin tubes of oil paint were heaped to one side, and I read the names as if greeting old friends. *Zinc White. Rose Madder. Aureolin. Cobalt Violet. Chromium Green Oxide.* And there, a sturdy wooden box with the lid flipped up, and blocks of familiar pigment slotted into dozens of little cubbyholes. A porcelain palette lay next to it, the white surface stained with old washes.

These must have belonged to the artist who had painted such exquisite beetles. I wondered who they were, and why they had left before finishing Halder's illustrations. Mrs. Kent had said that she hadn't done more than dust for the last year. Had it simply been left like this, untouched? And why had Halder waited so long to seek out a replacement?

The door opened behind me. I turned, finally catching a glimpse of the elusive Sally. She was a small white girl with mousy brown hair, who was probably older than twelve and younger than twenty. (Despite teaching girls for a number of years, I still can't tell ages apart after a point. They all just look incredibly young to me.)

"Are you Sally?" I ventured.

Sally let out a shriek and flung the sheets she was carrying into the air. "Oh! You *startled* me, miss!"

"I see that," I said, a bit more dryly than I intended. By the way she'd thrown the sheets, you'd think I had announced my intent to kill and eat her on the spot.

"'M not used to other people in the house, miss," Sally explained.

"The doctor doesn't have many visitors?" I asked, helping her to gather up the linens.

"Oh no, miss. Not often." She screwed up her face in thought. "Last one was another doctor, I think? Only not a doctor at the hospital, but like the doctor here. All bugs and such. Why, he had a box of grasshoppers in his luggage! *Live* ones!"

"No family, then?"

"Oh no, miss. Doesn't even put up a Christmas tree for the season, 'cause no one visits. But I go to the Kents for Christmas, so that's all right."

I filed this away while helping her make the bed. No family, and apparently few friends. Given his manner, I couldn't say that last surprised me much. Though if he was like most naturalists I know, he probably kept up dozens of correspondences with other people in the field.

Sally showed me where the catches were on the doors to the balcony. The windows were already open, letting a breeze swirl through the room.

"Will there be anything else, miss?" she asked. Judging by her hopeful air, I was providing rather more entertainment than her usual cleaning. I was sorry to disappoint her, but I already knew that I couldn't compete with live grasshoppers in the luggage.

"I'm afraid not. I don't have much to unpack. Is there anything I should know?"

She sat down on the bed and gave this serious thought. "Mrs. Graham comes by for the laundry on Tuesday, so you'll want to leave yours in the basket on Monday night. And there's bugs in the water sometimes. They startle you if you aren't expecting it! But if you need water for drinking, you know, that's *definitely* got no bugs, there's a pump by the kitchen."

"That is good to know," I said gravely, wondering if everyone here was simply used to washing their faces with bug water and if I'd be used to it in a few weeks myself. But at least it did answer the question of insects in the coffee. I was starting to wish I'd had a second cup. "Do you stay here at the house, or do you go home at night?"

"Oh, I stay here, miss." She nodded so vigorously that strands of hair escaped her braid. "My family lives 'bout two miles down the road, and it ain't safe to walk through the woods at night."

"Because of—err—bears?" I asked, racking my brain for something suitably dangerous. Surely there weren't enough humans in this part of the county to be significant, and I hadn't gotten the impression that Sally was religious enough to share Asa Phelps's fear of meeting the Devil.

She gave me a pitying look for my ignorance. "On account of the blood thiefs, miss."

"Blood . . . thieves?"

"Blood thiefs," she agreed. "They steal your blood and leave you all drained out and dead and limp." She demonstrated, letting her head flop to one side and her arms dangle.

"And what do they look like?"

She shook her head solemnly. "Nobody knows. My cousin says he seen one and it was like a great big bat, but he's a liar. If he'd seen one, it'd've stole his blood too."

I rubbed my temples. First Phelps and the Devil, now this. Apparently the woods of central North Carolina were a hotbed of the supernatural. "Are you teasing me, Sally?"

"What? No, miss!" She looked shocked by the idea. "Not about the blood thiefs. My mama wouldn't let me take the job unless I stayed here because of them. You can go ask her."

"No, no, I believe you." I believed that she believed it, for what that was worth. "We . . . err . . . don't have those in Wilmington."

"No, but you got sharks," Sally offered generously, "so I s'pose it evens out."

She took her leave and I unpacked my suitcase, still shaking my head. It really didn't take long. I stacked my sketchbooks by the studio table and placed the *Botanica* on the shelf, then found myself wandering aimlessly from window to window, looking out onto a short swath of grass and a deep sea of trees.

The room still did not feel unoccupied. It felt as if the owner had gone away shortly before, taking some of their personal effects, but planned to return. Everywhere I turned, I saw my predecessor's hand. The gorgeous golden light from the windows streamed over objects arranged on the broad windowsills—interesting rocks, an empty snail shell, a long blue feather that might have come from a jay. It was so clearly an artist's space.

Now, however temporarily, it was mine.

I checked the books scattered about the room, hoping desperately for an anatomical guide to insects. Instead I found novels. The bedroom yielded nearly a complete collection of Brontë, and *The Last of the Mohicans* lay open facedown on the desk. I picked the book up and attempted to close it, but it had lain open so long that the spine had warped.

You're stalling. Get to work.

"Well," I said, sitting down at the desk and placing the beautiful carrion beetle illustrations against the carved backstop. "Let's see if I can figure out how you did this . . ."

I stopped painting that evening when the light was no longer good enough to trust my eyes. I massaged the backs of my eyelids, opened my eyes, and looked from the illustrated beetle to my own attempts. I certainly hadn't managed to duplicate my predecessor's skill, but after a half dozen experiments, I thought that I had worked out how they had managed the gorgeous tinting of the burying beetle's shell. Resisting the urge to overwork the paint was key. That's always the problem with watercolor, of course. You have to know when to stop. The temptation to add just one more wash is so strong sometimes— *If I just add a little bit more, I can fix all the things that aren't quite right yet.*

What actually winds up happening is usually that everything gets darker and muddier. Watercolor pigment is water-soluble—obviously—so if you add even a little water to an area that's already dry, it rewets all the paint you've already laid down. Add even a fraction too much and everything runs together into soup. Gouache is the same, except that it's opaque where watercolor is transparent. Combining the two can work beautifully, or you can accidentally overwork an area that was *almost* perfect and turn it into sludge.

I cleaned my brushes and sighed. I always told my students to use a quarter of the water they thought they needed and to practice patience above all else. I then failed to heed this advice myself. *Do as I say, not as I am actually doing right now . . .*

I picked several dead mosquitos out of the basin, washed my hands and face, and went down to the kitchen to see about dinner.

Delicious smells wafted through the corridor as I approached the kitchen. When I stepped inside, I found Mrs. Kent bustling, which is rather like puttering but conducted at twice the speed and with far greater efficiency. Sally was sitting at the table, alongside a short, wiry white man with thinning hair.

"Hello," I said. "Am I late for dinner? I'm sorry, I lost track of time."

"You're just on time," said Mrs. Kent, lifting the lid from a pot and stirring the contents. "We eat a bit late in summer, since the doctor doesn't take his tray until after dark."

The man at the table rose and extended a hand. His hair was dark blond, grizzled with white at the temples. *More yellow ochre and some raw umber. And white gouache, I think, I'm not going to mask out individual white hairs, that way lies madness . . .*

"I'm Jackson Kent," he said, interrupting my musings on color. "Rose's husband. You must be Miss Wilson."

Ah. Suddenly much was made clear about why Mrs. Kent might prefer to work for a man who loathed everyone equally, regardless of the color of their skin. I wondered where the Kents had been married, and why they had chosen to live in a state where their union was considered illegal. *But that is not my business, and if Mrs. Kent wishes to enlighten me, I'm sure she will.*

I grasped his hand and said, "It's a pleasure to meet you, Mr. Kent."

I hadn't quite noticed the tension in the room until it suddenly eased. *Ah. That was a hurdle that we all had to get over together, I see.* I took a seat at the table. "Do you work for Dr. Halder as well?"

"Oh, aye. Odd jobs and handiwork, splitting firewood, all that's needful." He sat back down. "And you're a painter, I hear?" He had a faint accent that might have been Scottish or simply from the mountains where so many Scots had settled.

"Scientific illustrations, yes. The doctor has retained my services to illustrate his book on insects." That sounded awfully stiff, so I added, "All thousand or so of them. I suspect I'll still be painting bugs sometime into the next century."

Mr. Kent laughed. "He's certainly got a lot of them on pins in the library. I suppose you've seen them already?"

"Not yet," I admitted. "I just got in yesterday. I imagine I'll be spending a lot of time there."

"Oh, aye. Well, when you do get up there, remember who had to haul every single case up to that room." He grinned. "And I've the backaches to prove it."

"Grab your plates," Mrs. Kent ordered. We dutifully filed past the stove, scooping up rice and ladling beans over the top. The smell of ham and onions mingled with beans made my mouth water. This was a far cry from the meals at the school, where I suspect that the headmistress feared excessive flavor might lead to insurrection.

I dug into my food like a starving woman. The beans had more spice than I was used to, but I didn't care. Jackson eyed the sweat popping out on my forehead and passed me the cornbread. "You might want this," he said, sounding amused but sympathetic. "Rose's food bites back."

Mrs. Kent sniffed. "It's an insult to the pig to turn it into something bland. If I was a pig, I'd want to know I died delicious."

I swallowed my mouthful of cornbread. "This is the best thing I've eaten in *years*."

She sniffed again, but I could tell she was pleased. "Just beans and rice, nothing special."

"It's amazing."

"Not the sort of food you're used to?" asked Jackson. I admired the tact of the question, which expressed curiosity without demanding details I might not want to give.

"Not at all. My last post was teaching art at a girls' school in Wilmington." I briefly considered how much to tell, but really, what was I hiding? *I don't think I've got what it takes to be an international woman of mystery. Actually, I'm not sure what it takes. Confidence? Sex appeal? Extra stockings?*

"Oh, out on the coast." Jackson nodded to me. "Been out there a time or two. Pretty country."

Sally piped up for the first time. "Aren't there awful hurricanes out there?"

"Sometimes," I said. "We got two or three bad storms a year. I was only there for a few years though. The old-timers told stories about hurricanes that leveled buildings and flooded the streets, but I never saw one myself."

"I'd be mortal scared," said Sally, sounding quite satisfied by the prospect.

"I was scared stiff the first time a hurricane rolled in," I admitted. "It gets so dark and so loud and you can't tell if it's rain or spray hitting the building." The older students, most of whom had grown up on the coast, had found my terror rather quaint. A sweet girl named Edith spent much of the first storm sitting with me and patting my hand whenever a particularly loud gust of wind came through. It was slightly embarrassing to be comforted by a girl half my age, but I was still grateful for the kindness. (She later went on to become a nurse, and the last I heard was working in a sanitarium for victims of consumption. I imagine she patted a great many hands over the years.)

"We only get the leftovers of your hurricanes," Jackson said. "A lot of rain and a few trees come down, but that's usually it."

"I can't say I'll miss them." I chased the last of the beans around with my cornbread. "I haven't been to this part of the state before. What do you have, if not hurricanes?"

"Summer," said Mrs. Kent darkly. "Gets so hot and muggy, you feel like you're chewing the air afore you swallow it. And then it's sickly season and we'll all be taking Jesuit's bark and hope the ague passes us by."

I grimaced. Malaria season was the worst of the school year, as our students would be struck down with various shades of fever and ague. Quinine—what Mrs. Kent called Jesuit's bark—helped a great deal, though getting the youngest students to take the nasty-tasting stuff was a trial. "I can't say I'm looking forward to that part."

"No one does," Jackson said.

"Had bilious fever when I was nine," said Sally proudly. "Said I was like to die, but I didn't."

"I'm glad you didn't," I said, and she giggled. "What else do you have here?"

All three of them chimed in, relaying tales of snowstorms

(rare) and tornadoes (slightly less rare). Plus cottonmouths, copperheads, and, of course, bears.

"Not that any of them are much trouble," Jackson assured me. "Bear'll run the other way nine times out of ten, and copperheads just freeze up and hope you don't touch 'em. People swear cottonmouths chase you, but if you get out of their way, they'll go right past you often as not. It's usually some damn fool who decides to kill it with a stick and then gets real surprised when the snake isn't keen on letting that happen."

I snorted. "I'm familiar with the type. Snakes don't bother me. My father had a friend who studied them."

"Around here, it's more bugs than snakes," said Mrs. Kent. "You put your hand down on a wheel bug, you'll know you've been somewhere. Feels like somebody hit you with a hammer and kept on hitting. Some big centipedes too."

"A centipede stung me once," said Sally. "Felt like a hot wire. And it hurt for *days*."

"I suppose I'll be expected to paint all of them eventually," I said with a sigh. I wasn't looking forward to the centipedes. I had told Halder the truth, I wasn't squeamish, but I object to things with so many legs that they look like they're flowing instead of walking. Particularly when they pack a nasty bite. (The centipede had probably bit Sally, since they don't actually have stingers, but being pedantic was no longer part of my job description.) I cast about for a slightly more palatable topic of conversation. "When I was riding in, Mr. Phelps said something about a place called the Devil's Tramping Ground."

"Oh, *him*," said Mrs. Kent, in a tone indicating that she thought more highly of the wheel bugs.

"It's a real place," said Jackson. "I can even take you out there sometime if you like. Can't say it's very interesting though. Just a big bare patch in the middle of the woods."

"My da said the Devil stomped around in a circle there and burned all the grass away."

"Phelps did talk a great deal about the Devil," I said, as neutrally as possible. Neither of the Kents struck me as intensely religious, but you never know.

Jackson scoffed. "Phelps hasn't talked about much else since he got religion a while back. Nothing wrong with Christian duty, but he's one of those more interested in hell than heaven, if you know the sort."

"Oh, I do." It was nice to have my suspicions confirmed, anyway. I don't usually dislike people immediately, but I couldn't say that Phelps had left a favorable impression. "He was actually claiming he'd seen the Devil in the woods here."

The pause that followed that lasted just slightly too long. "Man's a fanatic if you ask me," said Mrs. Kent, getting to her feet. "Sally, if you're done, it's time to get scrubbing on the dishes."

"Yes'm," said Sally. She stacked the dishes and carried them off to the scullery.

Jackson waited until she was gone, pulled a flask from his pocket, and poured a measure of amber liquid into his empty cup. "You imbibe, Miss Wilson?"

"In very small amounts." I pushed my cup forward and he poured in just enough to cover the bottom. I took a sip. It burned savagely and I choked back a cough. "Good lord!"

"I make it myself," Jackson said. He eyed the contents of his cup appraisingly. "This batch is a little rough, I admit."

"That batch isn't fit for anything but horse liniment," said Mrs. Kent over her shoulder.

I tried a second sip. It did not exactly grow on me, but my throat had already endured the worst, so it went down easier.

"So I shouldn't worry about tripping over the Devil, but I should worry about tripping over your still?"

"Oh, aye, nothing in these woods any scarier than that." He paused, his smile slowly fading. "At least, not anymore."

I looked up, startled, but Mrs. Kent was already turning.

"Don't go filling her head with that old nonsense," she snapped. Jackson held up both hands in surrender and she grumbled at him, then turned back to preparing the tray for Halder's supper.

I raised an inquiring eyebrow at Jackson. He grimaced and shook his head, then leaned forward and poured me another thimbleful of moonshine. Even after the burn had faded, even after I sought the bed in the little room off the studio, the question stayed with me of what Jackson had been about to say, and why his wife had been so quick to stop him.

Falling asleep that night was difficult. I had been too tired the night before to notice, but now I lay in bed, listening, and the unfamiliarity of it all lay over me like a blanket.

It had been some years since I slept in a room alone. At the school, I had shared quarters with the French instructor, a lively young woman named Esther who was always moving, never alighting for long. There was always cloth rustling, feet tapping, fingers drumming. She even slept restlessly, tossing and turning and wrapping the bedclothes around herself in a hopeless tangle. It was strange not to hear that now, and instead to hear the swelling chorus of frogs and katydids, punctuated by the distant call of a barred owl.

The irony was that I knew those sounds too. Once upon a time I had known them as well as I knew my own name. Hearing them now, so long after Father's final illness and my time in Wilmington, felt like coming back to a childhood home gone unfamiliar and strange.

Relax. It's just an owl, not blood thieves. I snorted. Sally's mother was probably hoping not to have an extra mouth to feed in the evenings, and had spun up a story to suit. Presumably if there *was* a mysterious creature draining the blood out of people locally, it would have come up over dinner. Though I wasn't surprised that Sally hadn't brought them up in front of the others, since

Mrs. Kent clearly wasn't the sort to suffer nonsense, judging by the way she'd cut her husband off.

The floorboards creaked. I came instantly alert, wondering if someone had entered the room. *Oh god*, please *let it not be Halder, please let him not be that sort of employer,* I need *this job—*

A weight landed at the foot of the bed, stalked regally to the midpoint, flopped down, and began to purr.

"Smiley, you wretch," I said. "You scared me."

Smiley, showing no remorse whatsoever, wriggled around until his back was pressed against my hip and went to sleep. And after a few minutes, feeling oddly reassured, so did I.

CHAPTER 4

I slept until a decadent eight in the morning and rose feeling well-rested. For all my sense of intruding, the studio felt like a home. Not my home, but someone else's—well-used and well-loved. I dressed and wandered through the outer room, running my fingers over the painting desk, picking up random stones from the windowsill, turning them over, then setting them down again. I wondered if the previous tenant had collected them because they had some sentimental quality, or if she had simply thought that they were pretty. (I was nearly certain that my predecessor had been a woman. What clothing I had glimpsed in the wardrobe bore that out. Somewhere there is undoubtedly a man who prefers green suits printed with pink rosebuds, but in my acquaintance, they are few.)

Eventually my stomach growled and I went down to breakfast.

"Mrs. Kent?"

"Hmm?" Her back was to me, as she scrambled what looked like vast quantities of eggs.

"The studio I'm in—who was in there before me?"

The housekeeper paused for a fraction of an instant, then resumed whisking. "Can't rightly say," she said. Her tone was unexpectedly cool.

"Oh, I'm sorry, I didn't realize . . ." I started to wave my hands apologetically, realized that she couldn't see me, and let them drop into my lap. "I thought you'd been here when it was occupied."

Mrs. Kent shrugged, then slid eggs onto a plate and put it

down in front of me and turned back to her cooking. I got the distinct impression that I was intruding on her work, bolted my eggs and coffee, and slipped away.

It took me three tries to find the library, since I had forgotten to ask Mrs. Kent for directions and I didn't want to bother her again. I wandered the hallway near Halder's rooms, hoping that I wasn't about to open the door to his bedroom. Fortunately, after a locked door and a linen closet, I pushed open the third door and stepped into a large room lined with floor-to-ceiling cabinets, each with dozens of shallow drawers. I recognized the style immediately and laughed at myself for thinking that a library would be full of books.

This was a library of insects. Extremely shallow drawers at the top of each cabinet gave way to slightly deeper ones lower down, though none were deeper than the width of my palm. Each drawer had a small label in the corner. I pulled a drawer out at random, revealed dozens of brown and green beetles pinned to cork under a sheet of glass. Family *Scarabaeidae*, subfamily *Cetoniinae*, genus *Cotinis*, a large label informed me helpfully. Some of the beetles had cream-colored stripes around the base of their shells, others had subtle brown stripes across their backs. All of them shimmered as I tilted the drawer lightly, the green glittering brightly, then dulling back down depending on the angle.

I slid the drawer back in. The label in the corner read SC-C. S for Scarab, C for Cetoniinae, C for Cotinis? I selected another drawer, this one labeled LL-L and tugged it partway out, then laughed with delight. *Stag beetles.* I always loved stag beetles. Our giant native variety likes damp, decomposing wood, which is also what many of our native orchids like, so I had encountered them numerous times while out with Father. The male stag beetles look terrifying, with their huge mandibles like nutcrackers, but their actual bite is more like a pinch—startling if you aren't expecting it, but thoroughly underwhelming given their fierce appearance. (Mind you, I've known people like that too.)

I turned slowly in a circle. There were a good thirty cabinets surrounding a large central table with books stacked upon it. I spared a sympathetic thought for Jackson's back, lugging all that furniture into place, but mostly what I felt was glee.

I spent a happy hour pulling out drawers and inspecting the contents. The collection was mostly of American insects, so I recognized many old friends (and occasionally old enemies). Beetles, weevils, dragonflies, damselflies . . . crane flies, with their legs mostly detached and scattered on the floor of the tray . . . Not all of the collection was in terribly good repair, alas, nor were the labels as thorough as one might wish. One drawer, marked simply L, held dozens of loose, translucent envelopes that slid and slithered across one another as the drawer moved. Each one contained a single dried butterfly. A few of the envelopes had scrawled writing on the outside—I recognized Halder's cramped handwriting—but the majority were blank.

Collected, and then he told himself he'd organize them later, I bet. Every naturalist I've ever known had done it at one time or another, and then discovered their memory was not so good as they thought, and they no longer had any idea under what circumstances it had been collected. The good ones learned. The other ones . . . well, possibly they papered their butterflies and shoved them in a drawer to deal with later.

Still, it wasn't my place to judge Halder's collection methods. I had a job to do. I consulted the first name on my list of illustrations. *Cochliomyia hominivorax. Now let me see, that'd be . . . err . . . something-something, dash C.*

Um.

It occurred to me that what I really, really needed was an index.

The next hour was much less happy than the first. There wasn't an index. What had initially looked like a promising stack of books turned out to be the collected periodicals of a journal called *The American Entomologist*. I flipped through and found that it was very much not the sort of publication that would (to take an example *completely* at random) tell a layperson what the metathorax was.

I sat back with a groan. Halder probably hadn't bothered to index it because he knew where everything was. He only needed the shorthand labels to make things easier. Probably one cabinet was flies and one was ants and one was beetles and . . . well, no, probably more than one had to be beetles. There are a *lot* of beetles in the world.

And honestly, that sort of loose organization would have worked fine for me, *if* I had any idea what sort of insect I was looking for in the first place. But what was a *Cochliomyia hominivorax*? Was it a beetle or a butterfly, an ant or an antlion? I had no more idea of that than of where a metathorax went.

No, if I wanted to find the damn thing, I was either going to have to ask Halder, or start pulling out drawers.

I took a deep breath, squared my shoulders, and started pulling out drawers.

Two hours later—some of which was spent finding a stepladder so that I could reach the collections at the top of the cabinets—I located *C. hominivorax* in a narrow tray labeled DC-C. I pulled out the drawer, stared into it, then closed my eyes and leaned my forehead against the cool wood of the cabinet, not sure whether to laugh or cry.

They looked *exactly* like houseflies. The only reason I knew they weren't is because houseflies are *Musca domestica*, and the only reason I knew that was because Father used to feed them to his Venus flytraps, and *every single time*, he would announce, "*Musca domestica* for your enjoyment, ladies." (Possibly this tells you something about my father.)

I sighed heavily and descended the ladder, clutching my tray of not-actually-houseflies. I set it on the table and stared at them. There were larvae in there as well, larger than the adults as often seems to happen. They were lined up neatly along the bottom, preserved in tiny glass bottles, small to large. The largest of the larvae were most of an inch long and had an odd spiral ridge that ran their entire length. It was like looking at a small, fleshy screw.

"Delightful," I muttered. Well, that was tomorrow's problem. At the moment, I had a fly to paint.

The study table included a magnifying glass. I fetched my sketchbook and my pencils and my tiny plein air watercolor palette, and set to work. After a time, I selected one specific specimen, lifted it carefully from the tray, and examined it under the magnifying glass. Except for a distinct blue tinge, it still looked like a housefly to me. I wished I had better light, but Halder had been very clear that removing specimens from the library was a sin tantamount to murder.

There is a certain intimacy to examining a study specimen. You are studying parts much more closely than the animal presumably ever did on its own. Eventually you start to assign a certain amount of personality to them. (Well, I do, anyway. Other people may not.)

Hominivorax . . . hominivorax . . . "I shall call you Rex," I told the specimen.

"Pleased to be working with you, Miss Wilson," I answered for him, in a high buzzy voice. "I look forward to a fruitful collaboration."

(Look, if you can't amuse yourself by making the specimens talk, you're in the wrong field.)

"So do I, Rex." I sketched out the arrangement of his legs. "I don't suppose you'd like to tell me what your metathorax is?"

"I'll never tell!" Rex squeaked.

"You're a cad."

"What are you gonna do, kill me and put me on a pin?"

"No, I'll—"

A cough came from the doorway. I looked up guiltily to see Mrs. Kent standing there, watching me as if I had lost my mind.

"Err," I said, hastily setting the fly down.

"I came up to see if you wanted lunch in the kitchen or if I should bring you up a tray," she said.

"Oh. Uh. I'll come down in just a minute. Let me just . . . err . . . finish up here."

She nodded, so clearly *not* commenting on my behavior that it was practically a comment on its own. The floorboards creaked as she made her way back down the hall.

"This is all your fault," I muttered to Rex, and imagined a squeaky snicker in return.

Painting Rex the fly took me nearly two days. It shouldn't have, but I was most of the way through when I stopped to compare my work to my predecessor's burying beetle, and had to start over in despair. In the end, I did not so much finish as realize that I had passed the point of diminishing returns and was now just making things worse.

This sort of thing happens a great deal in illustration, and I had been doing it long enough that I usually knew when to stop. Unfortunately, between the new position and the terrifyingly high bar set by the previous painter, I had listened too much to my own anxieties.

It's as good as it's going to be. I need to stop. If this is not the quality that he wanted, he may fire me if he wishes, but I cannot do better than this.

I was gloomily aware that I had failed to meet the standard set by my predecessor. Even if I hadn't been, a quick glance at the pages on the worktable would have shown me. My fly was competent and workmanlike, but it did not look as if it might suddenly walk off the page.

I pinched the bridge of my nose. I could not *force* myself to be a genius. If artists could do that . . . well, we would be a very different breed.

The hallway leading to Halder's office seemed twice as long, and yet I was still at the door far before I was ready. I knocked and stepped inside.

"I have a sample for you, Doctor," I said. My voice didn't shake. I was rather proud of that.

"Very well. Let's see what you have." He held out his hand and I offered him the page, my hand trembling in a way that my voice had not. Fortunately, he didn't seem to notice.

He gave Rex a cursory glance, grunted, and pulled out his own magnifying glass. I clasped my hands behind my back to keep from wringing them, digging my nails under the opposite cuffs. My fingers felt like ice against my wrists.

"Bristles on the meron," he murmured, "longitudinal stripes on the thorax . . . yes. Competently done, Miss Wilson. Maintain this standard, and we shall have no difficulties." He held the page out to me. I blinked at him, then down at the fly.

Some part of me wanted to ask if he was certain, or if he was looking at the right image. Did he not *see* how shoddy it was compared to the work of my predecessor? Couldn't he *tell* that this was merely competent?

If it had been anyone else, I would have thought that he was lying to spare my feelings. But this was Halder, who, so far as I could tell, possessed the personal warmth of a guinea worm.

"Make certain that you do not confuse the larvae with any other fly," he added, not looking up. "The screwworm is distinctive and must be illustrated with great accuracy. The mechanism of its burrowing is one central to my thesis."

I swallowed. So this was the adult form of a screwworm,

the bane of livestock throughout the region. I had not realized. "This is the variety that attacks cattle?" I asked.

"Cattle, sheep, horses, us—anything that it can lay eggs in. *Hominivorax* is not picky about its diet." He smiled crookedly. It was not a pleasant smile. "It is one of the few insects that we know of that prefers to devour the living but will feast on the dead as well. It is a delightfully efficient little beast. The female lays eggs in nostrils, eyes, and open wounds, and once the larvae hatch, they burrow as deeply as they can, seeking live flesh. You have perhaps half a day to wash the eggs away before they hatch. I have heard of newborns suffering infestations in the stump of the umbilical cord when they were not bathed properly in the first days after birth."

"Good god," I said, appalled. Rex was apparently a bloodthirsty little monster.

"Cleanliness is next to godliness, Miss Wilson, or so they say. But foulness provides rather more opportunity for scientific inquiry." His smile grew, showing teeth. "You are most privileged, Miss Wilson. Your work may contribute, in some small way, to my life's dream of the eradication of monsters that have preyed upon us for centuries. Now, was there anything else you wanted?"

"No, Doctor," I murmured, and fled, feeling my skin crawling as if there were already eggs laid upon it.

Painting the *C. hominivorax* larva was, in some ways, much easier than the adult fly. In other ways though, it was obnoxious. Alcohol from the preservation process tends to bleach everything out, so I could never be sure of getting the colors quite right. Sure, it was white and fleshy, but was it the *correct* white and fleshy?

It's possible to preserve many insect larvae by pinning them, but since you have to remove the internal organs to keep them from rotting, they tend to collapse. Then you must reinflate them, using one of a number of patented caterpillar inflaters.

It's worth it for things like caterpillars, where the color patterns are so important, but hardly anyone bothers with maggots. (I learned this, incidentally, over the course of a ten-minute lecture from Halder when I went to ask about the colors. I went back to my rooms and said, "Patented caterpillar inflater," out loud several times and laughed so hard that Sally came to check on me.)

Nevertheless, after a great deal of lifting pigment and dabbing tiny smidges of gouache, I had something that bore more than a passing resemblance to the screwworm larva. I presented it to Halder, my stomach knotting almost as badly as the first time. *This is it, this is the one, he's going to look at it and think it's just a blob and . . .*

"Acceptable," Halder said. "You need not bother with the eggs of this species." He gazed at the image thoughtfully. "Do you know why it's called a screwworm?"

"Uh . . ." I glanced at the page in his hand. "Because the spiral ridge resembles a screw?"

Halder grinned unpleasantly. "Indeed it does. As it burrows, those ridges anchor themselves in living flesh using tiny bristles. They become nearly impossible to extract. After a week, they burrow outward and fall to the ground, where they pupate into the next generation." He reached out and tapped the jar on his desk. I glanced toward it and realized that the grubs inside were now familiar. Dead screwworms. Hundreds of them.

"Ah," I said.

"Most interestingly, killing the host does not kill the screwworm. It will simply continue to eat. Few other parasites survive the death of their host in such a way."

"Fascinating," I said faintly.

"It is my great hope that if I can fully understand the life cycle of these species, it will unlock new ways to deal with them. I have already determined the optimal way to extract them from living flesh with the least damage. My monograph on the subject is even now in circulation. But to learn more, one must study them exhaustively."

He took my illustrations, rose, and locked them in the cupboard in his office. I felt a brief, nonsensical pang at seeing my work squirreled away like that. *Don't be absurd. What are you going to do, hang your art of screwworms on the wall? Show it off to Mrs. Kent?*

I made a checkmark next to C. *hominivorax* and started on the next name on the list.

Esther, my old roommate, had asked me once if I liked painting. I must have looked at her oddly, because she colored up and said, "I don't like teaching French. I *know* French, but I don't *like* it."

I told her that I loved painting, and then, out of both truth and sympathy, admitted that I didn't like teaching it very much. Esther fell back into her chair with exaggerated relief and embarked on a tirade about how people don't understand that being good at something does not mean that you have any skill at teaching it to other people. She was quite right, of course, but the question that stuck with me was the first one—did I *like* painting?

Despite what I told Esther years ago, I didn't always know the answer. Some things I loved painting. I could be on my deathbed and I would still leap up at the chance to paint a pitcher plant. The veins, the little translucent windows, the lids with their flares and ruffles . . . I found them endlessly delightful. Sometimes I even dreamed about doing a book of my own on the topic, though finding a publisher willing to risk money was the hard part.

Other things . . . well, I was good at painting, and I liked doing something I was good at. But with some subjects, it felt more like a bodily function than a grand passion. I didn't love it. I didn't hate it. It was just what I did.

The insects rapidly began to feel like that. I got up in the morning, I ate, I hunched over a tray of pinned flies, I sketched them out, I applied color. I could not have said that I was enjoying the work, but it was a great deal better than teaching had been. Occasionally I would manage a particularly fine sheen on a wing, and I would feel a certain artistic smugness. This would usually last until I glanced at my predecessor's carrion beetle paintings, which took any of my pretensions and stomped them flat. I would go down to lunch. I would present Halder with the painting. I would start the next one.

Halder seemed content with my work. I started to think that perhaps he was simply not very exacting, until I handed him a *Necrophila rufithorax* where the elytron was not sufficiently truncated—at least, that's what I think he yelled—and he flung it back at me with a curt order to do it again, correctly this time. I slunk back to the studio, feeling about three inches tall, and spent an entire day doing sketches of the sample beetles in the case, wondering what an elytron was. I thought it might be the wing case? Their wings varied a bit, as it turned out, so I simply picked one and set about duplicating it exactly. Apparently the second time, it was sufficiently truncated, because Halder grunted, "Better," and went back to his papers.

I still had no idea what a metathorax was.

My only break in the routine came on Sunday, when Mrs. Kent went to church. She told me what time we were leaving in the morning, with an obvious assumption that *of course* I was coming, so I put on my best remaining dress and was ready at the appointed hour. (Sunday service was mandatory at the school, of course. I had rarely gone to church when Father was alive. "Nature is better than any sermon," he told me frequently, "and how better to honor the Lord than admiring His creation?" This was solid transcendentalist philosophy, though the fact that it allowed him to sleep in on Sundays and then go looking for interesting plants in the afternoon was not entirely lost on me.)

It was a Black church, and Jackson and I were the only white people there, but everyone greeted me kindly. The service itself was brutally long, by my (admittedly lax) standards, but afterwards, there was an immense community meal. Two older ladies, hearing that I was working for Halder, made pained noises and urged me to sit right down next to them, poor child, how *was* I holding up?

Their sympathy was far more comforting than I expected. Mrs. Kent was one of those aggressively competent souls who make you feel less competent simply by comparison, and while Jackson was entertaining company, I only saw him at dinner and sometimes not even then. Having two people ask, with every evidence of genuine interest, how I was managing in that big empty house with that *peculiar* man—good heavens, the stories they could tell!—and nobody but Rose Kent to talk to—not a *word* against Rose, no, certainly not, but such a *serious* girl . . .

"Not that anyone wouldn't be serious," the one on the right said, "with her poor mother going the way she did."

"Lost her memory," the one on the left said to me, "the poor dear. Would get lost in her own house by the end. Of course poor Rose couldn't move her, so she was stuck there, working for that doctor. Even after his poor wife—"

Her companion slapped her on the arm with a napkin, interrupting the torrent of *poors*. "Jackson, good to see you!" she sang out.

"I see Miss Wilson has found the two loveliest ladies here," Jackson said, sitting down at the table opposite me. Both of them laughed and all three embarked on an intense discussion of the weather as it related to gardening, which was doubtless satisfying for the participants, but left me with a severe case of *gossipus interruptus*.

Even after his poor wife what? *Died? Left? Ran off to Paris to become a burlesque dancer?*

. . . Was drained by blood thieves?

Since I wasn't going to get answers, I settled on getting a second helping of pulled pork, which was almost as satisfying.

I hadn't realized that I'd been feeling lonely and a bit cast down until we left and I realized that I felt better. (It didn't hurt that I was stuffed full of incredible food.) I leaned back against the bench of the wagon and closed my eyes, soaking in the spring sunlight and thinking that I had probably made the right choice in taking this job after all.

The sunlight, alas, did not last. Rain blew up that night and continued for three days. I huddled in the studio while rain splatted against the windows and wind rattled the doors. It was not nearly as windy as Wilmington had been, so the rattling didn't bother me, although the thrashing branches on the nearby trees rather did. Jackson assured me that this "warn't nothin'" and then regaled me with tales of past storms that had brought down massive oaks and how he had personally had to chop apart a tree with a trunk "near as tall as Sally here."

Sally giggled. Jackson mimed swinging an axe. "Took two days," he said proudly. "Had to cut it in two places and then hitch up Buckshot and roll the damn thing out of the way."

"And spent four days afterward laying around moaning 'cause you couldn't lift your arms over your head," said Mrs. Kent tartly, sliding hotcakes onto her husband's plate. "Don't think I've forgotten that bit."

Jackson blew her a kiss and grinned, unrepentant. I felt a stab of envy for them both. It would be nice to have someone else who was always on my side. My father had been, of course, but years alone had only softened the edges of that pain, not erased it. I lingered in the kitchen, running my finger around the edge of my coffee mug, reluctant to leave that oasis of light and warmth for the cold, watery light of the studio.

Jackson pushed back from the table, then paused. "Oh, Miss

Wilson. I'll be going into town once I can ride instead of swim, and if there's aught you need me to pick up for you at the general store, just let me know."

"I would love that," I said, "but I'm afraid I . . . err . . ." I lifted my hands helplessly. I didn't have enough money for more than penny candy, and probably not much of that.

"Which reminds me," said Mrs. Kent, wiping her hands on her apron. "It's the end of the month tomorrow, and you're due your pay."

"I am?" I said, heard the questioning note in my voice, and tried again. "I mean, I am, yes." Jackson chuckled at that, but his wife gave him a quelling look.

"You are, and don't think I'll let that tightfist upstairs forget it," she said. "Jackson takes the wage money out of the bank when he's there, so if there's something you want, he'll bring you the change."

"Without so much as a broker's fee," he promised.

"I would *love* enough fabric for a new dress," I said, with real longing. "It doesn't have to be fancy, but just so I'm not wearing the same two all the time."

"Pfff," said Mrs. Kent. "Is that all? If you don't mind dressing like Sally and me, there's still uniforms in storage from the days when we had a full staff here." She eyed me. "You can probably alter one or two to fit you, if you're decent with a needle, and if not, I know a lady who can do it for a fair price."

"I can do it."

"Then find me when I'm finished here, and I'll take you to see what we've got."

An hour later, Mrs. Kent led me to a back corner of the house, lighting candles as we went. It was clear that this was not regularly visited. The air smelled of floor wax. We stepped into a storeroom which, while neatly kept, was clearly where household goods went to die. There were neat rows of storm windows lining one wall and folded stacks of furniture covers, but there were also chairs that needed the seats re-caned, spare tin ceiling tiles, and enough chamber pots to accommodate a small weak-bladdered army.

Mrs. Kent threaded her way through these piles to a closet with double doors. The smell of mothballs rolled out, and she lifted a candle, revealing long shelves covered in fabric.

"Good heavens," I said blankly, staring at the rows of folded dresses and aprons. "You could dress every girl back at the school twice over."

"Supposed to be a dozen servants here," said Mrs. Kent, "just for the house itself." She leaned against the doorjamb. "That's why the whole place is in dustcovers. Can't keep it up, just with me and Sally. It's all we can do just to air everything and make sure it doesn't go to mold and mildew."

I shook my head. "It's such a big house. Why aren't there more people?"

Mrs. Kent snorted. "The doctor hasn't got that many friends, nor family either."

"Yet he built this place . . ." I glanced over my shoulder, down the hall, at all the closed doors. Behind them, furniture slept under sheets and wallpaper faded quietly in the sun. "I wonder why?"

"It wasn't *his* money that built it," Mrs. Kent muttered, then snapped her mouth closed as if she regretted saying so much. "Anyway, pick out anything close to your size and leave it outside your door. I'll see that it's washed and ready for altering." She turned away, her heels clicking on the boards, before I could ask whose money *had* built the house, and where exactly that money had come from.

"Jackson?"

Rain had given way at last to a clear, pleasant morning, and I tracked Mr. Kent down in the vegetable garden just outside the formal grounds. He looked up from where he was staking up tomato plants that had flopped over in the rain. "Hey there, Miss Wilson. Thought of what you need from town? I'll be going this afternoon."

"Indeed." I proffered a short list.

". . . Ah," he said, making no move to take it. "Should have warned you, miss. I'm not much good with my letters."

"Oh!" I put a hand over my mouth, embarrassed. "I'm sorry!"

He chuckled. "No, no, no need to fash yourself. My letters are bad but my memory's top-notch. Just you tell me what you want and I'll go looking."

"Socks," I said with a sigh. "I cannot knit socks to save my life. Tooth powder. And . . . er . . ." I scuffed one foot in the rich earth just off the garden path. A small green weed had poked its head up, and was promptly flattened, although it looked like plantain, and nothing keeps plantain down for long. "If they happen to have some penny candy . . ."

"Miss Wilson, I am *shocked*." He put his hands on his hips. "Are you telling me that our fine young scientist has a sweet tooth?"

"Not at all. I'm . . . err . . . conducting an experiment. On the effects of candy on mood." I caught the edge of his grin. "It's a *very* long-running experiment." Back in Wilmington, there had been a fine candy shop two streets over, and it was a rare week that I didn't acquire at least one peppermint stick. In all other respects, I was eating infinitely better now than I had been, but I did miss the occasional taste.

"Happy to oblige," he said cheerfully. "Socks, tooth powder, penny candy. Anything else?"

I considered. This was the first time I'd spoken to Jackson without his wife present, after all. "Actually, I had a question. I think the first night I was here, you said something about there not being anything scary in the woods *anymore*. What did you mean by that?"

"Ahhh." Jackson pursed his lips. "Old gossip, mostly. You sure you want to hear about it?"

Under his reluctance, a born storyteller was clearly dying to hold forth. I leaned against the garden gate. "Absolutely. I don't know these woods all that well, and anything you can tell me . . ." I trailed off, leaving a hopefully inviting silence.

He did not so much fill the gap as leap into it with both feet. "First thing you should know—my grandma, she was from the old country. Knew all the *real* old stories. At least, she said they were old stories, and nobody argued with Gran."

I raised my eyebrows, wondering what this had to do with inhabitants of the local woods. "They must have been fascinating," I said politely.

"Oh, aye, they were. But they weren't about ghosties and goblins and little people, if that's what you're thinking." He grinned. "She knew plenty of those too, but so did everybody else. You can't throw a rock out Asheville way without hitting an oldster who wants to tell you about leaving milk out for the other crowd. No, Gran told other stories. Like about Slith the thief and what happened to him, and the house where they hang two criminals from hooks and every now and then they come and take one down, when they find somebody who's done something even worse, and they put that one up on the hooks instead. Or the village where they take turns bleeding people to feed the old women during a famine, so that the Mother of Winter won't take one over."

I must have looked aghast at this, because Jackson lifted a hand and laughed self-consciously. "You see what I mean? They used to give me nightmares, some of 'em, but Gran said that just showed I was sensible. My mam didn't see it quite the same way, always tried to stop me from listening, so of course I snuck off every chance I got to listen, didn't I?"

This, at least, struck me as entirely logical, even if I didn't see how it related to whatever had gone on in the woods. "I certainly would have."

"There, you see? Girl after my own heart. Thing is . . ." He glanced toward the house, as if expecting his wife to appear and scold him. Not seeing her, he pulled a cigarette out from behind his ear and lit it. "Well, maybe ten years back, some bad stuff started happening. Felt like it came straight out of one of Gran's stories. The war'd been over a few years by then, and Rose and I had just moved back here to take care of her mam. Animals started turning up dead, all cut up strange, and then every now and then a person'd turn up that way too. They thought it was some kind of animal, maybe a cougar, but it sure wasn't like any cougar I ever heard of."

"Cut up strange *how*?" I asked.

He spread his hands helplessly. "Looked like somebody took a sharp knife and went to work. You'd find 'em up in a tree, head down, like somebody was draining 'em out. Cougar will drag things up into a tree sometimes, and they like a throat bite, so okay, not the worst suggestion. 'Cept I never heard tell of a cougar that hamstrung its dinner first. And they definitely don't bite out both wrists and then the neck too."

"Good god!"

"Yeah. People were spooked." Jackson gestured with the cigarette, the red ember tracing a line through the air. "Lotsa bad blood got riled up. Some people thought it was the Klan, but it wasn't showy enough for them, you ask me."

"So what was it?" I asked, ignoring the whisper in my head saying: *Blood thieves, Sally told you, they drain your blood away . . .*

Jackson shrugged. "Never found out. You ask me, it was something smart though. It'd get real bad for a little while and people would get themselves all worked up in a frenzy, then it'd ease off, like maybe whatever was doing it had gone off somewhere else. So everybody would start to relax a little and then a season or two later, dead animals would start turning up again. Kept happening over and over. Not just like dogs or pigs either, but wild stuff. You'd come across deer or even possums like that, except most of the time you couldn't be sure because the vultures would get to 'em first, and after that, ain't nobody gonna be able to tell how they died. Some people started to wonder if maybe there wasn't a lot more of it happening than we knew about."

I considered this. That certainly didn't *sound* like a cougar, granted, but then again, people are notorious for thinking that wild animal bites are actually knife wounds, and a lot of them don't understand that when, say, a fox kills a rabbit, there's rarely much blood. It was entirely possible that there'd been one or two real attacks and then a whole string of panicky encounters with perfectly normal carcasses.

"Anyhow." Jackson flicked the cigarette away. "It made me think of Gran's stories. Lot of 'em were about blood. People who maybe weren't all the way human, who fed on blood. They used to say that if you ate a wolf's brain, you'd get the ability to change your skin for his, but you'd have a hunger on you ever after. And even around here, there were stories about dead people coming back for the people they loved, and drinking them dry so they kept coming back."

My expression must have been obviously skeptical, because Jackson snorted. "I know, it sounds like a lot of hogwash. The missus gets mad if I bring it up. But I saw some of those bodies and I don't mind telling you, there was something very strange going on there."

"Oh?" I asked, trying to keep the disbelief out of my voice.

"Indeed there was. The deer were funny enough, but there was an old woman named Martha Glint. Nasty piece of work, and I can't say I was terrible broken up. Never forgave any Black soul for bein' freed, and the stories about what she did to people before the war would turn your stomach. Found her myself, halfway up a tree, white as a sheet, with her throat tore out and one wrist bit near through. And hardly any blood on the ground under her either."

I winced at the image. "Still," I said, after a moment, "she could have bled out somewhere else and been dragged there. And cougars do stash their prey in trees sometimes."

"Funny sort of cougar that unbuttons a lady's collar and folds back the cuffs on her sleeves though."

I stared at him, silenced.

"Oh, aye," Jackson said. "There was a bit of a fracas not long after that. Coupla men—that Phelps fellow was one of 'em—found two people living rough in the woods out Bynum way. White kids, barely outta their teens I'd guess, but real strange-like, they said. Real bad. Caught 'em in the middle of draining out a deer, and from what I hear, it wasn't the meat they were after."

I saw the Devil in these woods, Miss Wilson . . .

"They strung 'em up, but that wasn't enough. They put stakes in 'em like they used to do in the old days when they dug up a coffin and found somebody in it looking a little too pink-cheeked and rosy. Then they buried 'em deep. And after that, bodies stopped turning up, so seemed like maybe they got the people responsible."

"You don't sound so sure about that," I said.

Jackson dusted off his hands and lifted the latch on the gate. "I don't know to say otherwise. I didn't see what those men saw. For all I know, that couple was sittin' on top of a barrel of blood and pickin' their teeth with the bones. All I know is that afterward, Phelps took to the Bible like some men take to the bottle."

There was a "but" hanging in the air so obviously that it might as well have been written in letters of fire. I obliged. "But?"

"Seems to me that something smart enough to lay low for a season or two when things got too hot might be smart enough to move on completely in a case like that." Jackson grinned like a fox, all sharp teeth and faded red hair. "Anyhow, that was 'bout three years ago. Wouldn't fret yourself now. Much."

I recognized the grin as that of a storyteller who knows that he's succeeded in filling his audience with nameless dread. I scowled at him, which only made the grin spread wider. "Time to head into town," he said. "Socks, tooth powder, penny candy. Right?"

"Right." I followed him out of the garden, mind still churning with stories of blood and predators that could unbutton a collar. But I wasn't superstitious, and I certainly didn't believe in blood thieves. The fact that Sally's mother still thought they might be about didn't prove anything. "It's a shame that there wasn't a naturalist around to get to the bottom of it," I murmured.

Jackson shut the gate and turned back to me. "Oh, but there was," he said. "Wasn't just Phelps who was in at the death. Dr. Halder was there too."

CHAPTER 5

The clear weather seemed to be sticking around and I seized the opportunity to work on the balcony. It was a beautiful workspace. Seated at the table, all I could see were tree branches and a sea of leaves, which rustled and sighed and shifted like women rearranging green petticoats. The overhanging roof kept direct sun at bay for most of the day but it was bright and open and airy.

Sadly, the improved light made me stare at my current illustration—*Nicrophorus marginatus*, the margined burying beetle—and realize that all the colors were much too bright, the shell was more blue than black, and that I was an utter fraud at all forms of artistic endeavor. (This is a normal part of the illustrator's process, but sadly, knowing that does not always help.) Only great discipline and the knowledge that Halder probably wouldn't notice kept me from wadding the painting into a ball and flinging it into the woods.

I got out my sketchbook and studied my notes, returned to the library to study the beetle, went back to the balcony, looked at my sketchbook, looked at my paints, and wondered if it was too late to run away to join the circus.

It wasn't just the paint. I couldn't stop thinking about Halder and blood thieves in the woods. Or the Devil, if Phelps was to be believed. I told myself fiercely to concentrate on the task at hand. *Margined burying beetles. Focus on margined burying beetles.*

The beetles didn't put a stake through whatever they were

burying. *A stake! Jesus, Mary, and Joseph, you'd think this was the 1600s. And Halder* let *them?*

I wanted desperately to ask him about it, but I couldn't figure out how to bring it up. If I just asked him outright, he'd know that Jackson or Sally had told me. Would he be angry? Could it rebound on them somehow? I had no idea, but Halder hadn't exactly impressed me as a bastion of good cheer. If it was something he was ashamed of (and how could he not be ashamed? Letting superstition run rampant like that—staking the bodies, for god's sake) he might take it out on his employees. We were so isolated here, I didn't dare risk jeopardizing the only friendly faces I saw regularly.

At that moment, as I slumped despairingly against the worktable, an insect landed on my left wrist.

For a moment I thought it was a giant bee. It was at least an inch long, black with rusty yellow patches. I froze, not wanting to prompt it into a sting. But as it turned, I saw the enormous compound eyes and realized that it was, in fact, a fly.

"Now you're an odd beast," I murmured. What was it? I was vaguely familiar with giant robber flies, which look similar, but it didn't seem quite the same. *Halder would probably be able to tell me, if I can catch it. But will he be annoyed or happy to be asked?*

I suspected that Halder would be only too glad to display his expertise, but of course, I had to catch the creature first. I had been cleaning my brushes in a jar of water on the table. I reached for it very slowly, not wanting to startle the insect, and emptied it as quietly as possible, trying not to move my wrist.

The fly rubbed its front legs together thoughtfully. Its yellow patches were as fuzzy as any bumblebee, shading to a deep red at the back of the head. Its abdomen was glossy black, and I still didn't know where its metathorax was, or if it even possessed one. As I slowly lifted the jar, it pressed its abdomen against my wrist several times, as if dancing.

I slapped the jar down, mouth over the fly, and crowed with triumph. "Got you!"

The fly jumped up, buzzing against the glass, then dropped back down. It was only a moment's work to ease my hand out and slide my sketchbook underneath, though I was surprised by how strongly it flailed against the glass.

I might be an utter failure as an illustrator, but by god, I was sneakier than a large fly. I took my captive into the house and made my way to Halder's study.

"Hmph," said Dr. Halder, peering through his glasses at my captive. "Oh, a *Cuterebra*. Botfly. Also called 'wolf worms.' Parasitic on mammals."

"Parasitic?" I asked, looking dubiously at the fly through the glass.

"Oh yes." He grinned unpleasantly. "Nasty fellows, botflies. They lay their eggs in burrows—the ones that don't lay eggs on their hosts directly—and then the larva hatches out, waits for a host to walk by, latches on, and climbs inside. Mouth, nose, anus, open wound, they don't discriminate. Once inside, they wander until they find a spot just beneath the skin and begin to feed on the host's fluids. Proper little monsters, they are."

I stared down at my wrist in sudden horror. Had it been laying eggs on me? Were tiny maggots even now making their way across my skin?

"Deer botflies, now, they don't even wait for the animal to pass by—the female ejects her larvae directly into the nasal passages of the victim, where they form clusters at the base of the tongue. This, however, is likely *Cuterebra emasculator.*" Halder tapped the glass. "Forms enormous warbles on the sides of squirrels that hang there like grapes, each one with a single large maggot inside. Then one day the larva squirms loose and turns into a fly, who goes off looking for a mate, lays eggs, and then *her* larvae find a victim for their appetites."

"Blood thieves . . ." I murmured, half to myself.

Halder pushed his glasses up, giving me an odd look. "Not blood," he said. "They feed primarily on the lymphatic fluids."

I have a very strong stomach—all scientific illustrators must, I think, as we work so often from study skins and preserved specimens that reek of formaldehyde—but the description of warbles hanging like grapes from a squirrel, and the thought that I might wind up with one actually *on me* . . . My mouth flooded with bile. "Excuse me," I said in a strangled voice, and lunged for the basin in the corner, scrubbing frantically at my wrist where the fly had touched me.

Halder laughed. It was the first time I think I'd heard him laugh, high and braying, like a soprano donkey. I hated him for it, but I didn't stop scrubbing. It was a small comfort when his laugh turned into a coughing fit. *I hope it carries you off, you miserable old sod.*

No, I don't, I need this job. Damnation.

"You needn't worry," he said, once he'd recovered, and I'd scoured both arms from fingertip to the elbow. "This species don't usually latch onto humans."

"It's the *usually* part that worries me," I snapped.

Halder snorted. "Now, *Cuterebra emasculator*, as it happens, is a particularly fine example of human idiocy. Described in the middle of the century by that overrated hack Asa Fitch. 'The country's first professional entomologist,' they call him. They'd have been better served by amateurs!" His fist thumped down on the table, making the papers on it and the jar with the fly both jump. "The fool named it 'emasculator' because he said the maggots chewed the squirrel's testicles off. They do no such thing, as he could easily have seen if he'd taken five minutes to catch a male squirrel with a warble on it! And yet those fools at the Megatherium Club still hold Fitch up as the greatest man since Thomas Say!" He thumped the table again.

"I know of Say, of course," I said cautiously, "but I cannot say I have ever heard of Asa Fitch." (This was true, although I admit that I mostly knew about Thomas Say, famed naturalist, because one of my father's friends had named his bull snake Tommy in the man's honor. I decided not to mention that to Halder.)

The doctor harrumphed, but seemed mollified. He gazed back down at the fly in the jar, which seemed to cheer him. "You might illustrate the *Cuterebra* next," he suggested. "Since you have such a fine specimen to work with."

My skin crawled at the thought, but what could I do? "I'll do that," I said grimly.

Halder's grin spread on either side of his weevil-like nose. "There's a stack of killing jars in the library."

I nodded, collected my specimen, and fled the room.

The botfly bumped against the glass. I glared at it. "All right, then," I told it. "I suppose it's you and me now. Let's get this over with . . ."

Ironically, the next wild creature to alarm me was a member of my own taxonomic class, *Mammalia*. I was hunched over a sheet of watercolor paper, trying to add fractional amounts of deep red into the botfly's fur, when I heard a scuffle of bark from the nearby trees.

I glanced up, expecting to see one of the countless gray squirrels that made their homes overhead, and instead found myself gazing into the masked face of a raccoon.

I started back, then hastily set the brush down before I could splash Tuscan red across a nearly finished illustration that had cost me so much labor. "Well, hello," I said, amused. "What are you doing out so early?"

The raccoon stared back at me, clinging to the trunk of a sweet gum tree. Leaves cast a shifting shadow across its mask. I could not quite make out its eyes.

Slowly, as we studied each other, my amusement began to lessen. I'd encountered any number of raccoons before, of course. You can hardly wander the woods on the East Coast without meeting a few, and they love nothing more than to get into trash and make a dreadful mess. I had no fear of them, but a healthy respect. Despite their adorable looks, they have a savage bite if they feel threatened. Most of the time though, they'll go out of their way to avoid conflict. (Well, unless you're a chicken. They adore conflict with chickens, and the chickens rarely come off well.)

Something about this one looked . . . off.

Its fur lay in stiff clumps along its sides and chest. I would have guessed that it had been in the water recently, but it looked greasy rather than wet. Was it sick?

Rabies? While you do sometimes see raccoons out in the daytime, an unhealthy animal out during the day set off alarm bells. There was no way that it could make the jump from the sweet gum to the balcony, but I eased myself to the edge of my chair anyway, ready to dodge back if it made any threatening moves.

It didn't. In fact, it didn't move at all. It just clung to the tree and stared at me.

At least it looked like it was staring. I couldn't see the shine of its eyes, so for all I knew, it was taking a nap in my direction.

Or maybe it doesn't have eyes. Maybe they're gone. Or maybe it never had any and it's just got blank fur growing over the sockets . . .

That was not a thought that I enjoyed having. I could see it all too clearly, a skull like one of the ones in the studio, but with smooth bone where the orbits should be.

Stop that.

I wasn't usually this fanciful. It was probably just left over from dealing with Halder and the dreadful botfly, and from hearing Jackson's stories about bloodless bodies in the woods and God knew what else. It was ridiculous, scaring myself with things like that when rabies was scary enough already. I *knew* it was ridiculous. Rabies drove you foaming mad until you died in agony.

I wouldn't be able to see foam at this distance. All I could make out was a pale blob on one side of its face, which might have been a scar or a patch of sunlight or a piece of bark stuck to its fur.

I was *almost* certain it couldn't make the jump from the tree to the balcony.

"Right," I said. "I'm just . . . going inside for a moment." (Yes, it was very silly. I knew that even at the time. The raccoon certainly wasn't going to be impressed with my bravado. It was purely childhood logic at work: as long as I didn't run, it wouldn't be able to chase me.)

I stood up, nonchalantly gathered up my paints, balanced the half-finished fly atop them, and retreated at a decorous pace into the studio. When I closed the door, I could see the raccoon still facing in my direction. It hadn't moved at all and I still couldn't make out its eyes.

The next morning, when I came down to breakfast, there was a stranger at the table. She had the round, slightly jowly face that can be any age between forty and seventy, and I couldn't tell what race she was. Generally around here that means people assume you're Black, but I found myself reluctant to make that assumption either.

"Hezekiah Kersey," she said, waving the edge of a shawl at me. She was bundled up in shawls as if it were January instead of the first week of May. The shawls were all bright colors, red and green and purple, so she glowed like an orchid in the dimness of the kitchen. I would have to use color straight out of the tube to paint the fabric, and layer the shadows carefully so as not to dim their richness. "But you can call me Ma Kersey. Ev'rybody else does, whether I birthed 'em or not." She aimed a swat in Jackson's general direction as she said it, which he ducked, laughing.

"You're not old enough to have birthed me, Ma."

"Flatterer." She had two gold teeth that showed when she smiled.

"Sonia Wilson." I extended a hand and she took it. Her grip was solid but brief, not trying to prove anything, maybe not thinking that anything needed proving.

"I hear you've come to draw up more pictures for the doctor's book."

I didn't bother to ask where she'd heard that. Plenty of people gossip, but a certain sort of person can snatch gossip right out of the air, like a flycatcher bird grabbing an insect on the wing, and neither the gossip nor the insect knows what hit it. "I am. Lots of paintings of flies at the moment." I tried to sound rueful and amused, even though I was still feeling a little unsettled from the *Cuterebra* yesterday. It had taken a very long time to finally die, and no matter how much I told myself that some of the ether in the killing jar must have evaporated, I didn't quite believe it.

"Mmm." She leaned back in her nest of shawls and studied me with dark, sharp eyes.

Mrs. Kent slid a poached egg *and* hotcakes *and* bacon onto Ma Kersey's plate, *and* there was real maple syrup on the table. Mrs. Kent clearly thought highly of this guest. I used the syrup very sparingly, aware that I did not rank nearly so high, but the taste was like winter sunlight on my tongue.

"You cook just as good as your mama did," Ma Kersey told Mrs. Kent, who ducked her head, looking both pleased and slightly annoyed, as if she didn't want that to mean something. I ran the last bite of hotcake around my plate, trying to mop up any remaining molecules of syrup.

Ma Kersey leaned back in her chair with her coffee cup balanced atop her belly. I thought she was a big woman, but it was hard to tell under all the shawls. She caught my eye and grinned, gold teeth flashing. "Lumbee," she said.

"Pardon?"

"I'm Lumbee. You had that look on you, trying to figure out who my people are. There's your answer. Came from over Robeson way, followed a fellow here." She took a sip of her coffee and added meditatively, "He's dead."

"I'm sorry," I said automatically.

"That makes one of us. Sweet as sugar for six months and mean as a snake for the next six years." She held out her coffee cup into the air next to her with the absolute certainty that someone would fill it. Jackson hurried to do so. "But you," Ma Kersey said, "you're from out by Wilmington, I hear."

Again, I didn't bother wondering where she'd heard it. "That's right."

"Like it out here, do you?" Her eyes bored into me like surgical instruments, pulling out bits and holding them up to the light. "Or are you missing home?"

I had a distinct impression that there was a right and a wrong answer to this question, without knowing what they were. *Who is this woman?* I sipped my own coffee to buy some time while I formulated an answer. "I'm missing it less than I expected. I traveled a lot when my father was alive, so I'm used to being in new places." That didn't sound enthusiastic enough, so I added, "It's so incredibly green here. It feels so alive."

"That it is," said Ma Kersey, "that it is. Alive and all of a piece. You shoot a rabbit on one side of the county and the grass on the other side knows about it by nightfall."

Completely unscientific, but something about the way she said it gave me pause. *Alive and all of a piece. Huh.* But it was the mention of rabbits that really caught me. "That reminds me of something I've been meaning to ask . . ." I said.

Ma Kersey raised her eyebrows. "Well, go on, child, ask away."

"When I came in on the train, there was a sign saying 'Home of the World-Famous Chatham Rabbit.' Why are the rabbits here world-famous?"

"Ha!" Ma Kersey slapped a shawl-covered knee. "You haven't made your rabbit pie for the girl yet, Rose?"

Mrs. Kent pulled a face. "No, 'cause the boy who usually sells 'em to me started selling 'em in town instead. I pay more money, but I only want two or three, not thirty. They pot 'em up and ship 'em on to Raleigh now."

Ma Kersey nudged Jackson. "And what're you doing, young man, letting your wife's larder sit empty?"

"Fixing up the fences to keep the rabbits *out*," Jackson said plaintively. "Doesn't do much good to catch 'em *after* they've eaten all the veggies up first."

The old woman gave Jackson a stern look, though I could see the edge of a gold tooth showing as she did. Jackson hung his head. "Yes ma'am," he said. "I'll go catch some rabbits directly."

"Good man." Ma Kersey nodded and turned back to me. "Got a *lot* of rabbits out here," she said. "Used to eat it four, five meals a week sometimes. Big ones too. After the war, a lot of fields stood empty, and there's nothing a rabbit loves more. Out in Raleigh they say the best rabbit comes from Chatham County. With the railroad come through, I hear they even ship 'em clear up to New York!" She shook her head. "Suppose if you're in the city, it seems fancy."

Mrs. Kent moved to refill her coffee, but Ma Kersey put her hand over the cup. "Nah, time I was moving on. Just came by to drop off that stuff and get a look at the new girl." She looked me up and down again. I was suddenly glad that I was wearing one of the dresses that I'd altered, even if the fabric was a good decade old.

"It was a pleasure to meet you, Ma Kersey," I said, rising when she did.

"Likewise, I'm sure." Despite the twinkle in her eyes, I suspected that she hadn't made up her mind about me. That was a trifle worrying. Women like Hezekiah Kersey are good to have on your side. The alternative doesn't bear thinking about. *Oh god, what if she tells everyone I'm a snob and turns people I haven't even met yet against me?*

I stamped down my anxiety. "I hope I'll see you again," I said, which was the truth.

"Oh, I'm sure you will." She swatted at Jackson again, then took his arm and let him escort her out of the kitchen. I waited until I heard the door close before glancing back to Mrs. Kent.

"Whew." The housekeeper leaned against the wall, dabbing at her forehead with her apron. She caught my look and said, "Don't let her scare you, now. That was by way of a courtesy call. She mostly came so she can tell everybody that I didn't forget how to cook."

And you were scared that she might think otherwise, I thought, though I wasn't fool enough to say it out loud. "She's a bit . . . intimidating."

"Lord, you can say that again. And the biggest gossip in the county. Knows everybody's business practically before they do. But I tell you this, what she doesn't know about doctoring and delivering babies ain't hardly worth knowing." Mrs. Kent plucked the syrup from the table and tucked it into a cupboard.

I went back to the studio in a thoughtful frame of mind. *All of a piece . . . hmm.* I thought of the story Jackson had told me about those bodies found in the woods, strung up and drained of their blood, and wondered what exactly Ma Kersey might have been able to add to it.

"Doctor?"

"Eh?" Halder looked up from his work, clearly annoyed at being disturbed. "What do you want?"

I left the door ajar behind me, feeling the need for an escape route. "I'm afraid I've run into a problem with the *Cuterebra* illustrations."

The corners of the doctor's mouth drew down. "What problem?"

"It's *Cuterebra approximata*."

"The deer mouse botfly," said Halder. "What about it?"

"I can't find a specimen in the library."

"*What?!*" He rose halfway to his feet and I took a step back, startled. "What do you mean, you can't find it? It's in there! Are you blind?"

I swallowed, my mouth dry. I had gone through every drawer that ended in -C, hunting for it, but had found nothing, not even an unlabeled specimen that looked vaguely like a botfly. "It is not in with the rest of the *Cuterebras*," I said, in as neutral a voice as I could manage.

"Of course it is," he snapped, pushing back from his desk. He brushed past me, moving more quickly than I had ever seen him move, and stormed toward the library.

I had placed the tray of botflies on the table. Halder went to it and looked down, breathing hard. Surely the walk could not have exhausted him so much? Was he so angry?

This is it, this is where he fires you, you should have checked again, he'll point right at it . . .

But he did not. Instead he stared down at the case, his fingertips moving over the glass. "Oh," he said, in a much different voice. If it had been anyone but Halder, I'd have said he sounded sheepish. "Damn it all. The carpet beetles got that one."

I winced. Entomology may not be my strong suit, but every naturalist has heard of carpet beetles. They will happily devour clothes and bedding, but they positively *adore* taxidermy. One of my father's rivals had lost half his collection to them. "He didn't deserve that," Father had said, even though he loathed the man in a cordial academic fashion. "Nobody deserves that."

I could only imagine the havoc the beetles might wreak in a collection such as this one. I winced. "You had carpet beetles?"

"About a year ago," he said, almost absently. "Normally I'd have caught it earlier, but I had other things on my mind." He shook himself. "Base the illustration on the life studies, then."

"Errr . . ." I swallowed again, worry giving way to confusion. "I haven't done any life studies of *approximata*, Doctor."

He swung around and stared at me. His eyes seemed oddly cloudy behind the enormous lenses. "No," he said slowly. "No, what am I thinking? Not *you*." His gaze sharpened. "Wait here," he snapped, and stumped out of the room again.

I waited, baffled, beside the case of botflies. Like the one that I had caught, they were all thick-bodied, fuzzy creatures, looking halfway between a fly and a bumblebee. Deceptively fluffy and innocent for something that would burrow under your skin and drink your vital fluids. Some had deep red eyes, others black. I had used colored pencil to get a properly grainy look on the compound eyes. Most likely that detail would not come out in the actual plates made from my illustrations, but that was beyond my control.

Halder returned with another folio, much thicker than the one he had shown me before. He thrust it at me, and I took it, startled. "In there," he said, sounding irritable. "There's sketches of it. Draw from those."

"Yes, Doctor."

He stared at me broodingly. I wondered if he was actually seeing me, or if his mind was still on the carpet beetles that had devoured his specimens. Then he sniffed, turned on his heel, and stalked away.

I spread the contents of the folio out on the table. They were sketches, bound together with loops of string punched through one side. As I had already guessed, they belonged to my predecessor.

Insects marched and flew across the pages in an endless

parade, notes written in the margins in a small, feminine hand. Perhaps forty pages in all, the sketches ranging from quick gesture drawings to extremely detailed studies. I found the original sketches for the carrion beetle that had so impressed me, and a dozen more besides, for illustrations either never completed or that I had not seen.

Will you think less of me if I say that I was oddly relieved? The sketches were very good, but they did not have the almost supernatural quality that her paintings did. I could look at these drawings beside my own and not feel like an imposter.

The greatest gift, however, was not this boost to my confidence, nor even the studies for the deer mouse botfly, which I found near the end of the folio.

No, it was a hasty sketch of a bee, with a line pointing to a segment labeled "metathorax." The *backmost* section of the thorax.

If the artist had been in front of me, I would have thrown my arms around her, kissed her cheeks, and called her sister. As it was, I slumped against the table, feeling wrung out with sudden relief. "Thank you," I said to my absent predecessor. "Thank you, thank you, *thank you*."

The light was starting to fade. I returned the botflies to their drawer, took the sketches, and went to back to the studio. I felt the previous resident's presence in the room, as always, but this time, thinking of metathoraxes, I didn't mind at all.

CHAPTER 6

Another Sunday came and went, with food and sympathy and a sermon that lasted nearly two hours. "Young preachers," muttered the woman in the pew behind me. "Swear they forget that some of us got to pee on the regular." Out of the corner of my eye, I saw Mrs. Kent's lips start twitching at that. The food continued to be extraordinary and I continued to be pathetically grateful to talk to people that I didn't see every single day.

That afternoon, I decided that I would go absolutely mad if I went back to work on the latest insect and went out in the garden again to sketch flowers. I could actually feel my jaw unclenching as I worked. *I should do this more often.*

"Why plants?" Esther, my roommate at the schoolhouse, had asked me once. "Why not something interesting?"

"Plants are interesting," I said defensively. "They have evolved many fascinating mechanisms for—"

"Why not *people*?" she clarified. "You're good enough that you could paint people and they'd pay money for it. Or, I don't know, horses or dogs or something like that. Things people *buy*."

"People buy pictures of plants."

"People buy pictures of *flowers*," Esther pointed out with ruthless accuracy. "Roses and peonies and whatnot. You're painting *weeds*."

At the time I had been doing a watercolor sketch of the crumpled leaves of a broadleaf plantain, which is indeed a weed. Its flower spike is greenish-purple and you have to look closely to even see the flowers themselves. "I like plants," I said, knowing that she was right and that it would have been sensible to paint some peonies and see if I could sell them on my day off. "For one thing, they stand still while you're working, unlike *some* people." Which sent her off in a peal of laughter, because of course she was a terrible model, endlessly fidgeting, and my attempts to sketch her would end up with five different lines of mouth and ten different sets of arms.

"Fine, fine. You win. Enjoy your weeds."

What I didn't tell her, then or ever, was that plants were easy because they didn't have to like you. People have to like you if you're going to paint them. Animals, despite all the claptrap about the unconditional love of pets, have to like you. You have to move right and act right and have the right expressions or else they get skittish and start eyeing you as if you're plotting something nefarious.

Plants don't care about any of that. You can show up in a plant's life for two hours and then go away and the plant goes on about its business without any change. You can't say the wrong thing to a plant or startle it by sitting still for an hour and then moving suddenly.

And they *are* fascinating. Not just things like my Father's Venus flytraps, which even Esther could appreciate, but the little low plants that hardly anyone cares about. When hairy bitter cress goes to seed, if you touch it, the seeds explode in all directions as if propelled by tiny springs. The maroon bells of pawpaw stink of carrion to attract flies that normally feed on rotten meat. (Halder probably knew all those flies by name.) Some people hang chicken bones from the pawpaw branches to attract more flies and get more fruit, so in spring the trees look like grisly wind chimes.

Unfortunately, it was hard to get a publisher to bite on a book of illustrations of things like that. Nice ladies don't write odes to flowers that smell like rotting flesh. Esther was right, I'd probably have better luck with a book of peonies, or of different types of roses. Something that people could cut out and frame and hang on the wall. It was just that other people had already done that, so there was no reason for a publisher to take a chance on me. I had to find a different angle, and the angles available to respectable single women without a patron were extremely limited.

Still, if I did enough illustrations of various flowers, maybe I could figure something out. And here I had access to some marvelous materials, and if I used the paper and paints meant for the insects to draw some plants . . . well, surely Halder was unlikely to notice or care.

Two days later, I found something that Halder cared a great deal about, purely by accident.

I had been drawing blowfly maggots, which was exactly as thrilling as it sounds. They were mildly disgusting, but mostly they were dull. I couldn't even muster the enthusiasm to give them names and do voices for them. When I found that I was missing a maggot specimen, I consulted my predecessor's notes, then stared at the ceiling for a few minutes, thinking, *Somehow my life has led me to this point.* Then I pushed back from the table and went to ask Halder for direction.

"Eh?" His eyes sharpened on me. "What did you say?"

"The first instar of *Calliphora vicina*," I repeated patiently. "Either it's mislabeled or it's identical to *C. vomitoria*, but since the notes say that they're two different—"

Halder's fist slammed down on the desk. *"How do you know what my notes say?!"* he bellowed. Mottled red suffused his face, and for a moment I was afraid he was having an apoplectic fit.

I lurched back in my chair, astonished. "I . . . but . . ."

It's just a maggot! I wanted to yell. *Why are you this upset over one maggot?* But of course the answer was that he was a naturalist and careers can be made or lost on the back of a single maggot, so I bit my tongue. Hard.

"Are you *spying* on me, girl?" He pushed himself to his feet, leaning over the desk. "Did someone set you on me? The Megatherium Club?!" Drops of spittle struck my face.

"You gave me the sketches!" I said. It came out as a squeak. I didn't fear him physically—much—but his rage was shocking to see. "It was in the sketches, next to the drawings . . . you *told* me to use them . . ."

Halder stared at me. "The sketches," he repeated. I nodded vigorously, wondering if I should get him a glass of water or flee the room.

He dropped back into his chair, the flush slowly fading from his cheeks. After a moment, he said, "*Vicina* is identical to *vomitoria* until it pupates. All the *Calliphora* blowflies are like that."

"Okay." I was torn between anger at him and an intense sympathetic embarrassment *for* him. Had he forgotten that he'd given me the sketches? Why would he be so upset at the thought of me seeing his notes anyway? I remembered how he had pulled the few sketches he had given me from a locked safe. Odd, even for a naturalist. You only did that if there was something you didn't want people to see. "I'll arrange the plate to show that. I just wanted to make sure I hadn't missed something important."

He nodded curtly, pressing a hand to his chest. Dear god, maybe he *was* having a fit. Should I do something? But what? All I could think of was to get Mrs. Kent, but what was she going to do? For that matter, what was I going to do? Was he going to remember that he'd been angry at me for no reason, or just that he'd been angry?

Maybe I could distract him? I scrambled for a topic to divert his ire. "Errr . . . what is the Megatherium Club, sir?"

Halder flushed again, but his gaze was turned elsewhere. "Damned fools. A drinking club disguised as a naturalists' society. People advancing not because of their wits, but because they'd raised a glass with the right people forty years ago. Pah!" He looked at if he wanted to spit.

"There is no excuse for such nepotism," I offered, even though it sounded to me like Halder mostly resented the fact that he hadn't been invited.

"Entirely correct, Miss Wilson." He shoved his spectacles up his nose. "Nevertheless, I *shall* be vindicated. I have learned things about parasites that will revolutionize the field, and someday, the world shall wonder at it."

I bowed my head in acknowledgment. Halder waved an irritable hand and I slipped away, feeling as if I'd run a mile in uncomfortable shoes. I had, of necessity, gotten used to being yelled at in the last few years. Headmistress Silverton had a tongue like a greenbrier whip. But in her defense, it was usually for actual reasons, even if they were extremely minor. She had never accused me of spying on her.

Then again, naturalists are far more paranoid, as a group, about their work being stolen than headmistresses are. It is not as if one can copy a dozen schoolgirls and beat the originals to publication.

I shook my head and went back to painting maggots, telling myself that there was nothing unusual about Halder's paranoia, and almost, *almost* succeeding.

I stayed up later than usual that night. Even after I blew out the candle, I sat in the dark studio, staring out the window, where the year's first fireflies were beginning to call to each other in voices of flickering light.

Normally watching fireflies made me unaccountably happy, as if I were a small child again. Now I just felt weary and hopeless. Halder's anger must have shaken me more than I expected. Why?

You got comfortable. He was pleased with your work and you started to think you were safe. But all it takes is an angry whim and you'll be gone, out the door, onto the street.

The trees outside were Payne's gray with hints of ultramarine where the moon touched them, the shadows almost black. Black pigment is usually a poor choice for painting shadows. It flattens them out, and shadows are rarely flat. They're deep and layered and there are hints of shapes in them, things to catch your eye and make you wonder what's there, and if maybe it's looking back at you.

My cousin says he seen one . . . Sally's story about blood thieves kept running through my mind. But it had been three years, Jackson said. And they'd caught the blood thieves and staked them through the heart and buried them out near Bynum. Miles away. The only thing outside worth worrying about was that possibly rabid raccoon, and it was almost certainly dead by now. By the time they wander around acting strange in daylight, they aren't long for this world.

The shadows in the studio were thickening. I glanced over my shoulder, then looked resolutely away. The whitewashed walls were bright in the moonlight, but darkness had pooled along the floor, at the foot of the bookcases, and grew like a stain behind the wooden chest in the corner. My sense of intruding in a stranger's room was stronger than ever.

It wasn't my room, was it? It belonged to some other woman that Halder had employed. Had he driven her away with his temper? Had he fired her? Was she destitute somewhere, or had she washed up at a girls' school, teaching watercolors, not for love or skill but because watercolors were something that young ladies were supposed to learn, like music and deportment?

I realized that I was close to crying and bit my knuckle, angry at myself. *Don't let the old bastard get to you. Mrs. Kent warned you what he was like.*

Yes, and she'd warned me not to think he'd marry me either.

The thought wrung a laugh from me. God! I'd sooner wed the *Cuterebra*.

I pinched the bridge of my nose until the feel of impending tears had been driven away. *Don't be ridiculous. Do you think good scientific illustrators fall out of trees? It took Halder a year to replace your predecessor. He won't be in a hurry to replace you.*

I didn't know if that was true or not. What I did know was that Halder did not seem to like anything that upset the routine of his days. Mrs. Kent said he always ate the same breakfast at the same time.

The frogs were calling. I picked out chorus, bronze, and one tree frog calling, *HNEEEEEEE!* in a high, nasal whine that drew a reluctant smile from me. I propped my chin on my hand, staring into the dark.

One of the fireflies drew my eye. It somehow seemed to be blinking wrong.

Wait, is that a firefly? The frequency seems erratic.

It took me a moment to realize that I was seeing a light in the woods, and what I had mistaken for blinks was the shadow as it moved through the intervening trees.

I watched it, baffled. Mrs. Kent? But it was going in the opposite direction of the Kents' house. I racked my brain for a possible destination. Jackson had told me there was a stream back there, but I hadn't ever visited it. And I already knew Sally didn't go home.

The Devil walks these woods at night, Phelps had said. Did I believe that?

No, I didn't believe it. The Devil, if He existed, lived in the hearts of men. *And anyway, I doubt Satan needs to carry a light.* There was the old story about Stingy Jack, who wandered between heaven and hell, carrying a lit coal in a turnip, but I had significant doubts that an immortal Irishman was loose in the Chatham woods. And I really didn't believe in blood thieves, who were probably cougars anyway, and cougars definitely didn't carry lights. Which meant that there was a real human out there on the property doing . . . something. But what?

I couldn't think of many good reasons for someone to wander around the woods in the dark. Halder might go checking for nighttime insects, I supposed, but surely Halder was asleep by now. Searching for a lost animal? Could one of Mrs. Kent's chickens have wandered off?

Well, it was none of my business, of course. *I had no reason to go wandering through the woods at night.*

An unexpected pang of relief went through me at that thought. I zeroed in on that feeling, isolating it and pinning it to a card like one of the beetles downstairs. *Why am I relieved? I can't actually be* scared *of the woods, can I?*

I had spent half my life wandering through the Carolina woods. When I was seven years old, I caught a copperhead and brought it to show my father. The woods were *mine*, not like property but like family. I certainly wasn't going to be put off from them by a religious zealot's ranting about the Devil, or Jackson's stories about blood thieves or cougars or whatever they were supposed to be. I was most definitely *not* scared.

The light paused for a moment, then moved on.

Possibly if I had already undressed, I would have decided that I didn't have anything to prove. But I had only taken off one boot, and it was the work of a moment to shove my foot back in and hurry downstairs.

The back door was latched from the inside. Not Mrs. Kent, then. I dithered for a moment about continuing on, but curiosity has always been my besetting sin. I unlatched the door and slipped out.

A gibbous moon illuminated the landscape, which was good because I hadn't grabbed a light of my own. For a moment I thought I'd lost the trail, but then I caught a bright flash between the trees, and scurried after.

The light bobbed along ahead of me. It was going very slowly, and I had no problem following it, even in the relative darkness. I set my feet cautiously, wary of ankle-breaking holes.

After a few minutes, it occurred to me that I was also trying not to make any noise.

It's not that I'm scared of the woods. But you don't know who has the light, and people are much scarier than trees.

Just as I thought that, I stepped on a sweet gum ball that rolled under my foot. (If you have never stepped on the spiky seedpod of *Liquidambar styraciflua*, you cannot know the depth of a Southerner's loathing for them.) *Damnation,* I thought, barely catching myself before I fell. And then, belatedly, *Oops.*

The light stopped. A familiar voice called out, "Who's there?"

Halder?

Why is Halder *out here in the woods?*

Is he researching some kind of nocturnal insect? That seemed most likely. Regardless, I didn't particularly want to encounter the grumpy old bastard. He'd probably accuse me of spying on him again.

Which, in fairness, you kind of are *doing . . .*

I stepped behind a tree and waited. After a moment, Halder grunted and turned away, walking deeper into the woods.

Lucky escape. Well, you know what the light is now. Time to go back to the house and go to bed.

. . . And yet you seem to be following Halder.

I wasn't sure why I was doing it. It was definitely unwise. If he caught me, I had no idea how I'd talk my way out of it. And it was certainly no business of mine if he wanted to wander around his own property with a lamp after dark, collecting specimens for the killing bottle.

Nevertheless, I padded after him, setting my feet as carefully as I could. The ground was mostly pine needles and even last year's leaves were very damp from our days of rain, so there were no betraying crunches. Halder didn't turn around again. As we got closer to the stream, the frogs and katydids were calling so loudly that he probably couldn't have heard me if I shouted.

(and if something grabs you and hauls you into a tree and begins draining your blood, no one will ever know what happened to you.)

I scowled in the dark, annoyed with myself. *Don't be ridiculous. The blood thief was a cougar, that was all. Probably the last one in the county. Jackson was just scaring the new girl with ghost stories.* The only thing in the woods that I was scared of was Halder, and only in case he spotted me.

So why was I following him?

Because he's not catching insects.

The thought arrived with absolute certainty. I picked at it, wondering why I was so sure of that. Intuition, my father used to say, is just an observation that you don't realize you've made. What had I observed?

Halder stopped at last. I stepped behind another tree and watched as he shifted the lamp from one hand to the other, then set it down. He could do that easily because . . . *he wasn't carrying a net.*

That was the observation I hadn't realized I'd made. No net. No gear of the sort a naturalist would carry. Just a lantern.

As my eyes adjusted, I realized Halder was standing in front of a little low building, not much larger than a well house. I heard him mutter as he fumbled with the lock, then he picked the light up again and pushed the door open. It closed behind him a moment later with an oddly metallic clang. No light leaked under the door.

I was left alone with the frogs and the katydids and the dark.

After about five minutes, I was bored. Whatever curiosity had moved me was wearing thin. There was nothing to be learned here, and whatever Halder was doing inside the small building, it was his own affair. *For all I know, that's where he keeps his collection of pornographic etchings.*

I turned back. I was only a few yards into the trees when I

heard the door clang behind me. Shadows rose around me as the light swayed back and forth.

A thicket of saltbush proved just tall enough to conceal me. I waited until Halder had passed and followed at a distance. He was moving more quickly now, muttering to himself. I caught "... serves him right ..." and "... this long ..." and then, with startling clarity, "Keep *me* out of the Megatherium Club, will they?" but most of the words were lost, if they were even words in the first place.

When we reached the clearing around the house, I stopped at the edge of the woods and waited. If Halder locked the kitchen door, I was going to be in a tough spot ... but no. I suspect it never even occurred to him *not* to use the front door. He went around the front of the house, pausing only once to glance behind him. I waited in the shadow of the trees until I heard the front door close, and then gave it a few more minutes.

At last, when I judged it was safe—or at least when I was thoroughly sick of waiting and every mosquito in the county had arrived to feast—I slipped across the grass and into the kitchen. The house was dark and quiet. I made my way to my room, feeling a stab of panic whenever a board creaked underfoot.

But no one popped out of a closet to shout "Aha!" or point an accusing finger at me. I slipped off my shoes, washed my face and hands, and went to bed, still wondering what, if anything, Halder had been doing out there in the dark.

CHAPTER 7

Paint blobbed on the paper in front of me. I cursed and blotted at it, trying to stop it from running into the part that I'd already completed and ruining all my hard work.

My attempts were only partially successful. The first wash hadn't been completely dry and so it had sucked pigment from the fly's body into the head, turning the carefully rendered eyes into muddy pools.

I flung the damp blotter away and rubbed my face. It was one of those mornings when nothing seemed to be going right. I could not settle at anything and my thoughts ran in all directions, like a flock of pigeons scattered by a dog.

There was no mystery as to why, of course. I could not stop thinking about Halder's trip to the woods last night. I had never seen the man leave his room before, let alone go tromping through the woods. And what was that building he had visited? And why?

Curiosity had not so much seized me as engulfed me utterly, like a Venus flytrap closing on a small winged morsel. *Enough. Halder will get his painting a day late. I'm taking a walk.*

I snatched up a sketchbook and a pencil so that I could at least pretend to be working and stalked out of the room.

My spirits lifted once I was in the woods. I named each tree to myself as I passed it—*Quercus alba, Fagus grandifolia, Cercis canadensis, Pinus taeda*—and felt as if I were walking among friends. Sun turned their leaves to hot green stained glass. The early morning had been cool and humid and the afternoon looked to be warm and humid, to the surprise of no one.

I told myself that I was going to the stream to sketch. That I happened to be following the same route that Halder had taken last night was purely coincidental. It was on the way to the stream, that was all.

It was certainly even more of a coincidence when I saw the outline of a small building in front of me. "Goodness," I said aloud, as if I were in a play and an audience might be watching me. "What have we here?"

It was rather odder in daylight than it had been at night. I had thought that it was the size of a well house, but when I circled around it, I saw that it was longer than I had thought. The roof sloped sharply downward in back, giving the whole building the aspect of a triangle, like a slice of cake laid on its side.

The walls had been tightly caulked and there were no windows, but the strangest thing was definitely the door. It was made of metal and I could not see any hinges. In fact, when I approached, I realized that it had been framed with metal as well, even the bottom, which extended a good six inches up from the ground, like the door of a ship.

I walked around it twice, baffled. It reminded me of a bank vault, except that it was secured with a large steel padlock. If Halder was keeping pornographic etchings in it, he was taking no chances with thieves. *It can't be a still, there's no chimney. And if it's a garden shed, it's awfully far from a garden.*

I was just about to make a third circuit around the building when a man's voice barked, "Get back from there!"

I let out a yelp and spun around, my heart pounding.

Asa Phelps stalked out of the woods toward me and I exhaled with a whoosh. "Good heavens, Mr. Phelps, you scared the life from me." I put a hand to my chest.

His brow was furrowed and he scowled fiercely at me. "You shouldn't be here," he informed me.

"I'm *not* here," I said, nonsensically. "I mean, obviously I'm *here*, but I didn't come here deliberately. I was going to the stream and I saw this odd little . . . shed. Building."

Phelps's scowl lessened slightly. "The stream?"

"Yes?" I held up my sketchbook. "I was going there to draw. I thought there might be some interesting insects."

His face cleared. "Ah. Insects. Yes."

"I promise I'll be back well before dark," I added. "I remember what you said." *And thought it was a load of nonsense, but never mind that.*

Phelps nodded sharply. "Good."

"But what *is* this building?" I asked. "It's so oddly constructed."

The scowl did not quite return, but I could definitely feel it lurking. He looked reluctant to answer at all, looking from me to the shed and back again. Finally he muttered, "It's for gunpowder."

"Gunpowder?"

"And blasting supplies. Can't store it up by the house."

"Ohhhh . . ." I slapped my forehead. "Of course. And you wouldn't want it to get wet . . . yes, of course." I gave him my best smile. "I would never have thought of that."

He folded his arms and stared at the ground. "You should stay clear of it," he said. "It's not safe."

"No, of course not, Mr. Phelps. I shall keep that in mind in the future."

He grunted, still gazing at the ground as if it required intense concentration.

"Well," I said, when it became obvious that he wasn't going to either elaborate or leave. "It was lovely running into you. I'm going to go sketch some insects."

He touched the brim of his hat but didn't meet my eyes. "Miss Wilson."

I ambled toward the stream, swinging my arms like someone

with nothing more on their mind than sketching. I only glanced back once, to see that Phelps hadn't moved.

Gunpowder. It made perfect sense. *Except why would a reclusive collector of insect carcasses have that much gunpowder to begin with? And what was he doing in the middle of the night—reading it a bedtime story?*

I reached the stream, selected a rock, and sat down. The water flowed by, the sun sparkled off it, and dragonflies hummed and zipped over the molten surface. My sketchbook was open, but my pencil didn't move at all.

What had Phelps been doing here? I didn't think he lived nearby. He'd said that Halder's place was only "more or less" on his way. So why was he on Halder's property at all?

Halder doing something odd didn't surprise me. Naturalists are inherently odd. My father used to make up songs to sing to his pitcher plants. But Asa Phelps had been lying to me, I was certain of it. He was not a terribly good liar. He hadn't been able to meet my eyes when he did it. I was guessing he did not have much practice in the art.

What the devil is really in that shed?

There was a light in the woods again that night. I didn't follow it, but I sat up, waiting to see where it would go.

It vanished into the trees in the direction of the gunpowder shed. I lit a match and checked the wall clock, curious as to how long Halder would take this time, then snuffed the candle out again.

Not very long at all, as it turned out. I expected Halder to go around the side of the house again, but to my surprise, the light turned the opposite way, skirted the edge of the clearing, and went south. I lit another match once the light was gone. Eleven minutes. Halder had not stayed long, if he had gone to the shed at all.

Well, that was peculiar, but it was still none of my affair. Phelps had definitely been lying to me, but that did not mean that there was some great mystery afoot. It was pure curiosity that motivated me, and however valuable curiosity was for a naturalist, I couldn't allow it to jeopardize my work. A job like this came along once in a decade, if I was lucky.

I turned away from the window, padding on bare feet back to my bed, and threw one last glance over my shoulder.

The light had returned. It was going back the way it had come, along the edge of the clearing, toward the shed again.

No, I told myself firmly. *It is not my business. Leave it alone.*

I lay down on the bed and closed my eyes, determined to sleep. I had almost succeeded when I heard the distant thud of the front door slamming shut, as Halder returned at last.

Feeling both frustrated with myself and resigned to my own folly, I lit a match and checked the clock.

Whatever he'd been doing in the woods had taken him thirty-eight minutes.

"The damnedest thing," said Mrs. Kent the next morning as I came into the kitchen. She bobbed her head at me in acknowledgment, but didn't stop talking. "One of the hens missing like that."

"Huh," said Jackson.

I sat down and helped myself to biscuits. "You lost a hen?"

"My best layer too." Mrs. Kent pulled a face.

"Fox?" I hazarded. "Raccoon?"

"No, that's the strange part. She was inside the coop last night. I check on 'em myself every night before I go to bed, and she was asleep in the nest box. I know because I had to reach under her to grab the eggs, and she wasn't best pleased about it." Jackson passed the coffee over and I poured out a cup gratefully. Mrs. Kent pursed her lips, looking more annoyed than I'd ever seen her look. "I'm not saying one *couldn't* get into the coop, mind, but if they do, they sure don't take one hen and go back out again."

"Fox gets in the coop, it's a regular massacre," Jackson agreed.

"So I'm stumped," Mrs. Kent said. "She was just gone. And no feathers either."

That did surprise me. Even with my limited knowledge of chickens, I knew that if a predator grabbed one, it looked like a pillow exploded.

"Could it have been a thief?" I asked tentatively.

Mrs. Kent sighed heavily and slumped back in her chair. "Don't like to think that, but it could be. Can't imagine any of the neighbors would stoop to stealing chickens though."

"Might've been a tramp," Jackson offered. "Somebody just passing through."

"S'pose it could be." She stared broodingly into her coffee. "My best layer. How do they always know?"

I wondered for half a moment if Halder might have been responsible. The light had gone in the general direction of the Kents' house and the chicken coop. But I had a hard time imagining Halder stealing chickens—and anyway, they were probably technically *his* chickens, so why would he go skulking around at night after one?

"I could get a lock for the henhouse," said Jackson.

"More trouble'n it's worth," Mrs. Kent said. "I'd be going back and forth looking for the key. But if it happens again, maybe." She got up and went to the stove and began slapping ingredients around. It looked more like venting her feelings than cooking. I finished my biscuit meekly, refilled my coffee, and carried the mug upstairs to get back to work.

There was no light in the woods that night. I had almost succeeded in convincing myself that there was nothing at work but a strange coincidence, until two nights later, when I saw the glow of the lantern moving between the trees.

Forty-two minutes later, the front door slammed as Halder came inside.

"Another hen gone!" said Mrs. Kent. Her bafflement was clearly about to metamorphosize into rage. I could practically see it, like a dark red butterfly fluttering around her head. "Not a sign of anything. No blood, no feathers, just *gone*."

Jackson had been attempting to placate her when I walked into the kitchen. It hadn't gone well. He had gone out to the garden and I took my plate outside and ate my breakfast there.

I had an idea. It was fairly strange and I didn't want to share it with anyone yet. Mrs. Kent didn't seem like she was in the mood to entertain speculation right now, so I dropped my plate in the scullery and slipped past the door without bothering her.

My idea was very simple. Actually, it was more of a question than an idea. *Was* it possible that Halder had been taking the chickens to the shed?

A good scientist tests their hypotheses. I checked the clock in the hall—7:25—and then scurried as quickly as I could outdoors, to the spot where I had seen the light last night. *Figure that took about a minute, maybe two. Now, the Kents' house is this way . . .*

I had to slow my usual brisk gait to allow for the darkness and Halder's slower pace. Still, it was no time at all before the Kents' cottage hove into view. It was a small, neat building, clearly built at the same time as the main house. When I had seen it that first Sunday, I had thought that it looked much friendlier and more lived-in than Halder's mansion. Chintz curtains framed the windows, and a hen had escaped the run and was scuffling in the dirt at the edge of the woods.

There was an elderly hound asleep on the porch. We'd been introduced before. If I were painting him, I'd lay in yellow ochre for the fur, then lift most of it back out again for his face, which had gone white to the eyebrows. He lifted his head when he saw me, then stood up, stretched arthritically, and ambled down to have his ears scratched. He ignored the chicken, who returned the favor.

"Sorry, boy," I told him. "Can't stay. I'm testing a hypothesis."

The dog indicated that he would like to test a hypothesis involving an old dog's ears being scratched. I groaned. "You're gonna ruin my science, boy." He leaned against my shins and began the slow melt that some dogs are capable of, in defiance of all laws of physics. I studied the henhouse. How long would it take to get in and grab a hen? I didn't want to actually test that part, because if someone showed up, I would have a devil of a time explaining myself. Three minutes? Five?

Probably depends on how comfortable you are with grabbing a chicken, and if you know the layout of the coop. Halder certainly knows where it is, but does he come here regularly enough to be quick at it?

It seemed unlikely. Mrs. Kent wouldn't have been so upset if chickens were vanishing regularly. And surely if you had a regular need for live chickens, and you already *owned* the chickens, you'd just give orders to the housekeeper to fetch one?

None of this made any sense. I tamped down my speculations. *First, figure out if Halder could have been the one taking the chickens. Then start worrying about causes.*

I realized with a start that I had been standing there, petting the dog and staring into space, and lost track of time. Had it been five minutes? Longer? I grumbled at my past self for selling Father's pocket watch, but in fairness, she hadn't known that she might someday be timing how long it took to steal a chicken.

I gave the dog a firm pat and stepped back. He heaved an enormous sigh and returned to the porch. I turned around and retraced my steps, past the house, in the direction of the alleged gunpowder shed.

I wasn't quite certain that I'd be able to find it again. There was no path etched through the woods, which argued against regular nocturnal visits, although given the carpet of pine needles, a path might not show up well. *You should have worked out where it was in advance,* I told myself irritably. *This will throw off the timing.*

If you keep going out to the shed, Phelps might catch you again and what if he tells Halder and Halder thinks you're spying on him and he turns you out and you've only made a month's wages and . . .

I clamped it down. If anyone asked, I was going to the stream. I had my sketchbook to prove it. And anyway, it was none of Phelps's business, and why was he even here?

My sense of direction was not so bad as I'd thought. I saw the shed roof through the trees and a moment later, I was standing in front of it. Once again, I wished for a pocket watch. I turned and made my way back to the house, finding a slightly shorter path this time.

When I finally got inside, the clock read 7:56. Thirty-one minutes. Allowing for the time it had taken me to get into position, it seemed that Halder would have had more than enough time to steal a chicken and take it to the shed, as long as he didn't spend more than ten minutes there himself.

I pinched the bridge of my nose. I'd successfully proved that Halder could be responsible. In fact, I was increasingly sure that he *was* responsible.

Now what?

CHAPTER 8

Two nights later, I put on my shoes, slipped out of the house, and waited. *And a pretty fool I'll look if Halder doesn't come out tonight,* I thought, leaning against a tree trunk. The moon was waning and the blue light it cast over the grounds was barely enough to see by. I needed some time for my eyes to adjust, since I didn't dare carry a lantern.

I looked up at the stars, trying to pick out constellations. Astronomy is the natural science that I know the least about. I could find Orion and the Big and Little Dippers, but that was as far as I went. My time in the woods was more usually spent turning over rocks than gazing up at the sky.

Probably for the best, given how hard it is to paint a good night sky in watercolor. There's something about the glow of stars that simply doesn't want to translate into paint. You can take the most spectacular night sky ever seen and on paper, it just turns into a sheet of muddy blue-black flecked with little white dots.

I heard a distant door slam and ducked hastily behind the tree I'd picked out. Light splashed around me, casting brief, fantastic shadows before moving on, then footsteps went past. I waited long enough for the sound to fade, then scurried after.

Definitely Halder. I could make out the familiar slumped form silhouetted against the lantern. He was moving quickly but kept throwing glances over his shoulder. He didn't slow down or swing the lantern around though, which made it seem more like a nervous tic than an actual attempt to spot pursuit. Still, I moved from tree to shrub to tree, trying to stay in cover in case he decided to actually stop and look. Fortunately, sound couldn't betray me, because the frogs were making a deafening racket, intermixed with the shrilling of katydids and the short, sharp chirps of some insect that I didn't know but that Halder probably did.

We reached the clearing that contained the Kents' small, neat house, and Halder hastily dimmed the light down to a firefly glow. He moved cautiously around the side to the chicken coop, holding the lantern so that it didn't shine into the darkened windows. I halted behind a loblolly pine and waited.

A whippoorwill called monotonously in the woods. Halder fumbled with the latch on the coop.

Something moved on the porch. I froze. So did Halder.

Claws scraped the boards as the old hound stood up, stretched, and came ambling down the steps.

Don't look in my direction, I prayed. *I'm not here. I'm not.*

He took a few steps toward my tree. I saw a flash of moonlight on white teeth as he yawned. Surely he must be able to smell me. If he came up to me, I had no idea what to do. Hold very, very still and hope that Halder didn't come to see what had attracted his attention? Try to run?

Oh please, please, go away, I can't pet you right now . . .

Then Halder got the door open and the old hound turned, attracted by either the sound or the movement of the light. His tail wagged amiably as he went toward the chicken coop.

Light gleamed through chinks in the boards, and a moment later, my employer emerged, holding a groggy chicken tucked firmly under his arm. The dog came up and sniffed at the dangling feet with great interest.

Halder reached into his pocket, pulled something out, and tossed it to the hound. Suddenly all business, the dog caught it neatly in midair and trotted back to the porch. I heard the creak as he flopped down and began chewing.

Very clever. Cleverer than I had been, certainly. I'd known the dog was there, but I hadn't even considered that he might give me away.

The light bobbed through the trees as Halder went back the way he had come. I gave chase, hearing the occasional puzzled *err-err-errrk?* from the hen. I felt a pang of sympathy for the poor chicken. I didn't know what Halder's plans were, but I suspected the bird's future was extremely limited.

The gunpowder shed loomed ahead. I slipped back behind the shrubs and waited. Halder set down the lantern, took out his key, and unlocked it, then picked up the lantern again and stepped inside.

He didn't shut the door behind him. He shouldered through some kind of drape and let it fall, cutting off both the light and a last, worried cluck from the chicken.

I swallowed hard. Did I dare get closer?

No! Stay here where it's—well, not safe, obviously, this is all a terrible idea, but if you go any closer you are absolutely going to get caught, you know *you're going to get caught—*

The problem with anxiety is that you get so good at tamping down that inner voice that sometimes you ignore it even when it's right. Halder had only spent about five minutes in the shed last time. I should definitely stay where I was.

Stop, stop, what are you doing, stop! I told myself as I slunk across the open ground. The moonlight was just barely strong enough to make out folds of material in the doorway. I touched it cautiously. Heavy oilcloth. Very heavy. Weighted at the bottom too, it felt like, and stiffened along the edges, forming a barrier just inside the arc of the door.

Okay, now you know what the drape is made of, for all the good it does, now you're going to turn around and go back to your hiding place . . .

It occurred to me that there was no light coming from around the edges of the drape. I leaned closer. It was certainly heavy, but it couldn't possibly seal so tightly that light couldn't get out, could it? I didn't hear anything from inside. The shed was so small, surely I should hear Halder moving, shouldn't I?

He wouldn't just be standing there in the dark, in total silence, holding a chicken. That made no sense.

None of this makes any sense!

Crouching down, I plucked the edge of the drape and lifted it a tiny fraction. Light failed to spill out from underneath.

My courage would likely have failed me at that point, except that I heard Halder's voice, much farther away than expected, saying, "Worked a treat though, didn't it?"

It didn't sound like he was in the tiny shed. It sounded like he was across a room and at the bottom of a flight of stairs. And who was he talking to?

Fear warred with curiosity and lost. I lifted the corner even higher and peered inside.

At last, I could see light. It was at the bottom of a flight of stairs that opened up in front of me. I saw the glow illuminating the edges of plain board steps, and what looked like an earth floor beyond.

Halder's voice drifted up the steps. "No. I don't."

I strained my ears, but couldn't hear any reply, not even a murmur.

A large insect climbed over my hand where it held back the drape and I jerked away, biting down a yelp. It was too dark to make out what species it might be. I shook my hand violently and it flew away into the dark. Moth, probably, or a large beetle. I lifted the drape again.

Below the shed, Halder laughed abruptly. It wasn't a nice laugh. As it died away, so did the calls of the frogs and the insects, leaving a dreadful, vulnerable silence.

I should probably have fled then, but my brain was churning with questions. What was Halder doing? Who was he talking to? What was going on underneath that shed?

Could there be a *person* down there?

I waited too long. The light swung suddenly, and I actually saw the top of his head come into view at the foot of the stairs before I jerked back, letting the drape fall. I scrabbled backward, heart hammering, tried to rise—and felt my feet go out from under me.

Stairs creaked as Halder climbed. Panic painted the inside of my skull a numb white. I crab-walked backward, hit something that I recognized as a fallen log, and flung myself over it, dropping flat. There was a gap underneath where the log lay across another one. If Halder happened to glance down, six feet to his right, he would almost certainly see me, but I had no more time to run.

The drape opened and he stepped out. I could only see him from the knees down. I wouldn't even know if he'd seen me until he shouted. Assuming he bothered to shout.

A katydid called, then another one, and suddenly the full night chorus was rising again. *Oh good,* I managed to think. *Now I won't even* hear *him coming.*

His feet turned back toward the shed, and he set the lantern down. I heard him fumbling with the drape, then the door swung shut, but the woods were too loud to hear the key click in the lock.

Don't look over here, I begged silently. *Don't look.* My dress was dark, true, but the forest floor was the color of old pine needles and the fabric would stand out like an ink stain against it, with my hands and face horribly bright by comparison. My only hope was that he wouldn't bother looking this way at all.

The songs of the frogs swelled louder as Halder bent down and picked up the lantern. I squeezed my eyes shut to stop any betraying reflection. *Please be blind from looking at the light. Please have no night vision. Please go away.*

A new sound threaded through the cacophony, thin but oddly tuneful. It took me a moment to realize that Halder was whistling.

Darkness touched the backs of my eyelids. I opened one a crack and saw the door of the gunpowder shed, closed and locked, bathed only in starlight. When I finally dared to lift my head, long after the whistling had faded away, I saw Halder's lantern far off through the trees, heading back to the house.

Well, I thought as the light bobbed away from me. Now *what do I do?*

Obviously I couldn't tell Halder I'd seen him, and I wasn't sure how to tell Mrs. Kent what had been happening to her chickens. *Your employer is taking them at night without telling you and putting them in a shed that's supposed to be full of gunpowder.* How did I even start that conversation? How could I explain that I'd been following Halder around at night? Why should she even believe me? How could I prove it, short of dragging her out to watch with me?

Sally was far too young. I could tell Jackson, but he'd naturally tell his wife. I could have sworn him to secrecy, I supposed, but going around swearing other woman's husbands to secrecy and asking them to come lurk in the shrubbery with me at night . . . No, that was not a road I wanted to start down.

I would have given a great deal for someone else to confide in. My friend Esther from the school hadn't really understood my devotion to science, but she certainly understood secrecy. We'd covered for each other regularly—me when she had slipped out to visit the synagogue, and her when I snuck out to mail letters to potential employers. Esther would have understood how bizarre the situation was, and she certainly would never have told Halder. But Esther was two hundred miles away in Wilmington and I couldn't think of anyone else to talk to.

Why on earth was Dr. Halder delivering hens to a small shed in the middle of the night? More importantly, *who had he been talking to?*

My mind seethed with possibilities, most of them bad. Maybe he was having a secret meeting with someone. The Klu Klux Klan had been active here for years, even if they were supposed to be as dead as the cougar now. I could just about believe Phelps was a Klan member, since plenty of the miserable bastards claimed to be religious, and that he and Halder were having a meeting, except that a meeting would take a lot more than five minutes and why would they need a live chicken?

It was possible that he could have been talking to himself. Plenty of people did. I did it myself, sometimes. He'd *sounded* like he was answering someone else, but it had been late and I had been very nervous. I might have misheard. "Worked a treat" was the sort of thing that you might say when you saw an experiment going well.

An experiment could explain what he was doing. He studied necrophagic insects, so it wasn't out of the realm of possibility that he was laying out a dead chicken to see how long it took maggots to devour it, or even just to collect the insects themselves for his collection.

But why the secrecy? Everyone in the house knew about his work. He could just have ordered Jackson to kill a hen for him and done it in broad daylight. And why put it inside a shed, where it would be harder for the bugs to get at the body?

I rubbed my forehead. A comparison, maybe? Rate of decomposition in a closed space versus outside with more insects? But again, why the secrecy?

I could easily believe that Halder would decide that he had to test a theory *right this minute.* Lord knows, Father would occasionally get an idea in the middle of the night, leap out of bed, and start rummaging through herbarium specimens. Halder was likely no different. And certainly having done so, it might not occur to Halder to tell Mrs. Kent, and leave her baffled as to where her chickens had gone.

But to keep going back at night? And taking even more

chickens? Was he feeding something? A colony of dermestid beetles . . . no, that made no sense, you could feed them just as easily in daylight. Was Halder working with a nocturnal species that fed on carrion?

A large insect *had* climbed over my hand. It could have been a beetle. Or a moth. Were there any carrion-eating moths? It wouldn't surprise me, actually; you see butterflies on carrion regularly, licking at salt. If there were necrophagic moths, Halder would be the person keeping them, Lord knows.

I could almost believe that Halder was keeping an insect colony down there, except for the way he kept looking over his shoulder when he went to the shed. He had moved like a man doing something illicit.

What possible illicit acts could you get up to in a shed, with a live chicken? I wondered, and then gave the equivalent of a full-brain cough and had to compose myself for a moment.

Well. All right. Leaving aside certain . . . err . . . exotic depravities, that is. I had a hard time picturing specifics, but I will admit that I didn't try very hard. You cannot grow up among biologists without a certain degree of open-mindedness, but there are hard limits.

Although in fairness, exotic depravities might explain both his reluctance to tell anyone and Phelps warning me away from the shed. But that assumed that Phelps knew what Halder did in the shed. Maybe Phelps had helped him dig the stairs out below?

I saw the Devil in the woods, Miss Wilson . . . and he was buggering a chicken.

I started giggling so hysterically that I had to shove my hand into my mouth to keep from alerting the house. What the fireflies thought of the shadowy figure making "huh . . . ahuh . . . ahaha . . ." noises, I suppose no one will ever know.

I slipped back into the house and went up to my room. Unanswered questions make an uncomfortable pillow, but at least

I'd managed to prove that Halder was doing something strange, even if I had no idea what. I just wished that I didn't have such a bad feeling about it.

I wished even more strongly that I could tell someone the next morning. Mrs. Kent had not taken well to the loss of *another* hen. She embarked on a savage spree of baking that left Sally and I tiptoeing through a house full of glorious smells and barely contained wrath. I bolted my breakfast—bacon and toast, not eggs—feeling horribly guilty. Even if I hadn't been the one stealing chickens, I knew what the problem was. I just couldn't figure out how to tell anyone what I knew.

I snuck down for coffee a little before ten and saw the tray that Mrs. Kent prepared for Halder. The usual poached egg was missing. I wondered if Halder would care. His housekeeper certainly did. Her jaw was so tightly clenched that I was afraid her teeth would splinter.

I lurked in the library, the door open, and eavesdropped shamelessly down the hall.

I couldn't quite make out what Halder said, but caught the end of Mrs. Kent's reply. ". . . Jackson into town to buy some."

Halder said something else.

"No, sir," said Mrs. Kent coldly. She sounded angry. Had Halder confessed? I wished I could hear what he was saying. I leaned out of the library doorway, straining my ears.

". . . going to stay up with a shotgun tonight. I'm about done with this."

I gulped. He definitely hadn't confessed. I inched farther down the hall until I could make out the doctor's voice.

"Yes . . . err . . . quite right," Halder was saying. He sounded as uncomfortable as I felt. "I'd rather not have anyone shot on the premises, however."

"Oh, he'll load it with rock salt," said Mrs. Kent. "I ain't looking to murder anybody. Just warning you in case you hear a gunshot."

"Yes, yes, *quite* right. Thank you, Mrs. Kent."

I lunged farther back into the library just in time to avoid being spotted. My heart pounded and I pressed my hand against my chest. I knew that there are people who enjoy eavesdropping and get a thrill from going through other people's medicine cabinets, but clearly I was not one of them. *I am really not cut out for all this sneaking around. I don't enjoy it at all. Actually, I feel sick.*

Judging by Halder's responses, he wasn't cut out for sneaking around either. He hadn't sounded at all like his usual abrasive self. He'd sounded worried. Guilty, even.

But they're his *chickens. He doesn't need to steal them. And scientists hardly ever feel ashamed about their work—quite the opposite. You can't stop them talking about it. And it's not like he'd feel guilty for sacrificing a mere chicken in the name of science. That one colleague of Father's electrocuted a* horse, *for god's sake, trying to prove something or other about alternating current.* So far as I knew, the only branch of science that didn't eventually wind up experimenting on living things was geology. A chicken was nothing.

Jesus, Mary and Joseph, maybe he *was* committing some kind of unnatural sex acts with the chickens.

No, no. He wouldn't have had time. Granted I had only a hazy concept of how that would even work, but it would certainly have taken more than two minutes, wouldn't it? There'd be cleanup. *Anyway it only started in the last week. The first time you followed him to the shed, he wasn't carrying livestock of any sort, and based on Mrs. Kent's reaction, this is a new turn of events.*

But if we've ruled out sex and science, what else is *there?* I had lived a fairly sheltered existence in some regards, but as far as basic human motivations went, I could only think of a few. Sex. Science. Money. Power.

I stared down at the tray of pinned insects in front of me

without really seeing them. Halder had money, and I had serious doubts that he could increase his fortune by depositing a single chicken in a shed nightly. Same went for power. It just made no *sense*.

Sighing, I pulled out my sketchbook and set to work on the next round of illustrations. It was clear that I wasn't going to solve this mystery any time soon, and at least I could work on earning my daily bread. Today was another *Cuterebra*. Halder had three trays of the damn things, one made entirely of C. *emasculator* specimens. This discovery had annoyed the hell out of me, given how long I'd struggled with the killing jar and the botfly buzzing against the glass, refusing to die.

No, money and power made no sense as motives for Halder. If he had more money, he'd spend it on dead insects, and he used the power he *did* have to annoy his assistant.

It was only later that I realized that I'd left off a very important motive, but by then, it was too late to do anything about it.

CHAPTER 9

"It's got to be a tramp," Mrs. Kent said at dinner, addressing the air over the stove. The rest of us were crouched like rabbits hoping to avoid the hawk's notice. The pot pie she had made was spectacular, with a crust that melted like butter. I wished that I was able to enjoy it. "No critter ever opened a lock like that."

I cleared my throat nervously. "Raccoons can be very—"

"No way one could've lifted that bar. And I know I didn't leave it unlocked."

None of us were foolish enough to challenge this.

"No feathers either," Mrs. Kent continued. "Just gone, same as last time."

"Maybe it was blood thiefs got it," Sally piped up.

Jackson winced. Mrs. Kent wheeled around, holding a wooden spoon like a sword. "Don't you talk nonsense, girl! That old business is done and over and no need to bring it back up!"

Sally fled. Jackson silently produced his flask and poured us both out a measure. Mrs. Kent went back to staring at the air over the stove.

"I'll go to town and buy you a padlock," Jackson offered again.

"I don't know what the world's coming to, when you've got to padlock the henhouse." Mrs. Kent finally abandoned her post at the stove and sank down at the table. She glared at the ceiling, possibly addressing God. "Dog didn't even bark."

"Dog's getting old," said Jackson reasonably. "I'll ask around, see if anyone's got any pups going begging."

My desire to defend the poor hound's honor was intense, but I bit my tongue hard.

Mrs. Kent put her forehead against her fist. "That dog's only seven years old, and I'm not raising another pup until I have to. If a tramp steals a chicken, fine, but you get a chicken-killing *dog* in there..."

Jackson, very wisely, poured her a small quantity of whiskey and slid it across the table. She sighed and her shoulders sagged. "Hatched every one of them out my own self," she said gloomily. I could have painted a portrait entirely in shades of Payne's gray and ultramarine, and called it *Discouraged Woman*. "Good layers, the lot. I don't begrudge anybody a meal if they're hungry, but if they were gonna steal chickens, couldn't they have grabbed one of the young roosters?"

I excused myself quietly. I could just about hold up to an angry Mrs. Kent, but a depressed Mrs. Kent was too much. Guilt gnawed at my guts like one of Halder's screwworms. I wanted to tell her, but how?

All this angst over missing chickens, I thought, staring out the window. Though it wasn't really about the chickens, was it? Mrs. Kent would have been annoyed if a fox had killed them, but not upset like this. It was clearly the notion of a *person* taking them that was upsetting her view of things. I could understand that. Either your neighbors were thieves, or there were strangers lurking in the woods who might not stop at chickens, and neither prospect was particularly appealing, was it?

I didn't go out that night. Neither did Halder, judging by the lack of a light. Presumably neither of us wanted to take a couple of barrels of rock salt... although Halder didn't *have* to, dammit, he *owned* the chickens, he could have just *said*...

You've been over this a dozen times already. You're not going to figure it out with the information you have available.

Clearly what was needed was more information.

I went out early in the morning, carrying my sketchbook. If

Phelps was lurking around the shed—*And why would he be lurking, what does he know, how can I find out?*—I would just tell him that I was sketching the building. Drawing architecture is excellent practice for any illustrator, which is probably why I hate doing it. Yes, you have to be precise with botanical illustration, but I've yet to meet an orchid with crown moldings and a dozen windows that need to be placed in correct perspective.

Still, I'd draw the damn shed if that's what it took.

The air was cool and humid, but I knew the temperature wouldn't last, even if the humidity did. Cicadas were already beginning their ascending buzz, summoning the heat. I threaded my way between head-high buckeyes, their flowers mostly spent and littering the ground beneath them with damp red trumpets.

No one awaited me as I approached the shed. I looked around, half expecting Phelps to jump out at me, but the woods were empty. I glanced over at the log that I'd hidden behind and felt a shudder that started at the hinge of my jaw and went down past my rib cage. That wasn't a hiding place in any sense of the word. I had gotten absurdly lucky. Halder must have been distracted, or his night vision had been ruined by lantern light, or perhaps, as the headmistress used to say, God sometimes looks out for fools.

The door was just as heavy as I remembered it, with the odd metal plates around the edges, and the cracks in the wood were still sealed up tight. Of course, if you were running an experiment with insects, you wouldn't want any to get in from outside, would you? The wrong kind of wasp could be just as dangerous as a fox in a henhouse.

I stifled a sigh. I was probably going to be embarking on wasps next. Halder had mentioned that I should keep an eye out for caterpillars with parasitic wasp larvae on them when I was out on the grounds. Those would be almost impossible to preserve on a pin, no matter how many patented caterpillar inflaters you owned.

The lock on the door was still very large and very solid.

I stared at it for a long moment, feeling as if there was something important here that I was missing. Shed. Door. Hasp. Padlock.

The lock is on the outside.

I grimaced. *Of course it's on the outside, you nitwit, how else would Halder unlock it?*

No, wait. If it had been a knob, not a padlock, he could have unlocked it from either side. He could lock it behind him when he went down. But he didn't. Why not?

Memory flared of a stormy night, and the girls telling ghost stories, scaring themselves into panicky giggling. The speaker with the candle held low in front of her, painting yellow-orange light on her chin and leaving her eyes dark, like empty sockets. "And the little girl laid down in the trunk to hide . . . and no matter how hard everyone looked, they couldn't find her. Hours went by, then days, then weeks . . . Everyone was frantic. It was like she vanished. They thought she must have been kidnapped and *murdered* . . . her mother died of a broken heart . . . then one day, when they were cleaning the attic, they opened the trunk, and there she was! When she closed the lid, the latch fell down and she was locked in. Nobody heard her screaming and she died all alone in the dark and her ghost haunted the attic for years afterwards, pounding on the walls, whispering '*Let me out . . .*'"

Gasps and more terrified giggles greeted this, and then the practical girl had said, practically, "Come on, they'd have smelled her when she started to rot."

Cries of "Ewww! Disgusting!" greeted this statement. The storyteller lowered her candle, annoyed. "They did not. It was cool in the attic and the lid kept the smell in."

"Nothing keeps a smell like that in," said the practical girl. In the doorway, I had stifled a sigh. It was impossible to explain to her that some people didn't want accuracy, they wanted a delicious frisson of terror. I knew I couldn't explain it, because I'd been like her myself. Instead I went in and shooed everyone to bed in case the headmistress came by to check for lights under the doors. Fear of the headmistress, at least, was far more real and solid than ghost stories.

Ghosts aside, the moral was clear about not closing doors that would lock behind you. The gunpowder shed was not nearly so small and cramped as a trunk in the attic, but it would still be a dangerous place to be trapped. It would be impossible to force the door with those metal plates. You could yell for days and, unless somebody happened to come along at precisely the right moment, nobody would hear you.

But I'd heard Halder talking to someone in the shed. And then he closed the door and locked it, with a lock that couldn't be opened from inside.

The second shudder went all the way down my spine, and I felt myself break out in gooseflesh despite the increasing warmth.

My god. What if he really does *have a prisoner down there?*

I took a step back from the door, holding my sketchbook up in front of me as if it were a talisman to ward off evil.

Could he . . . had he . . . could there be someone down there, right now, in the dark?

Stop that. I shook my head, summoning the spirit of that practical girl. *You thought it sounded like he was talking to himself, remember? And if there was a person being held down there, you certainly wouldn't throw live chickens to them every few nights. That's not how you feed a human.*

Besides, who would Halder want to keep prisoner? My employer flew into rages, certainly, but unless Fitch the entomologist had come to visit, I couldn't think of anyone. Granted, that wasn't proof. I had learned next to nothing about my employer, and certainly he could have murderous passions I didn't know anything about, but . . .

Maybe it's the previous illustrator, my treacherous imagination whispered.

Oh, come on. He isn't Bluebeard. And the studio's been empty for a year, Mrs. Kent said as much. Do you expect me to believe that he's kept my predecessor alive in a shed for a year by throwing them occasional live chickens?

When I put it to myself in those terms, it did seem a bit ridiculous.

It's just a damn padlock. People put them on things they don't want other people getting into. It doesn't mean there's anyone locked inside. You're piling up assumptions and you still don't have any more information than you did yesterday.

I walked around the back of the shed, where the roof dipped down so sharply. Yes, all right, the shape made sense now when I thought about a staircase going down. And when I looked in the direction of the stream, the woods did slope down in that direction, so maybe this section was high enough to hollow a space out above the water table. Given the red clay everywhere, I'd expect the room to be awfully damp and prone to flooding, but I was no architect.

Let's see . . . it looked like the stairs went down maybe six feet, so then the room should be straight down from about . . . here.

I stood at a spot just behind the back wall of the shed and studied the ground.

Yep, that was ground all right.

It didn't look like anything much. Pine needles, last year's leaves, a small rock with an even smaller tuft of moss. There was a rather sad *Polystichum acrostichoides* fern, which didn't look sturdy enough to hold up the weight of the Latin name. In a painting, I would have rendered the whole thing with a wash of yellow ochre, maybe with a hint of Tuscan red mixed in, and not bothered with details.

I stomped my foot, wondering if the earth would sound hollow, like a wall with an opening behind it. It sounded exactly like I would expect ordinary dirt to sound.

I moved over a dozen yards and stomped again experimentally. It also sounded like dirt. I went back to the original spot and stomped a few more times. Was it just slightly louder? Was there a tiny bit more resonance? I couldn't tell.

I lifted my foot to try again and a sound burst out of the ground that nearly stopped my heart in my chest.

It was a dry, rasping scream, the sound of a fiddle bow drawn inexpertly across the strings, and yet there was some quality to it that undoubtedly came from an animal throat. I leapt back, horrified, feeling as if I'd accidentally stepped on a cat's tail and heard it yowl—but of course there was nothing there, nothing but the ground and the dead leaves.

I looked around wildly for a source, feeling as if the familiar woods had suddenly turned alien and strange. I *knew* these trees and I knew what lived in them. I knew the cries of whippoorwills and owls, the shrieks of katydids and frogs, but I did not know this.

Another scream rose from the ground, practically under my feet, a sound of misery infinitely prolonged.

My nerve broke and I ran.

Fortunately, no one saw me bolt out of the woods and into the house. If Mrs. Kent had seen me tear past, I would have had to explain . . . what exactly? I heard a noise in the woods and it scared me?

I needed tea desperately. My hands shook a little as I filled the kettle. *Logically. Think logically. You are a naturalist, not a spiritualist to jump at knocking shadows. What does logic tell us?*

Logic was having a hard time telling me anything through the screaming of my nerves. I gritted my teeth. *What would your father think?*

My father had been a brilliant naturalist. He had taught me to look and see what was there, not what I expected to see. If there was some terrifying creature underground, he would have been . . . well, not the first to seek it out, since botany was his first love, but he certainly would not have shied away from it.

I took a deep, steadying breath and let it out again, trying to organize my thoughts.

Right. Logic. I can do this. I had heard a creature that didn't sound like anything I'd ever heard before. What did that mean?

The most logical explanation was that I was wrong, of course. *If you hear a horrible sound in the woods and you don't know what it is, it's probably a fox.* (Another of my father's pearls of wisdom.) So, yes. Probably I had simply startled, and been startled by, a fox.

And if it wasn't?

Well, it wasn't impossible that there was some creature down there unknown to science. Even in the enlightened age of 1899, we had not described everything that walked, crawled, swam, or flew beneath the sun. It was little more than a decade ago that a French priest had sent back the skin of the strange black-and-white bear from China, a beast entirely new to Western science. Such creatures existed.

But really, what were the odds that Halder was keeping a completely unknown species hidden away in a shed?

At least you know it's not human. That's worth something, isn't it?

Strangely, it was. The idea of a prisoner had been horrifying, and I would have had to do something about it. You can't just let people be kept in a hollowed-out hole in the ground. But doing something about it would have undoubtedly meant the end of my employment, and . . . well . . .

Fine. It's petty and venal and you feel bad about it, but it's still a relief that doing the right thing doesn't mean getting fired.

I would have done the right thing though. I would have.

. . . I'm almost sure I would have.

The nasty little anxious voice in my head whispered that I was almost certainly a terrible person who would choose the security of a job over the suffering of another human being. I shoved it back down. *I would not. Father would have disowned me.* He had been an abolitionist, descended from Quakers, and even if his faith in the divine had been overshadowed by his faith in plants, those particular beliefs remained strong.

I *would* have stood up for what was right. It's just that sometimes, it's a relief not to have to.

A shriek went up behind me and I nearly bolted out of the room.

(*it's here it's here it's found you*)

Then I recognized the sound of the kettle and laughed at myself. It came out as more of a croak, admittedly, but it still came out. I set the tea to steep, feeling foolish. If I was so nervous that a teakettle could practically send me into hysterics, I was clearly not what one would call a reliable observer.

Right. So there's an animal in the shed, and Halder was feeding it. That's all it was.

I wouldn't particularly want to be kept in a dark room under a shed, but Halder was a biologist. Perhaps it was a nocturnal species or a burrowing one, and preferred the dark. And as for the secrecy . . .

You know that it's got something to do with his parasite studies. You know it's probably revolting. I thought of the jar of screwworm larvae and shuddered. Was he infecting some unfortunate host with live ones? Possible. Unpleasant, yes, and I couldn't have done it myself, but . . . well . . . thousands of animals suffered screwworm infestations every year. It was an immense and intractable problem. Anything Halder could learn that might someday lead to a solution . . .

Regardless, I had my answer. I could stop chasing the doctor around the woods at night.

Thank the Lord for that. Just thinking about how close I had come to discovery made a shudder diffuse through my skin like ink in water.

When I dropped off the latest illustration the next day, I felt as if my guilt must be blazing like a brand across my face. Apparently it wasn't though, or maybe Halder was feeling just as guilty, because he took my painting after no more than a cursory glance. I stepped out, feeling lightheaded, as if I'd gotten away with something.

A week went by, with no more missing chickens, and no more lights moving through the trees. Either the threat of being filled full of rock salt by his own hired man was sufficient to dissuade him completely, or Halder had moved on to some other avenue of . . . whatever it was he was doing. Mrs. Kent returned to her normal self, and, after Jackson returned with a cage full of squawk and feathers, breakfast also returned to normal.

I was still deeply confused about the whole thing, but as the days passed, my concerns . . . well, "faded" was the wrong word. I dug them out and turned them over so often that they began to fray at the edges, becoming part of the background anxiety of my life. I had gotten so good at tamping down anxious thoughts that these were just more of the same.

Probably he was feeding some kind of carrion-eating insects in the shed, and was so paranoid about someone stealing his research that he had resorted to outlandish secrecy. Probably I'd misheard most of what he said, and he'd just been talking to himself after all.

Probably it had just been a fox after all. Certainly there were plenty of them around, feeding on the world-famous Chatham rabbit. And yes, it had seemed to come from underground, but I had been nervous and jumpy and the hardest lesson a naturalist has to learn is how desperately unreliable their own senses can be in the moment.

And even if neither of those things was true, there wasn't a damn thing I could do about it anyway. I was hardly going to pick Halder's pocket looking for the key. I didn't know how to pick a lock, unlike the heroines in the Gothic books scattered around the studio, who all seemed to have childhoods that involved picking locks with hairpins. And I certainly wasn't going to grab an axe from the woodshed and go try to hack the door down.

So I painted. I painted endless identical botflies, and when I had exhausted Halder's collection of botflies, I painted the bone skipper fly, *Thyreophora*. Halder had a single specimen collected from Austria, before they went extinct. It was a strange little horror with a brilliant red-orange head, and while I hate to think of any species going extinct, I admit that I was much more broken up about the great auk than the bone skipper.

Most of my painting was done outside. Granted, it took a while after the *Cuterebra* incident for me to be quite comfortable on the balcony again. But indoors was just as muggy and uncomfortable, and at least there was a slight breeze outside. After several days during which I encountered nothing more alarming than mosquitos and butterflies, I had relaxed.

Day followed day without much change. Sometimes it rained. This didn't make things any less muggy. Jackson found a hornworm caterpillar with a line of white capsules clinging to its back, courtesy of a parasitic wasp of the *Ichneumon* family. He gravely presented it to me, like a knight offering a sword, and I accepted it equally gravely.

"Your caterpillar, Miss Wilson."

"My gratitude, Mr. Kent."

Then we both began snickering, and Mrs. Kent, who watched the whole exchange, rolled her eyes and told us that we were both ridiculous and that caterpillars did not belong in the kitchen.

I did not use the ether bottle for this specimen. There was hardly any point—the average speed of a hornworm caterpillar is only slightly faster than a rock, provided the rock is not feeling motivated. It lived in a large jar on the studio table for two days, and I only bothered with the jar because Smiley was extremely interested in what I was doing.

When I was finished, I released the caterpillar back into the garden. There was no real reason to do so—it had been doomed from the moment that a wasp found it. The larvae would devour it from the inside, leaving it a limp little sack of green hide. Perhaps it would have been more merciful to kill it outright. I don't know how much pain a hornworm caterpillar feels, but surely that cannot be a pleasant experience.

Still, who am I to sit in judgment on when a caterpillar's life is worth living? Did the doomed relish the taste of a tomato stem any less thoroughly?

"Well done," said Dr. Halder, when I presented him with the illustration. "This has been drawn many times before, of course, but it is important to include it in my work as one of the classic examples of parasitism. Did you know that the wasp larvae will deliberately avoid the vital organs of the host as long as possible, in order to preserve its life, and thus, presumably, its freshness?"

I had not actually known that. I kept my face expressionless. "How do they know what organs are most vital to the caterpillar?"

"It is instinctual, of course. The wasps are hardly given an anatomical chart. They have simply evolved blindly over the course of millennia, growing more and more attuned to their hosts." He tapped his fingertips together. "We pity the caterpillars their suffering, but in truth, the wasps are trapped more than the caterpillars are. Their species is unable to survive without the specific host. Their fortunes are intertwined. Anything that wiped out the caterpillar would wipe out the wasp as well, but if the wasps were to go extinct, the caterpillar would neither notice nor care."

My suspicion was that Halder did not pity either caterpillar *or* wasp, but it hardly seemed politic to say so.

"Charles Darwin believed that the existence of the *Ichneumonidae* was proof that a beneficent God had not designed all of creation," Halder said musingly. "For surely He would not have deliberately created something that required such unspeakable suffering in order to survive."

I made a noncommittal noise. I was actually rather inclined to side with Darwin on this one, but I had no more wish to debate theology with Halder than I had with Phelps. Besides, Halder had not hired me for my opinions.

Still, it was something of a relief, when I went back to the specimens, to work on something other than caterpillars.

CHAPTER 10

Scritch . . . scritch . . . scritch . . .

Something was scratching to get in the bedroom door. "Dammit, Smiley," I muttered. I opened one eye, saw only the vague outline of my own hand on the pillow, and closed it again.

Scritch . . .

The sound was insistent, and must have been going on long enough to wake me up. I poked my head up from the nest of blankets, yawning. Moonlight was coming in through the narrow glass door of the bedroom. I squinted. Was that where the scraping sound was coming from? The door to the studio was open, and it sounded too loud to be coming from the hall.

Sure enough, there was a dark shape just at the door, right at shin level. As I watched, it stretched up on its hind legs and pawed at the glass.

"Smiley, you twit, did you get stuck on the balcony?"

Smiley reached up even farther and tapped the doorknob, which only proved that a cat could be highly intelligent and rather dim at the same time.

"It'd serve you right if I let you sleep outside," I called. "Maybe then you wouldn't lurk on the balcony and get cat hair in my paint."

Smiley obviously heard me, because this statement precipitated a whole volley of scratches. He actually hooked one paw around the doorknob and hung from it for a moment, as if trying to work out how to open the door himself.

I sighed. The last thing I needed was for the cat to figure

out doorknobs. One of my father's friends had a cat who could work doorknobs. There hadn't been a safe place anywhere in the house. He was particularly fond of barging into the water closet to stare at you while you attempted to attend to personal business.

"Fine," I muttered with ill grace, sitting up. "I'm coming."

I had one foot on the floor when I heard a quiet *mrrrp?* from the foot of the bed.

I looked down. Smiley looked back at me, probably wondering why I was disturbing his nest in the middle of the night.

The scratching from the door was suddenly very loud.

. . . scritch . . . scritch . . . SCRITCH . . .

I stared at the dark shape against the glass. It didn't look all that much like a cat, now that I was really looking. The ears were wrong and the legs were short and the tail was much too thin.

"Oh Jesus," I said out loud, "it's a possum."

My first instinct was actually to laugh. Possums are inherently absurd creatures. They try so hard to look scary with the hissing and all, but they're so bad at everything. I'd seen possums try to run away and run headfirst into trees. If you spend any time around them, you eventually realize this. "The Virginia opossum," my father once dryly said, "is the closest we have to a refutation of 'survival of the fittest.'"

"What are you doing?" I said to the creature, standing up and moving toward the door. "This isn't a good place for possums."

It stood on its hind legs and scratched at the door again, for all the world like Smiley trying to get in.

"Don't tell me that someone has a pet possum and lost it." I peered through the glass at it and it raised its head to look at me.

There was something on the side of its head. At first I thought it must be a trick of the moonlight or a distortion of the glass. But when I shifted to one side, nothing changed. A growth as large as my thumb hung from the right side of its face. Some kind of tumor?

"You poor thing," I murmured. Sympathy warred with curiosity, but neither were going to cause me to open the door. Letting wild animals into the house was a good way to acquire bites, fleas, or both.

It gazed at me with dark, strained eyes. The one on its right was half closed where the growth pressed against it. As I watched, it stretched up to claw at the door again, and I saw another tumor on its side, even larger than the first. *Is this some kind of disease in the local population? The marsupial equivalent of bubonic plague?*

"Shoo," I said, making flapping motions with my hands. "Get out of here. I'm very sorry for you, but I don't think I can help."

It ignored me and jumped for the doorknob again. This time it caught it in both paws and swung a hind leg up to brace against the doorframe.

The knob began to turn.

"*No,*" I said, grabbing the knob and holding it in place. "Stop it! I don't know why you want to get in, but it's not going to happen!"

I felt the knob try to twist in my hand. It was a strangely revolting feeling, as if the cold metal were some live animal sliding against my fingers. Except that I loved most live animals, and I didn't like this at *all*.

There was a latch somewhere. I hadn't bothered to throw it for days, since it didn't seem likely that anyone was going to walk through the woods to Halder's house, climb up the outside, and break in through my balcony. I hadn't figured on diseased possums.

The knob moved again as I felt up the frame for the latch. "Stop that!" I hissed at the creature. It ignored me.

I wasn't scared. That was the oddest thing to me, in retrospect. I was exasperated and baffled, yes, but it was a *possum*. Not even a particularly healthy possum. My heart was pounding, yes, but more from astonishment than fear.

At last my fingers found the sliding metal bolt. I threw it across the door and released the knob. It immediately turned all the way to the left and the door rattled against the bolt. The possum dropped back to the ground and stood for a moment. I could see its teeth in the moonlight as it opened its mouth. Was it panting?

In the hall, the clock tolled out midnight.

The creature stood up again and pushed against the door. I stared down at it. It couldn't *possibly* understand doors. Possums, in my experience, barely understood rocks. What was going on?

It can't be rabies. Possums hardly ever get it, and a rabid possum certainly wouldn't be thinking clearly enough to work a doorknob.

The door rattled against the bolt again as it pushed. Despite what I thought I knew, the creature was certainly acting as if it understood doors. It had turned the knob until it unlatched and now it was trying to open the door.

It occurred to me that if I hadn't woken up when I did, it would be in the room with me at this very moment.

I still wasn't exactly afraid, but prickles of unease went through me at the thought. I told myself that I was just concerned that Smiley would get in a scrape with it and get some disease, not that I was thinking of it snuffling along the baseboards or climbing the bedsheets. *Waking up to see the creature's lopsided stare, the strange growth squeezed against its eye . . .*

It hit the door with force this time, shoulder first. The door slammed into the bolt again, hard enough to rattle the glass in the casement. I jumped back, startled. Smiley made a low, grating sound, not quite a yowl, the sound of a cat that is contemplating violence.

"Go on," I said, a bit desperately. "Shoo! Possums do not belong here!"

It would be absurd to think that it listened, but the creature stopped. It gazed up at me for a long, long moment. There was a dark blotch at one end of the tumor that looked horribly like another eye staring back at me.

Then it turned and waddled away.

I sagged against the wall beside the window. "Jesus, Mary and Joseph," I whispered. "What was that all about?"

Should I go tell someone? But who would I tell? Mrs. Kent had gone home with Mr. Kent, and the only other people in the house were Halder and Sally. I couldn't imagine that Sally would handle an apparently crazed possum very well, and Halder would just yell at me for waking him up for a mammal. *Assuming he believed me in the first place. Probably he'd just tell me that possums don't act like that and decide I was a hysterical female.*

The frustrating thing was that he'd be right—not about the hysterical bit, but that possums *don't* act like that. I rubbed my temples. A new disease? Not rabies, but maybe something else. I knew that there were diseases in sheep that made them act strangely, although I'd never heard anything about trying to open doorknobs. Then again, I didn't know much about sheep. *God knows that there are enough diseases that make humans act strange, maybe there's some brain fever in possums now.*

The doors in the studio banged as something hit them.

Oh my god. I lunged for the next room, heart hammering, already dreading what I'd see.

Moonlight streamed through the studio's big glass doors, leaving enormous rectangles across the floor. The possum's shadow made a dark blot that stretched and twisted as it moved. It was already pawing at the doorknob.

I was halfway across the room when I heard the *click* as the knob unlatched.

My shoulder hit the door before it was more than an inch or two open, knocking the possum back onto the balcony. I held it closed, fumbling for the bolt. Double doors, damnation, where was it, it had to be here somewhere . . .

The glass rocked as the possum struck it. The force was

astonishing. I am not a small woman, but it actually shifted the door a fraction despite my weight.

The door bolt was clear at the top of the frame. Of course it was. The possum slammed into the glass again as I shot the bolt. My hands were shaking so badly that it took me two tries.

It seemed that I was afraid now after all.

I stumbled back, ready to throw myself at the door again if needed. The creature continued its assault undaunted, smashing itself against the glass over and over, *thud thud thud!*

"Surely it can't break the glass?" I said out loud. I think I was hoping to reassure myself, but my own voice rose at the end in a question, and I was not at all convincing.

I looked around the studio for something to block the lower panes, just in case it could. Easel, no—bookcase, too heavy, unless I pulled all the books out—trunk, *yes*!

The trunk weighed more than I'd expected. It occurred to me that I had no idea what was in it. Opening it would have felt like snooping, so I hadn't. But the thud of the animal's body against the glass gave me the strength of panic, and I grabbed the handles and hauled it step by step across the floor. The rug rucked up under it and the far end was probably leaving huge gouges in the wood, but I didn't care.

I dropped to my knees and shoved it into position. It blocked the lower panes on the doors and I could no longer see the possum outside. The sound of the creature hitting the glass was suddenly muffled.

I collapsed across the trunk, gasping, my forehead pressed against the lid. The carved wood made indentations in my skin, and my vision filled with gritty sparks. The thudding seemed to come from very far away.

Dear god, am I about to faint?

Don't be ridiculous. I never faint. It's simply not something I do. I clenched my teeth and breathed through my nose, and after a minute or two, the sparkles went away.

It took me a few more minutes to realize that the thudding had stopped. I lifted my head, listening.

Silence.

I could move the chest and look . . .

I could also run upstairs and throw myself off the roof, I told myself tartly. *Which would be just about as sensible.*

Did I really think that a possum was intelligent enough to give up attacking the glass and lie in wait for me instead?

Intellectually, it seemed unlikely. But everything this particular possum had done was wildly unlikely, and I wasn't going to test it now.

The wood of the chest was cool against my cheek. I knelt on the floor and waited grimly for the dawn.

"I know I sound like a perfect ninny," I told Mrs. Kent the next morning, as we climbed the steps to the studio. "But it beat itself against the glass so hard that I thought it was going to break the door. And this morning . . ."

Mrs. Kent's eyebrows had gone up when I started talking about the possum, and hadn't yet come back down. "No," she said, "no, I figure that would be upsetting, right enough." I had a depressing feeling that she was humoring me, but insisting that no, there *had* been a possum and it *had* been scary was going to make me sound like one of my old students panicking over a mouse. I clamped my lips together and led the way up the stairs.

I promise I'm not the sort of person who imagines things, Mrs. Kent. I'm a scientist. A rational observer. I have trained for years to try and see what's really there, not what I think should be there.

. . . And there was *a possum, and it* was *scary, dammit.*

When we reached the studio, she took one look at the chest in front of the door, then glanced back at me. I shrugged helplessly. I could feel the tips of my ears burning.

"Well, let's get this moved, then," she said, reaching down to take an end.

I grabbed the other, and was surprised by how heavy it was. Mrs. Kent gave me an appraising look. "You moved this all by yourself?"

"Yes," I mumbled. That was somehow even more embarrassing, since it meant that I had been gripped by the strength of panic.

Maybe she can't tell. My sleeves are loose, she doesn't know how much muscle there is under them.

The two of us wrestled the trunk out of the way. I could see twin gouges on the floor under Mrs. Kent's feet as she walked her end backward, but she didn't say anything.

And then— "Lord have mercy!"

I followed her gaze to the bottom of the door.

An irregular blotch of dried blood and pale hair clung to the glass, and a thin crack had run through the middle. From the correct angle, the crack looked almost like an eyebrow over a bloody eye.

Mrs. Kent went down to one knee to look at it. I knelt down beside her, not sure if I wanted to crow with triumph or wince because apparently it had been just as bad as I thought it was.

"Looks like it very nearly got in," she said. She sat back, shaking her head. "That's a new one. Never hear of a possum acting that way."

"Me neither."

She got up and unbolted the door, pushing the unbroken side open. I felt a panicky rush of adrenaline, as if the possum might really be lying in wait on the balcony, eight hours later.

Is that so strange? It could understand doorknobs. I had left that bit out of my account. Even though I was pretty sure that it was true, I was not willing to offer that testimony to the jury of Mrs. Kent's eyebrows. It had been much easier simply to say that it had been jumping at the door so hard that it jarred the doorknob.

"Well," said Mrs. Kent from the balcony, "it didn't get too far afterward, that's for sure."

I scrambled to my feet and found her staring down at the corpse of a possum. Its mouth lay open, the jaw misaligned, and its fur was matted with blood.

"Is it really dead?" I asked weakly, not wanting to get any closer. "I mean, it's a possum . . ."

"Since there's flies on its eyeballs right now, I'm thinking so, yeah."

God, she really must think I'm a ninny. Probably because I'm acting like one. I wiped my hands on my apron and stepped around her, then crouched down.

It was definitely dead. The tumor on the side of its face was strangely deflated, the skin hanging loose and bloody, like an empty sack. Fluid leaked from the closest eye, as if it too had deflated.

I fished a pencil out of my apron and used it to move the head to one side. The flies buzzed away in a panic, though I knew they'd be back within seconds.

There was another, similar hole on the back of its head, close to its spine. I wondered if there had been another tumor there, or what I had taken for a tumor, and I simply hadn't seen it in the dark. "If it did have a disease," I said, using the pencil to roll the poor creature over, "we should dispose of the body so that it cannot be spread." The creature's left side was clearly what it had been using to attack the window. Blood was crusted across its shoulder and I suspect that arm would have dangled if the body had not stiffened. The other lump, the one on its belly, had deflated much like the first one.

Mrs. Kent and I stared down at it, housekeeper and naturalist united in dismay. "I'll have Jackson burn it," she said finally. "And fix up the windowpane, though that'll take a few days."

"It's fine," I said absently. I set the pencil down beside the body. I couldn't imagine drawing with it again. "I'm sure it'll be fine. I don't think I'll be using the balcony for a while anyway."

Mrs. Kent left me alone with a promise to send Mr. Kent up directly. I knew that I should get back to work, but I was restless and unable to settle. Carefully adding leg hairs to paintings of nearly identical flies seemed rather less important than it had yesterday. So Halder got his flies a day or two later than I'd hoped. Would he notice? Would he even care? He wasn't going to praise me for having been early, that's for sure. I was already failing to meet the deadline he'd set my predecessor, and never mind that he hadn't bothered to hire a replacement for an entire year.

I paced through the studio, trying not to look at the cracked windowpane and failing miserably. When I found my gaze straying there for the third time, I turned away and told myself firmly to look at something else. Anything else.

My eye fell upon the chest, still standing in the middle of the floor. Why had it been so heavy, anyway? It hadn't really occurred to me to open it, since I still felt on some level that I was a guest in a stranger's room. But if it was full of my predecessor's things, those were more or less mine now anyway. Maybe it was more paints, or brushes, or boxes of paper. (Come to think of it, it was just about heavy enough to be full of paper.)

I knelt down and flipped up the latch.

As it turned out, I wasn't far wrong. The trunk was full of paper, though it was all contained between stiff covers. I picked one up and turned it over in my hands. The edges of the pages were wavey and stained from watercolor washes. *Are those . . . ?*

Sketchbooks.

The spine made a cracking noise, stiff from disuse, when I opened to somewhere in the middle. A page of faces looked back at me, quick gesture sketches with nothing like the precision of the insect illustrations. Yet I could see the same hand at work—something in the use of color, maybe, or an echo of a beetle's carapace in the line of a cheekbone.

I was startled to recognize Phelps among the faces there. But of course, Mrs. Kent knew him, so there was no reason that the artist wouldn't. *Asa Phelps* was written next to his image, in the familiar handwriting, reminding me irresistibly of the scientific names written under insects in the other sketchbook. *A. phelps, type specimen collected in North Carolina* . . . I snorted.

Then I turned the page and laughed out loud. There was Mrs. Kent from multiple angles, looking younger but with the same skeptical expression that I was learning so well. One had been worked into a watercolor study. The artist had mixed indigo into the shadows of her face and the hollows of her neck, a hint of warm yellow ochre into the highlights, so that she glowed on the page.

At the top of the page, the artist had written *It's Rose's birthday! Can't believe it's been another year already.*

I sat down cross-legged in front of the chest, possum forgotten, and paged through the sketchbook. Mrs. Kent again, with her husband this time, both of them shown laughing together, faces detailed, framed by quick lines that suggested arms around each other's shoulders. I'd never seen Mrs. Kent laugh like that in person.

The artist had captured Halder as well, in a dozen poses, mostly at his desk. The lines in his face were as deep as ever, and none of his expressions looked terribly pleased. The artist didn't seem pleased either, because they had crossed out several of the drawings and hadn't painted in any of them. Nor had they written anything next to the drawings, which struck me as odd, because the rest of the sketchbook was full of dashed-off comments, the sort that the artist never expects anyone else to read. Some of them were dated, most were not.

Wet today, stuck inside.

March 14th— Trillium up!

Went to town today. Horses outside general store.

Church very, very long today, saw these flowers outside, couldn't wait to draw them.

Ugh, can't draw at all today. (That last accompanied a handful of crossed-out sketches, and made me sigh with recognition. We all have those days.)

I turned pages slowly. Trees were interspersed with drawings of faces, sketches of hands, horses, wagons, even a remarkably detailed painting of an apple. Exactly the sort of thing that's in my sketchbooks, honestly. It felt familiar and slightly intimidating all at once. My predecessor was just so damn *good*. I took some small comfort that her drawing of trillium was not as good as one of mine would be, but her humans were a good deal better.

The last half of the book seemed to be full of sketches that could only be Smiley as a kitten. I turned back to the beginning, to the very first page.

Property of Louisa Halder
Halder House, Chatham

If found, I beg you, of Christian charity, to return this volume.

1893

I stared at the name blankly. *Louisa Halder? As in Dr. Halder?* Was I here to replace a daughter? A sister? A maiden aunt?

In my mind, I heard Mrs. Kent, the first night. "He won't marry you."

My god. Did he hire me to replace his wife?

"Miss Wilson?" Jackson's voice was muffled through the door. "Rose sent me up to deal with a possum?"

"Yes! Sorry!" I scrambled to my feet and opened the door for him. He glanced around the room with mild interest, including the stack of sketchbooks beside the trunk, but didn't comment. I was glad to see that he was wearing heavy leather gloves.

"It's on the balcony." I showed him the broken pane and then the pitiful body beside it.

"Lord have mercy." He squatted down and studied the smear of blood and hair on the window. "Never heard of a possum doing this. If it was stuck inside, maybe, trying to get out, but from this side . . ."

"Seemed more like it was trying to get in," I said, and then immediately wished I hadn't said that out loud at all.

"Yeah," he said, shoving his hat back from his forehead. "Yeah, it . . . yeah." He shook his head. "Right. Well, I'll take it away and then fix that window up for you. Rose said the body ought to be burned?"

"In case it has some disease," I said firmly. "And be careful handling it yourself, please."

"Right. I'll go get some burlap." He shook his head. "Poor devil. Wonder if it was trying to bash the wolf worm out."

I froze halfway over the threshold to the studio. "What did you say?"

"It had wolf worm." Jackson glanced up at me. "Three of 'em, looks like."

I did not want to spend any more time looking at that poor, bloodied rag of a body, but if there was an explanation for the creature's behavior, I had to have it. I stepped back out onto the balcony. "Wolf worm?" Why did that sound familiar?

"Here." He pointed to the deflated tumor on the side of the creature's face. The wound gaped like a small red mouth. "It was all curled up inside here, then it must have hatched out. And there's another one back here, right on the back of its head." The possum flopped loosely as he turned it over with his boot. "You see 'em on the squirrels around here sometimes. Doesn't usually kill 'em, but they're not usually right on the head like this." He scratched his head. "Might've been pressing on its brain or something."

"Ah," I said. I could hear Dr. Halder lecturing in my mind. . . . *a* Cuterebra. *Botfly. Also called 'wolf worms.' Parasitic on mammals.*

"Don't worry," said Jackson, seeing my expression. "They don't bother humans much."

"No, of course not," I mumbled, scratching at my wrist involuntarily.

He went off to get burlap. I went back to the sketchbooks, trying, with difficulty, to push the idea of the botfly out of my mind. *A thing hanging on the side of your head, pressing against your face and you can't get it out and it keeps growing and your skin stretches and it starts to cover one of your eyes and maybe you feel it moving, the swollen body wriggling against your skull and it's just a thin plate of bone between your brain and the larva that's drinking your fluids . . .*

I might start bashing myself against a window too.

With difficulty, I forced my mind away from that image. I picked up another sketchbook and welcomed the question of Louisa Halder's identity in its place.

This sketchbook was dated from 1897, and it was only partly completed. The first few pages were studies of acorns and oak galls and an elegant drawing of a sweet gum ball that almost made me like the damn things. Then more faces. Most of them were of a man this time, one I didn't know. He had a long, angular face and short dark hair. I don't know if he was handsome. Something about the line work made me think Louisa had thought he was.

Her son? I wondered. In the drawings, he looked to be about the age I was now. How old had she been? If she was Halder's age, she could probably have had an adult son. Would that make him Halder's son as well?

Well, if she was actually his wife, that would be logical . . . but was she? It *felt* correct, but just because it made *sense* didn't mean it was *true*, as any good scientist knew. How could I find out for certain?

Could I ask someone? Not Halder, who was so cagey about his illustrator. *1897 was a little over a year ago. Sally's probably too young to have been working as a maid then, but Mrs. Kent would surely remember . . .*

And there I stopped, because Mrs. Kent had definitely known Louisa Halder—the sketchbooks were full of portraits—but when I had asked her about who had used the studio, she'd said she didn't know. Had she lied to me?

No, she didn't. She said that she couldn't rightly say. Which I thought *meant that she didn't know, but that isn't quite the same thing. She walked right up to the edge of a lie, but she didn't quite go over.*

I sat back on my heels, baffled and annoyed. First Phelps and the shed, Halder and the chickens, now Mrs. Kent? Why were people keeping secrets about things that seemed so utterly innocuous?

Had Louisa died?

Halder had one of her sketchbooks in his office, the one full of insects, but he'd left these here. Had he not known they existed, or had he simply not cared?

Given that there aren't any bugs in these, he probably just didn't think they mattered. No, that was unkind. Perhaps he'd been grieving and simply shut the room up and tried to ignore it. Grief takes people strangely, God knows. I remembered how calm and efficient I had been when Father died, deciding what to keep and what to sell, as if my life and my future hadn't been buried in the ground alongside him.

Though it was strange, now that I noticed, that there were no insects in the books. Not even a bee or a butterfly crossed the pages. Flowers, yes, and studies of animal skulls and Smiley at various ages, but not a single insect.

Perhaps she drew them so often that she was tired of them. I could certainly understand that.

The door opened again as Jackson returned with a burlap sack and a shovel. I jumped up, sketchbook falling from my lap. "Jackson!"

He swung toward me, startled. "What? Is it the possum?"

"No, no." I shook my head. "No, I—I have a question."

"Sure, shoot." He opened the door and lifted the possum on the end of the shovel, then maneuvered it into the sack. "What's on your mind?"

"Who was Louisa Halder?"

"Ah." I couldn't see his face, but there was a world of meaning packed into that syllable, if only I could decipher it. He stood, holding the sack with its unfortunate contents. "She was the doctor's wife."

Ha! I was right. "But . . . ah . . . when I asked Mrs. Kent about who had lived here before . . ." I trailed off, realizing that could be taken as a criticism of his wife.

Jackson glanced toward the floor, as if seeing through the layers of boards to where Mrs. Kent was at work in the kitchen. "She ain't too keen to talk about it." He paused, clearly weighing up how much to say. "They were pretty good friends, Louisa and Rose. And I sure wouldn't go saying anything to the doctor. It was quite a . . ." He stopped, as if he'd thought better of what he was going to say.

"Quite a . . . ?"

Jackson shook his head. "Quite a *mess*. It's all done and dusted now though." His lips thinned. "I'd appreciate it if you didn't ask Rose about it. She still feels like she shoulda done more, and it puts her out of temper."

"All right," I said. "Err . . . did she die?"

"She left," said Jackson, "and who can blame her?" He glanced toward the glass door and the dead possum, and for a moment

I thought that would be his last word on the subject, but the soul of a storyteller is hard to keep down. "Been a bit over a year now, though she was unhappy for a long time afore that . . ."

The story was short and all too familiar. Louisa had come from money, but had fallen in love with a man of science and put both money and artistic talents to work in his service.

Eventually, though, Halder's bitterness was too much even for Louisa, and she fell in love with another man. "Saul, his name was. Saul Gregor. Bit of a drifter, but he'd come into town a year or so earlier, and took one look at Louisa and she took one look at him and they were in love like a storybook. I'm not saying she did anything wrong," Jackson said. "Don't think that for a moment. She was a real good woman and a friend of Rose's, and Halder's . . . well, you know Halder. All she really wanted was somebody who'd love her back, and here Saul thought she'd hung the moon and the stars."

"So she ran away with him?"

"Tried to." Jackson shook his head again. I could sense genuine regret behind the words. "She snuck out one night, without much more than the clothes on her back, and met up with Saul. They'd planned to run, of course. Only somebody tipped Halder off and Halder was waiting for 'em both with a rifle. I don't say he meant to use it, but Saul got between the two of 'em and Halder fired on him. Saul took a bullet and yelled at Louisa to run, he'd catch up, so she did. Only he didn't ever catch up." He sighed. "Rose saw the whole damn thing. That's why she doesn't want to talk about it."

I swallowed. This was more of a tragedy than I'd expected. Halder's rages had alarmed me, but it had never occurred to me that he might be a killer. "And he didn't get into any trouble with the law? No one arrested him?"

Jackson snorted. "Feeling 'mongst a lot of people in these parts was that Halder'd been within his rights to shoot a man running off with his wife. So the law was real careful not to ask any questions that would lead to answers they didn't want to hear. Saul never even got a headstone in the churchyard."

"What happened to Louisa?"

"She was brokenhearted and wanted to go back to find Saul, but I'm given to understand that some cooler heads among the womenfolk convinced her that would be a very bad idea." Jackson wouldn't meet my eyes, and I suspected that he knew more than he was saying. "Now, if you'll excuse me, I've got a possum to burn."

I let him pass. I had wrung as much information from him as I was going to get. Much more and I'd be going up against Rose Kent, which was the last thing I wanted to do.

Was it true? I didn't think Jackson would lie to me, but he'd certainly felt no qualms in spinning me a tale about blood thieves. I wouldn't put it past him to have embroidered a few details here and there, but which ones?

I ran a finger slowly over a page of the sketchbook, one with the unnamed man's face on it. Saul, the doomed lover. Though if he was dead and Louisa was still alive, I wondered, why did the studio feel so much like she was haunting it?

CHAPTER 11

"Dr. Halder?"

I was pleased with how light and calm my voice was. It was smooth and professional and there was no way that he could guess the questions that beat against the walls of my skull. *Did you really get away with murder?*

There was no answer for that question, but I had another, more immediate one. One that Halder was uniquely equipped to answer.

"Eh? Oh, it's you, Wilson." Halder sat back in his chair. Smiley slid past my ankles and circled the desk, clearly plotting what stack of paper to knock over first.

"I had a question, Doctor. A possum tried to get into my room last night."

"What?" He turned toward me, his eyebrows drawing low. "A possum? What are you talking about?"

"It was trying to break through the glass," I said. "I know that it sounds bizarre. It was very strange behavior for a possum. But this morning, when Jackson collected the body, he found three . . ." I took a deep breath. ". . . three deflated warbles. From botflies."

"It happens," he said gruffly, swinging back to his papers.

"I know it does. What I wanted to know was if it was possible that having two botflies like that on its head might have affected its behavior. Driven it to madness, like rabies."

This time Halder stared at me for quite a long time. My gut began to clench tighter as the seconds ticked by. Had I somehow offended him? He was so protective of his notes, had I somehow guessed at something that he thought was a secret?

"I don't . . ." he began, and then stopped. "That would certainly be unusual." He pinched the bridge of his nose tightly. "Describe its behavior to me again. Describe it *exactly*."

I obeyed. When I reached the part about it leaping at the doorknob, he muttered something to himself, then cut me off. "Where is the body now?"

"Err . . . Jackson was going to burn it."

For a moment I thought there might be another eruption of temper. His face flushed dark red that would have required multiple layers of crimson to capture. But instead of yelling, he leapt to his feet and sprinted out the door at a speed I would never have guessed him capable of, shouting for Jackson.

I followed, more than a little surprised. It had been an odd question, but that odd? I truly hadn't expected him to do anything but dismiss me out of hand.

Halder flung open the door and charged into the garden. "Jackson! Jackson, where are you?!"

We ran the man to earth at the far end of the vegetable garden. He had been building a fire of brush in the burn pit, and looked up in surprise at our shout. "Sir?"

"Give me that!" Halder shouted.

"Err . . ." Jackson looked down at the bundle in his hands. "Sir, it's a dead—"

"I know what it is, man!" Halder snatched the bundle away from Jackson and began to unwrap it, revealing the stiffened body beneath. "Where . . . there! Yes. Warbles, most definitely." He slid a finger into the opening in the slack skin and pulled it open, looking inside.

I took a step back. I know that rabies is transmitted by bites, and that possums rarely carry it in any event, but the sight of Halder's bare fingers in the bloody flesh was alarming.

Halder's face screwed up in concentration, then he turned,

looking around almost wildly. His eye fell on the lean-to that served as a potting shed, and he rushed to it and swept his arm along the table, knocking trowels, pots, and bits of twine to the ground. The crash of breaking ceramic did not even seem to register with him.

Jackson looked at the mess with resigned dismay. "Sir . . . ?"

I could have told him that it was no use. There was a light in the doctor's eyes that I knew well, though I had never seen it in Halder before. Scientific curiosity had set its claws in him and nothing short of an anvil to the head was likely to penetrate.

He laid the possum out on the table, wiping his fingers on the burlap. "Miss Wilson," he said over his shoulder. "Go to my study. There is a leather case by the desk there. Bring it to me at once."

I did not like the man, but his intensity was infectious. I snatched up my skirts and ran.

The leather case was surprisingly heavy and resembled a doctor's bag. I lugged it back down the stairs, to where Halder was practically dancing with impatience. He snatched it from me and opened it up.

The kit inside was a cross between a surgeon's and a butterfly collector's. He pulled out forceps and metal probes, then a small, sharp scalpel, and set to work.

Jackson edged away, but I found myself at Halder's elbow, peering down at his work. He cut away the leading flap of the warble and peeled it back, revealing a round hollow in the jaw muscle and the skull beneath. "There," he murmured, half to himself. "The larva was up against the bone, and—*there!*"

He grabbed a metal probe and poked it through a small, neat hole, just behind the eye. I swallowed and told myself that I was fascinated.

"Intrusion into the brain," Halder breathed. "The hole is located where the larva's head would be, but how could it have penetrated bone?"

He turned the possum, looking for the warble on the back of

the skull. Rigored as it was, the body did not wish to achieve that angle. "Miss Wilson!" he barked. "Hold the specimen steady!"

Nature, I told myself. *This is an act of nature, and I am a naturalist.* I picked up the burlap to wrap around my hands—I was not risking my fingers so close to a scalpel, no matter what Halder thought—and took hold. It might as well have been a wooden carving of a possum.

Fully rigored, I thought absently, as the doctor began carving into the warble at the back of the skull. *Usually achieved within three hours of death, lasting up to eighteen hours. Of course it would be stiff by now, it beat itself to death last night.*

Something itched at my mind, but Halder let out a sudden cry of triumph and snatched up another probe. "Look!" he said. "Look, there! It has burrowed through the bone and deeply into the brain!" He tilted the possum and slid a probe in, far deeper than I would have guessed possible.

"I did not think botflies did that," I said.

"They don't!" He beamed at me, his insectile face suddenly transformed. "This has never been recorded before! Never!"

I don't delude myself that Halder thought I was in any way worthy of sharing this discovery with him. If I hadn't been there, he would have told Jackson, and if Jackson hadn't been there, he would have told the cat. This was scientific enthusiasm, pure and simple.

He withdrew the probe, made a note of the depth, and began hastily scrawling down measurements on a pad from the bag. I set the body down with some relief.

"Could this explain its strange behavior?" I asked.

"What? Oh yes, yes. Well . . . possibly." He frowned down at the possum. "There are parasites that change the host's behavior, certainly. The wasp *Ampulexa sinensis* stings a cockroach in the brain and renders it docile. It leads the roach back to the burrow by its antenna, and then lays its eggs in it. And of course that Wallace fellow was terribly excited about his *Ophio-*

cordyceps fungus and the ants. Though those are much more directed. This may simply have been pressure on the brain causing strange behavior . . ." He trailed off, scribbling more notes and muttering to himself.

I suppressed another shudder. I had heard of the *Ophiocordyceps* fungus discovered by the famous Alfred Russel Wallace—there were still fights in nature journals about it now, twenty-five years later—but I had not heard of the wasp. While I had never previously empathized with a cockroach, it was much too easy to imagine oneself being helplessly led around, then lying passively in the dark while *things* hatched inside you and began to gnaw . . .

"Miss Wilson!" Halder barked, and I looked up, grateful for the interruption, if not his tone. "Are you certain that the warbles were present last night? And that the larvae had not yet evacuated?"

"Completely sure," I said. "I thought they were tumors."

"And it did not occur to you to capture the beast?"

I drew myself up. "Dr. Halder, I believed it might be rabid. And when it stopped beating at my door, I assumed that it had left the balcony. I did not realize that it had simply dropped dead a few feet away."

Halder sighed, much put-upon. "No, of course not. It would be too much to hope. I must show Sanders. He knows his mammals, he will be able to tell me . . . Jackson, prepare the wagon— No, never mind that. Saddle my horse. I must be in Raleigh at the earliest possible moment, before the body has a chance to decay any further!" He wrapped the bundle back up and made for the house, clutching the dead possum to his chest as if it were an infant.

Jackson gazed after him, glanced at me, and shook his head. "The man's completely mad," he said.

"Probably." I didn't feel like getting into a discussion over the joys of discovery. Mostly I felt an overwhelming need to wash my hands. Possibly with lye.

I went inside and scrubbed myself nearly raw with water that only had a few beetle parts floating in it. Partway through, I heard the sound of hoofbeats, a trot breaking rapidly into a gallop, as Halder made for Siler City and the train station. In the hall, the clock struck eleven.

The itch in my memory suddenly blossomed. I had staggered downstairs not long after dawn, and had found Mrs. Kent. Call it seven in the morning. She had insisted that I eat, and I had obeyed, not wanting to seem any more hysterical than I already did. She had finished cooking, then agreed to go see the door. Had that been about eight? And it had taken at least an hour for Jackson to arrive, while I perused the sketchbooks. Yet when he had nudged it with his boot, the body had been as limp as a dishrag.

I had heard the clock toll midnight while I was frantically throwing the lock on the door. No matter how I calculated, the possum had been alive on the balcony until almost dawn, separated from me by no more than a pane of glass.

The time of death hardly matters, does it? It didn't get in, and what's an hour or two either way?

Yet despite that, it troubled me to think of the poor mad thing lying outside the door all night. Both because it had been suffering, and because I could not escape the feeling that it had been waiting for me to unlock the door so that it could finally get inside.

I went back to my room in a mood that had passed through pensive and come out the other side. Possums with wolf worms in the brain. Halder's excitement. The sketchbooks.

Dear Lord, the sketchbooks.

I picked one up, flipped through it, and set it down again. *Louisa.* What had become of her? Had she died? Had she gotten away safely? Had Halder really killed her lover?

Who might know more? If Mrs. Kent didn't want to talk, who would?

The image of Ma Kersey dropped into my head, fully formed, like a page ripped from the gossip rag of the gods. *I would bet my eyeteeth that she knows what happened to Louisa. Possibly before Louisa did.*

I snatched up my own sketchbook and went to find out.

"You want to see Ma Kersey?" Mrs. Kent gave me a wary look, as if a rabbit had just announced its desire to pay a visit to the wolf. "What for?"

I'd run the housekeeper to earth two doors down from the studio, where she was determinedly airing out a guest bedroom. Furniture huddled under sheets like the ghost of occupations past.

Fortunately, I had already thought of an answer to this question. "I draw plants," I said. "Well, I used to. For my father, you see. I like them a lot more than bugs."

Mrs. Kent smiled, though she still looked a trifle puzzled. "I can understand that. Plants, eh? Flowers and such?"

"Yes, but also . . . here, it's easier to show you." I fetched the *Botanica* from my room and opened it to my favorite page, the jack-in-the-pulpit. A strange little vase of a plant, with dark streaks running up from the base, and the spadix tucked inside like a tongue in a toad's mouth, and another illustration alongside it, of the bright orange fruit that clung to it later in the year.

Mrs. Kent gazed at it for a long time, turning the pages almost reverently. "So this is what you do . . ." she murmured.

I felt a sudden stab of embarrassment. Had I really not shown her any of my work? No, I hadn't. However good a job I did on the screwworm larvae, it wasn't the sort of thing I could imagine showing Mrs. Kent, and I've never been the sort of person to show off my sketchbooks. And yet she was, by leaps and bounds, the closest thing I had to a friend in this place.

I cleared my throat awkwardly. "Yes. That's what I've been doing in the studio all day. Only bugs, not plants."

"Virginia bluebells," she said softly, running a fingertip over the page. "These were my mother's favorite."

I had no idea what to say.

"You have quite a gift," said Mrs. Kent, handing the book back to me. She cleared her throat and straightened her back, apparently realizing that she'd been poring over the book for the last few minutes instead of working. "What's it to do with Ma Kersey though?"

"Plants," I explained. The deception, which hadn't bothered me in the slightest five minutes ago, suddenly seemed like a betrayal. Nevertheless, I had started down this road, and suddenly changing my mind would sound even stranger. "You said she was good at doctoring. A person like that uses a lot of herbs—they always do—and I wanted to ask her about some of what she uses. Father was very interested in things like pollination and seed dispersal, but he never cared much for things like medicinal uses. I did. Do."

Mrs. Kent nodded. "Ah, yeah, herbs. She does a spring tonic that'll curl your toes and chase the winter right out of your bones." She fanned the air with her apron. A little breeze forced its way through the sluggish heat and stirred the furniture covers. "Right. She's not hard to find. Just go left as you come to the road and go about a mile down, maybe a little bit more. You'll cross two roads, and then there's an itty-bitty drive with about five houses on it. Hers is the last one in the row." She paused, eyeing me up and down. "She likes people to ask her for advice. She'll probably be happy to tell you. But I'd take her a little gift anyway, just in case."

I set out the next morning with a satchel I'd borrowed from Jackson slung over one shoulder. Despite leaving early enough that it was still cool, I can't say that it was a particularly pleasant walk. The weight of the *Botanica* made the strap dig into my shoulder after the first half mile, and the road itself was in dismal repair. The recent rain had turned parts of it into sucking mud, and I had to switch which side I walked on multiple times to avoid puddles that resembled small inland seas.

Oh well, it's still more comfortable than riding in Phelps's wagon, I thought, *with all his talk of devils in the woods.* Presumably he'd been referring to the blood thieves? I suppressed the urge to look over my shoulder. There was nothing out here. It had been three years ago. I'd been roaming around at night myself, and the only thing I'd seen was Halder, who had been quite alarming enough, thank you.

The distance was more like a mile and a half, all told, but the right-hand side opened up after a while, into fields that had been cleared for farmland.

My mind kept returning to the possum, to the hole drilled into its skull . . . I ordered myself to think about something else.

Fine. Is Halder really a murderer, do you think?

This was not an improvement. I tried to distract myself by identifying the plants that sprung up along the verge—dock and bitter cress, garden vetch, crownbeard and speedwell. On the side partly shaded by the woods, burgundy wood sorrel put up tiny flowers. When I ran out of new plants, I went to birdcalls. The scolding of a Carolina chickadee, the liquid trilling of a hermit thrush, the white-throated sparrow that calls *Old Sam Peabody, Peabody, Peabody* . . . from low to the ground.

It was with some relief that I reached the turnoff. The row of houses was just as described. Ma Kersey's house stood a little apart, surrounded by a garden that did not so much grow as rampage in all directions. A few chickens ran screaming from my approach, and a rooster stood on top of a ramshackle henhouse and shouted insults at me in Chicken.

Unlike her birds, Ma Kersey was delighted to see me, or at least did a pretty good imitation, and professed equal delight with the gift I brought her. I had spent part of the evening carefully drawing a rabbit, based on a few quick sketches I'd done of one that had been hanging around Jackson's garden, made larger and fluffier with imagination. I wrote *World-Famous Chatham Rabbit* underneath, which she read aloud when I presented it to her with some trepidation. (It's always awkward to give people art that you've made. It feels egotistical, as if you think so highly of yourself and your skill that you expect other people to be impressed as well. Even now, when I make my living with that skill, I can never quite shake the feeling that people are humoring me like a child when I give them something I've drawn.)

When she had finished admiring the rabbit, she put the drawing up on a high shelf, looking down over the room, then put on the teakettle.

"How you settling in?" asked Ma Kersey. She cocked her head to one side, eyes bird-bright. "How do you like them woods?"

"I love the woods. I grew up tromping through them with my father, painting things."

"Mmm."

I wasn't sure if that was an invitation or not, but I decided to treat it as one. "Though I heard something about some . . . err . . . bad things that happened in the woods years ago," I said cautiously, "but that was a long time ago. Errr . . . blood thieves?"

Ma Kersey's bright little eyes narrowed. "Jackson's been telling you tales, has he?"

I gulped. I didn't want to get him in trouble, and I had a feeling that Ma Kersey could make quite a lot of trouble if she chose. "He didn't mean any harm. I'm sure he was just trying to put a scare in the new girl."

"Mmm." Ma Kersey poured the tea. "Wasn't just a story. Some bad things went on back then."

I was beginning to regret starting down this road at all. Despite the goodwill the Chatham rabbit had won me, the old woman's tone was, if not hostile, at least chill. "Well," I said hastily, "he said they caught some people and it all stopped happening."

"The three-month babies," she said.

"Beg pardon?"

"Brother and sister, they were." She shook her head. "Old story. Old gossip. Never mind it. It's over now. For good, I hope. What's this you're wanting to know about plants?"

The phrase "three-month babies" had lodged like a thorn in my brain, but I shook it off and explained about medicinal plants, passing the heavy copy of the *Botanica* to her. Ma Kersey read the title aloud, and began to page through it. When she reached a plant that she knew, she told what she used it for, and she knew a *lot* of uses. I hastily pulled out my sketchbook and began taking notes. It was unlikely that there would ever be another edition of *Botanica*, but there have been a few books published by female naturalists over the years, and books on herbs and home remedies seem to be of greater interest to publishers. Perhaps my hasty deception might prove truthful after all.

My hand nearly cramped by the time she had finished telling me all the uses for dock leaves, and I stopped and shook it out. I was sneakingly grateful when she reached my favorite section of the book, page after page of terrestrial orchids. Few of them have any medicinal use that I know of. Ma Kersey looked through them appreciatively nonetheless—crane-fly orchid, rattlesnake plantain, wake-robin, pink lady's slipper. "Mmm-mm-mm," she said. "You drew all these, huh?"

"Every one. Though it took a long time."

"I'll just bet it did." She sat back, pushing the book back toward me. "And now you're drawing for the doctor's book, are you?"

I didn't think I'd get a better conversational opening than this. "I am. Though that one's partly done already." I licked suddenly dry lips. "Halder's wife, Louisa, was the illustrator before me."

"Oh, *Louisa*," said Ma Kersey, shaking her head. "Poor unhappy soul."

"I heard that she left . . . ?" I let the last word trail off.

Ma Kersey pounced on it like Smiley on a piece of string. "Left! Ran for her life, more like. Oh, it's a sad tale, it is." She poured herself out more tea. "She was younger 'n you when she married the doctor. Not that he was as old then as he is now. They were married a good fifteen years. Probably felt like fifteen hundred, so far as Louisa was concerned."

"The doctor can be difficult to get along with," I said.

"The doctor's a horse's ass, if'n you ask me."

"That too," I admitted. She cackled. I plunged onward. "Although I didn't figure him for a murderer, but Jackson said . . ." I let the word trail again, and Ma Kersey obligingly picked it up.

"Saul, yep. Damn shame. Odd fellow, but a good one, and he loved Louisa something fierce." She sighed. "Suppose if I was being charitable, I'd say the doctor didn't mean to kill him, but I doubt he shed many tears when he did."

So it was true. He really had killed Saul. I had no idea how to feel about that. Aloud I said, "Dear god. Poor Louisa."

"Ayep." Ma Kersey gestured with her cup. "Anyway, she ain't been seen around these parts since, and if she's smart, she won't be. Halder's still got all her money, and maybe she could get a divorce and try to get some of it back, but I wouldn't give a plug nickel for her chances."

This struck me as extremely depressing. I clutched the *Botanica* against my chest, appreciating the solid, grounding weight. "And you're sure she got away? *Really* sure?"

I hadn't *really* thought Louisa was chained up in a shed being fed live chickens at random intervals . . . at least, I was pretty sure I hadn't . . . but it would be nice to be sure.

Ma Kersey gave me an odd look. "Sure as sure can be. Why?"

I had no good answer. I ducked my head and said, "Just . . . I worry about things." Which was certainly *a* truth, if not quite *the* truth.

She drummed her fingers on the table for a moment, studying

me. "You ever start to worry about Halder, you tell Rose," she said abruptly. "Or come tell me."

I nodded, though the mention of Rose brought another question. "Jackson said that Mrs. Kent . . . Rose . . . was Louisa's friend. But how can she still work for Halder?"

"Ahhh . . ." Ma Kersey shook her head. "Don't judge her too harsh. Her mama was in a bad way right then. She'd got old and her mind wandered 'til she could get lost inside her own house. Rose didn't dare move her. Probly she always meant to leave, as soon as she could. And then her mama dies and it's hard to think about moving right then, and pretty soon it's another year past." She poured out more tea, even though it was growing cold. "And she keeps lookin' for another place, but there ain't so many people around here who'll hire a married couple who ain't the same color. Halder's a mean old bastard, but he ain't stingy and Louisa got away safe, so maybe it doesn't seem so urgent now."

I felt my shoulders sag as I pictured Mrs. Kent, hating Halder and unable to leave because her mother was dying. I'd sat in a tiny little bedroom myself, listening to my father drown in his own lungs. I'd have worked for the Confederacy or the Devil if it meant I could pay the doctor. "God," I muttered. "How awful."

"It ain't easy to swallow some things down. Makes you feel like maybe you aren't who you thought you were. She's got a good husband though, and that's got to count for something. I'll send you home with some of my tonic for her." Ma Kersey stood, and I took it as a sign that the interview was over. I gathered up my books, thanking her again for sharing her knowledge with me.

She waved her hand. "Ain't nothing. Told plenty of people over the years." She gave me a sly grin. "Couple of 'em brought me rabbits, but none so fine as that one."

I was turning to go when another thought occurred to me.

"Ma Kersey?"

"Eh?" She paused, the shadow of the door falling over half her face, a study of light and darkness.

"You said earlier . . . ah . . . something about 'three-month babies'?"

"Ah. Them." A gold tooth flashed from the shadows. "Never were right, not since the day they were born. Their granddaddy was a preacher. Not a kind man, but he thought he knew his duty." For a moment, I thought she would stop there and wave it off as old gossip as she had earlier, but then she heaved a great sigh, closed the door, and sat back down. I perched on the edge of the chair, waiting.

"Those two. Sad little things, they were. Brother and sister. I delivered them, you know. Their mama didn't want to tell nobody about it. Strange, that was. Not that young women don't get in trouble sometimes and try to hide it, the Lord knows, but this was a different kind of trouble, though I was too stupid to see it at the time."

"What kind of trouble?"

She picked at the corner of a shawl with her fingernails. "Swore up and down that she'd met the father not three months earlier. I thought, fine, she just doesn't know how to count, or maybe there'd been somebody six months afore that. Or maybe she just didn't know what she was doing would lead to a baby. Wouldn't be the first girl who thought you couldn't get pregnant afore you were married or if you were standing up or some damn fool thing like that. But afterward, I thought yeah, maybe it *was* only three months. Wouldn't surprise me now. Those babes weren't right from the first."

I pinched the bridge of my nose. This was making even less sense than I'd expected. "Weren't right?"

"Not shaped right. Not moving right. Eyes all sealed shut like a kitten's, and a mouth full of milk teeth like a kitten too." She made a small, exasperated sound. "But I've delivered more babies than I can remember, and they don't all come out right. Sometimes they don't grow right inside and they don't live more'n five minutes. Got twins that were all grown together once, and more'n a few with some extra bits here and there. You ever seen one of those two-headed calves in a jar? People're no different, really." She grabbed the teapot from the side table and poured us both another cup. I accepted the one that she thrust at me, even though it was tepid by now.

"Anyway, those babies weren't like that. They weren't like a person gone wrong. It was like they were supposed to be some other thing entirely." She took a sip of tea, then stared at it in disgust, nose wrinkling. "Shit."

"It's fine—" I started to say, but she snatched the cup out of my hand and dumped it out.

"Never mind the damn tea. I need something stronger anyway." She retrieved a flask from somewhere under the shawl, and poured a small amount of the contents into my cup, then slugged some back straight from the bottle. The smell alone made my eyes sting. I lifted my cup and let the alcohol just touch my lower lip, which promptly began to burn. Jackson's moonshine clearly had nothing on Ma Kersey's.

"Drink up, it's good for you. Practically medicinal." She gazed past me at nothing. "Not like a person. That's what I've always thought," she said moodily.

"Err . . ." I tried to find my way back into the conversation. "Thought what?"

"Those babies. They were like a whole 'nother sort of animal. Wrong for one of us, but maybe right for one of them. And maybe they did only take three months to get born." She put back more of the moonshine. I tried letting a drop trickle between my teeth, and immediately regretted it.

"Did you ask their mother about it?" I asked, when I could breathe again.

"Couldn't. She didn't survive. You see that much blood going in, you know you can't save the mama. Would have been better if I couldn't save the babies either, but that's the sort of thing you don't know 'til later." Ma Kersey shook her head slowly.

"Not sure she would have made it anyway. Wasn't hardly anything left of her once them babies came out, like carrying 'em had hollowed her out. Most women gain weight, but not her. Wrists like sticks and her skin hangin' loose as an old coat."

In my mind's eye, a green caterpillar clung to a stem, its body sagging as white wasp larvae devoured it from the inside. I took a larger swallow of liquor, not caring about the taste any longer, hoping the burn would drive the image away.

"Anyway, her granddaddy took 'em and said he was gonna raise 'em, learn 'em their Bible, made sure they had clothes on their backs. Not that they were simple, nothin' like that. But strange, everything about them was strange. Their eyes were shut but with eyelids so thin you could see 'em watching you through the skin. Really watching too, not just staring the way any baby does." Ma Kersey swirled the moonshine as if it were the finest brandy instead of a bare step up from wood alcohol. "Always meant to go back and check on 'em, but the next thing you know, the court strikes down the Rights Act of '75 and things go completely to hell here." She snorted. "All of us had a bit on our minds, you might say."

"Understandable," I said, a bit faintly. I had been born the year after the war ended. Fortunately, my father had been engaged in an extensive survey of wildflowers in New England when everything came to a head. We'd moved back while the ink of the South's surrender was still wet on the page. But I was old enough to remember Reconstruction, and how things had seemed to get better, and then suddenly it was all gone again.

Ma Kersey wiped her mouth. "Anyway, lost track of them and their granddaddy, but I didn't think much of it. Lost track of plenty of people after the war, after all. Didn't even occur to me they might be behind all the killings, I'll tell you that."

"Jackson said they were pretty bad," I said hesitantly.

"Bad enough. When they finally did catch 'em, I still didn't think of it at first. Shouldn't have been more'n about twelve, and what those men caught sure looked older. But later I got to thinking, if it only took 'em three months to get born, maybe it didn't take 'em that long to get grown either." She stood up, and this time it was clear that the interview was over. I went meekly to the door.

"What happened to their grandfather?" I asked.

Ma Kersey's voice followed me down the steps. "It was pretty clear he'd been keeping them locked up. Inside an old shed on his property, like dogs."

CHAPTER 12

It doesn't mean anything, I told myself on the long walk home. *It's not as if it's the same shed.* Jackson had said that the two responsible for those strange murders had been caught and killed over near Bynum, which I was pretty sure was thirty-odd miles as the crow flies. Just a coincidence. Hell, not even as much as a coincidence. *There are lots of reasons people have sheds. Some of them aren't even particularly nefarious.*

Anyway, the story was absurd. Or, not absurd exactly, but there were obvious explanations. The children Ma Kersey delivered doubtless had some deformity. It's tragic, but it happens. And she'd said herself that the culprits caught in Bynum had seemed much older than the children she'd delivered would have been. She'd probably conflated the two out of guilt for not following up on those babies during the war, particularly if it turned out that their grandfather had been mistreating them. Which is also tragic and also happens.

This was depressing. I tried to turn my thoughts to other things, which wasn't hard. There was enough to turn my mind into a perfect froth of anxiety.

I couldn't imagine how Mrs. Kent must feel. Trapped in a situation she must hate, with a man she'd watched shoot her friend's lover . . . God. I wondered if there was anything I could do to help, but my mind was a perfect blank. I couldn't even help myself.

I exhaled slowly as I turned up the rutted drive to the doctor's house. The doctor, who'd shot a man in . . . if not cold blood, at least something like it. And here I'd been stalking him through the woods, thinking that at most he'd fire me.

Lord, maybe I *should* leave. Now would be a perfect time. Halder was gone to Raleigh. I could leave without explaining myself to anyone but the Kents.

Leave and go where?

It had been nearly two months. Surely my position at the school had been filled already. Respectable but penniless young women were in near-endless supply, as the daughters of war widows sought employment. Headmistress Silverton only needed someone with enough skill to teach the basics of watercolor to her students. I had been almost absurdly overqualified for my post.

I had enough money to take the train . . . somewhere. Perhaps a town where a friend of my father's had lived. I knew a few who would likely put me up for the night. Perhaps if I stayed with one of them, made myself useful in small ways, they would keep me on.

Which was exactly what I had tried to do after my father's death. It had landed me in Wilmington, with a man who studied seashells. His wife had been in a family way, and I had seen a future as an unpaid nursemaid stretching ahead of me, a fate which she desired no more than I did. She had found me the spot at Silverton's school, for which I was grateful. I was unlikely to be as lucky a second time.

Halder had not offered me violence. Indeed, it seemed that his violence had been reserved for Louisa's lover. I could not forgive that, but I also did not imagine for a moment that he felt any jealous passion for me.

In another year though, I could save enough of my wages to travel for several months. I could write to Father's friends and perhaps this time some of them would remember to write back. Or if I could see the project through, if Halder's book did well, perhaps I might even make enough of a name for myself as an illustrator that I would not be dependent on their charity.

(another year working for a murderer)

I don't like it, I told myself, *but not working for him won't bring back the dead either.* And wondered if Mrs. Kent had said the same thing to herself a year ago.

I was glad to reach the house, to take a long drink of water still cold from the well. I handed off the jar of tonic to Mrs. Kent, who took it with a smile. I studied her form as she turned to put it away, feeling the guilt lodged in my skin like a parasite.

You're trapped here too. And it's worse for you. And I didn't know.

"You all right?" she asked. "That old woman didn't tear any strips off you, did she? She's got a tongue on her, but you shouldn't take it too serious." She frowned. "You look a bit flushed."

"I'm fine," I said, ducking my head. "Just tired from the walk, that's all."

I could hear Ma Kersey as I climbed the stairs. *It ain't easy to swallow some things down. Makes you feel like maybe you aren't who you thought you were.*

I stared at my paints for half a minute, then went outside to find Jackson and ask him what his wife's favorite flower was.

I entered the kitchen the next morning to find two men sitting at the table, and that was sufficiently odd that I paused in the doorway. The tension in the room was so thick that you could have sliced it and fried it up like bacon. Mrs. Kent was pressed back against the stove in a way that put me in mind of an animal at bay—still dangerous, perhaps even more dangerous, but, for the moment, cornered.

What on earth *is going on here?*

"Good morning," I said cautiously, half afraid that the phrase was going to precipitate a hail of gunfire. It was that kind of tension.

Mrs. Kent looked up and met my eyes, and relief flashed so

clearly and unexpectedly across her face that it got me moving again.

"Morning, Miss Wilson," said Jackson heartily. He met my gaze as well, but instead of relief, there was something sharp and worried around his eyes.

Then the other man turned—his back had been to me—and Asa Phelps said, "Morning, Miss Wilson."

"Mr. Phelps," I said. "How unexpected." I stepped around the table to take the chair next to Jackson. Somehow it seemed important to range myself on the side of the Kents against the intruder, although I wasn't quite sure why.

Mrs. Kent brought a plate of bacon to the table. She put one hand on my shoulder as she leaned over to set it down, and gave two quick, sharp squeezes. Clearly a warning, but of what?

Phelps, either oblivious to the tension or unconcerned by it, helped himself to the bacon. I tried to eat a biscuit, but my mouth had gone dry and it stuck in my throat like heavy clay.

"So what brings you by, Mr. Phelps?" I asked, when I had drunk enough coffee to dislodge the biscuit.

He shrugged. "The doctor asked me to keep an eye on a few things while he was gone."

I felt myself bristling at the implied insult. "I'm sure Jackson's more than capable of keeping an eye on things."

"I don't doubt it," said Phelps in his dolorous voice. "But the doctor insisted." He met my eyes squarely and held them uncomfortably long, until I looked down at my plate. "How are you settling in, Miss Wilson?"

None of your damn business, I thought, feeling unaccountably hostile. I gave him a shrug of my own. "It's been nearly two months," I said. "I figure I'm pretty well settled by now."

Phelps nodded solemnly and pushed his chair back. "Fine cooking, as always, Mrs. Kent."

She gave him a bare nod. He tapped a finger to his brow in my direction and went out. I heard the side door slam a moment later.

Both of the Kents sagged in clear relief.

"What was *that* all about?" I asked, taking another slice of bacon.

"Didn't have time to warn you," said Jackson. "Phelps don't know we're married, and we ain't looking to tell him."

"Ohhhh . . ." It was amazing how people who'd turn a blind eye to a mixed couple living in sin would become outraged if they got a church sanction on it. I could just hear Phelps holding forth about miscegenation and the curse of Ham. He was practically the type specimen for that species.

Still, that didn't quite explain the relief that I'd seen from Mrs. Kent when I walked in. "He sure won't hear from me," I promised. "But what's he doing here, anyway?"

"No idea," said Jackson. "The doctor didn't say a thing to me about it."

"Mmm." I remembered meeting Phelps out by the gunpowder shed. Had the doctor hired Phelps to tend to his mysterious animals?

"He asked about you," said Mrs. Kent unexpectedly. She wiped off the chair Phelps had vacated, as if he might have left some residue behind, then sat down.

"*Me?*" I paused with my coffee cup halfway to my lips. "What about me?"

"Where you came from. Who your people were. That sorta thing. Normal enough." Jackson frowned. "Course, when *he* does it, it sounds like he's getting ready to accuse a body of witchcraft."

"And whether you were a 'moral and upright woman,'" said Mrs. Kent, lip curling.

I set the coffee cup down with a thump. "A *what*? What business is it—I mean—*what*?"

"Mayhap he's sweet on you," said Jackson. "And just bad at showing it." He considered. "Very, very bad."

"Gah! I'd sooner wed a toad. No, I actually rather like toads."

I tried to think of a creature I didn't like. "A botfly. Or a hookworm."

"Jackson's a romantic," said Mrs. Kent tartly. "Me, I think Phelps was just being nosy, or worse."

"Worse?"

Her lips turned down at the corners. "Don't know. I don't like him and I don't trust him. I was glad you showed up when you did. He could just as well ask you to your face, but did he?"

I stared into my coffee, wondering if Phelps somehow knew that I'd followed Halder to the shed those times. *No, that makes no sense. He wasn't there. When you've got a secret, you worry everybody else knows about it, that's all.*

"Told him you were so moral and upright that you didn't even drink," said Jackson, patting his flask. He winked at me.

I groaned, thinking of the horrible possibility that Phelps was looking for a wife. "I'd almost rather you told him that I was a degenerate," I muttered.

"Oh, well. If he asks again, I'll tell him I found you smoking, cursing, and playing cards."

I rolled my eyes, took my plate to the scullery, and went to fetch my sketchbook, hoping that time spent outside would shake the dread that followed me like a shadow.

Mrs. Kent's favorite flower, according to Jackson, was sweet shrub. I knew it well. *Calycanthus floridus*, also called Carolina allspice. It's a big, suckering shrub that likes to send out runners and form thickets, and there's not all that much to recommend it, except for a month or so in late spring when it flowers. The flowers are deep, dark burgundy and they smell like nothing else in the world. If you've smelled them, then you know exactly what I mean. If you haven't, then the best that I can say is that they smell like how berries and cream tastes.

I wanted to paint something for Mrs. Kent, in gratitude for all the meals and what was, in her rather brisk way, a great deal of kindness. Her favorite flower seemed like a good choice.

It was coming on toward May and there was a thicket of sweet shrub down by the stream that probably still had some flowers. I could have used the illustration in the *Botanica* for reference, but I never quite felt that particular image did justice to the flower. I took my sketchbook and a little knife to cut a branch, and tromped down to find some reference material.

I don't know if I believe in fate. I don't think I do. Things just happen sometimes, and you can drive yourself mad thinking of all the ways that they might have happened differently. If you'd turned left instead of right. If you'd said yes instead of no. If you'd gone to visit your father's friends in Richmond instead of Wilmington. But even below the level of conscious choice, there's another level, where dramatic things happen because of facts that should be utterly insignificant.

If Mrs. Kent's favorite flower had been marigolds or wake-robin or wild violets, I would not have gone to the stream, and everything that happened after would have happened differently or not at all. But she loved a shrub that smelled like berries and cream, so off I went.

I spent about two hours at the stream, drawing. By the time I set back toward the house, I had three pages of sketches and a cut branch emitting the spicy halfway-cinnamon smell of sweet shrub bark.

The woods were dense with new growth, much of it still pale green. I gave a wide berth to a stand of poison ivy that straggled up a chestnut tree, the thick stem covered in hairy rootlets like a millipede's legs. The swamp jessamine had stopped blooming by now, but the cross vine was still putting out blazing coral trumpets. Coral is a marvelous color in nature and a damnably difficult one to render on the page. You need red and pink and orange in the right proportions, all in washes thin enough for the white of the page to shine through and keep it bright.

My mind was running through the paints back in the studio, wondering if there was anything that might make a good coral, while my feet took the most familiar path through the woods. I saw the shed up ahead, just as Phelps stepped out of it.

If I hadn't spied on Halder, if I hadn't been nursing a nervous guilt, I would have said nothing. Probably I'd have turned back and hoped he didn't see me at all. But it seemed imperative that he not think that I was suspicious, so I called out "Mr. Phelps!" in hearty tones the moment I saw him.

He jumped a foot in the air. I can't tell you the satisfaction that gave me. *Moral and upright woman, my aunt Fanny.*

"Miss Wilson! You—err—startled me." Phelps hastily pulled the door closed and fumbled with the lock.

"I was just cutting some sweet shrub," I said gaily, waving my branch in his direction. A touch of malice led me to add, "But don't worry, Mr. Phelps. I took your warning very much to heart."

He blinked at me. "My warning?"

"About the gunpowder."

"Oh . . . err . . . that warning." Phelps glanced back at the shed, as if it might rise up and declare him a liar on the spot.

"And the other one too. I never go out in the woods at night."

"Very wise." He moved hastily away from the shed. "Please allow me to walk you back to the house."

"Certainly." A thrill of adrenaline shot through me. Had I heard what I thought I had? I was nearly certain of it, but I couldn't stop to check now.

Phelps walked beside me, his shoulders slightly hunched, like a shabby vulture. I glanced over at him. "Jackson told me about what happened in the woods three years ago," I said. "The murders."

"Oh." His voice, never particularly expressive, became as flat as paint. "Yes."

"It must have been quite horrible."

Phelps grunted.

"I'm so glad that you all were able to put an end to it."

His shoulders hunched even deeper. The house appeared through the trees before us, and Phelps made for it, stretching his legs slightly so that I had to hurry to keep up.

At the edge of the woods, he paused and turned to me.

"It is the duty of good men to kill monsters, Miss Wilson," he said, in his flat, solemn voice. Then he tapped the brim of his hat and stalked toward the stable. A few minutes later, I heard the sound of his horse trotting away.

That sound, however, was not nearly so important to me as the one that I *hadn't* heard.

When Phelps had shut the door to the shed, in his haste, he had closed the lock without looking. And I hadn't heard a *click*.

CHAPTER 13

This time, I took no chances. No more following people through the dark and diving for cover. I armed myself with a candle and matches, though I didn't dare light them in the woods. It seemed unlikely that anyone would see it, with the doctor gone and Phelps thankfully not staying at the house overnight. Nevertheless, I did not want to get into the shed and find myself stumbling around blind.

Could it really be unlocked? Really? Was I finally about to learn what Halder was experimenting on?

Don't get your hopes up. You might just have missed the click, that's all.

But if you didn't, then you'll know soon.

Dusk spread ultramarine shadows under the trees, then deepened into dark. I paced the studio restlessly, unable to settle. *Soon. Soon.*

I thought I had successfully buried my curiosity, but apparently I had only shoved it down to fester into obsession. When I caught a glimpse of myself in the mirror, I looked almost feverish. Two spots of color burned high on my cheeks, a rose madder wash on cold white skin.

Soon.

I waited until I heard Mrs. Kent leave, waited a little longer, then slipped out the door and into the woods.

The walk to the shed took far too long, and I forgot it all instantly the moment that I arrived. It was a dark night and the shadows were thick around the shed. At least, I thought it was dark? My vision seemed odd somehow, the edges bright with pinpricks of light, but it didn't make it any easier to see.

Calm down. Your heart is pounding like you've been running.

I shook myself. Regardless of the darkness, it was easy to make out the heavy lock. I put out a hand, my heart in my throat, and tugged down.

It opened without a sound.

My god, my god, it's open, it's really open!

With nerveless fingers, I slid the lock from the hasp and hung it back on the door. I stepped over the threshold, swung the door shut behind me, and stood in darkness. When I reached out, the fabric of the drape caught my fingers.

Steady . . . steady . . .

I took the matches from my pocket. *You're going to feel awfully silly if you light that thing and the room really is full of gunpowder. Unless you drop the match and then you won't feel anything for long.*

Ah yes, that rare gunpowder that eats live chickens, I snapped back at myself, and lit the match, then the candle.

The space between the drape and the wall was only wide enough for the door to open. Behind the door was a peg with something hanging from it, something so oddly incongruous that I paused with my hand on the drape. It looked like a lady's hat with a veil. *Huh. That's strange.*

Unlike everything else about this situation, which is totally normal.

I pushed the drape aside. The stairs yawned below me. Something flickered in their depths, and for an instant I thought there was someone else down there, until I realized I was looking at a reflection. The early summer rains had left at least three inches of water on the floor of the hollowed-out room.

There, I told myself triumphantly. *No one stores gunpowder in ankle-deep water.* Fortunately, I was wearing my sturdy boots.

I hitched my skirt up to keep the hem dry and descended the staircase.

The first thing that came into view was a wooden table. It held a chipped enamel pan and what looked like a pair of rusted forceps, but nothing else of interest.

My last step onto the floor splashed instead of squelched. Someone had laid boards down over the clay. It felt surprisingly solid underfoot. Burlap had been tacked up over the walls and boards covered the ceiling as well, braced and re-braced.

I had only a moment to take that in, however. My attention was immediately claimed by the second table in the back of the room.

The one with the corpse laid out atop it.

It was very obviously a corpse. No living human, even in the farthest extremes of starvation, could look like that. The ribs were etched so deeply that I could have fit my hand into the grooves between them. Skin and hair still clung to the body, otherwise I would have called it a skeleton.

Strangely, I was not frightened. I had seen skeletons before. Art students use them to study anatomy. I took a step forward, the water splashing around my feet, and lifted my candle higher.

It—he—looked desiccated, despite the thick humidity of the air. I thought of mummies pulled from Egyptian tombs. His skin had shrunk so tight against the bone that I could see the sunken depression between the bones of his forearms, leading down to the delicate bones of . . . the wrists, bound with iron manacles . . .

I swallowed hard.

My first attention had been for the corpse itself, not its surroundings. But now I looked and fear coiled up from my belly and took me by the throat.

The body lay spread-eagled on a wire mesh, heavy and widely spaced, like a fence panel, framed with wood. Iron shackles, dripping with rust, enclosed his wrists and ankles.

Oh god, I thought. *Halder, what have you done?*

If I had found that he was using human corpses in experiments with insects that ate carrion, I would have been horrified, yes. But the dead were dead and long past harming, and, God help me, I would have understood *why* he did it.

But the dead don't need to be chained down.

I wanted to turn away. No, I *wanted* to run screaming. My vision swam.

Stop that. You are a naturalist, are you not?

This isn't natural! I shouted inside my skull.

No. But you are a trained observer. So observe, *damn you, and quit cringing.*

My breathing steadied. I straightened my shoulders. *The dead are dead. Now the living have to take notes.*

The corpse had been male, in life, though what remained was shrunken almost to nonexistence, and his face was stained with black around the nose and mouth. His hands had shrunken so far that he could have pulled loose from any ordinary shackle. In life, the fetters must have been cruelly tight. But his fingers . . . what was wrong with his fingers?

They looked impossibly long and deformed, curling back on themselves. So did his toes. I took another step forward, saw the sharp edges, and realized that I was looking at fingernails that had grown and grown and grown and never been trimmed.

Jesus, Mary and Joseph. How long was this poor soul here?

The wire platform was about waist high, but there was a solid wooden shelf a few feet under it. A wide metal trough covered half of it, perhaps to catch the prisoner's waste. I saw flashes of white in the candlelight and leaned down.

Chicken feathers.

I had no time to dwell on what that might mean, because

in bending down, I saw what lay on the underside of the wire mesh.

My first wild thought was that someone had poured wax over the body and that it had dripped downward, forming swollen droplets that hung from the underside of the corpse in pale swags. Then I saw the dark ovals on each swelling, the blunt black ends of larvae burrowed beneath the surface, and I knew.

I did not scream. I did not even flinch. I simply stared.

The botfly larvae had grown atop one another in places, dozens of fat warbles hanging together like bunches of sickly grapes. Under the corpse's hips and lower back, they were so thickly clustered that they formed a mass as large as a man's head. All the flesh that was missing from the bones hung below the mesh, filled with squirming, parasitic life.

I might have stood there, frozen, until dawn, if not for the candle. Hot wax burned a trail down my hand and I yelped and dropped it.

The flame hit the water and went out.

Panic leapt up and grabbed me by the throat. The blackness that engulfed me was a hundred times deeper and darker than anything aboveground. I went to my knees in the water, groping across the surface for the candle, because if I couldn't find it, I was going to be blundering through the dark, looking for the exit, and what if I *didn't* find it, what if I got turned around and went toward the body instead, what if I reached out and my hand closed over the warbles, the soft flesh stretched tight around the dark body within, what if it *moved* . . .

Stop that! I screamed at myself. *Stop that!*

My petticoats were soaked with water. It sloshed over the top of my boots. It was freezing cold, much colder than it had any right to be, but I kept sliding my hands across the surface, feeling desperately for the candle, terrified that I was making ripples that would send it floating even farther away.

And then my fingers touched something smooth and cylindrical and I felt it bobbing away and snatched it up. Found the wick. Nearly cried with relief.

I was groping in my pocket for matches when something buzzed against my face.

I batted it away with a shriek. It was big, the size of a bumblebee, and on some level I knew exactly what it was, but if I let that thought come up to the surface, I was going to pass out right here in the black water and then it would come and lay eggs in my skin and . . .

The match flared up. My hands shook so violently that I had to move two steps and brace myself against the wooden table before I could light the candle. Cold fabric clung to my legs and I realized that I was weeping.

I lifted the candle just as the corpse opened its eyes.

When the hurricane's eye had passed over the school, the howling winds dropped away and we sat in sudden, impossible silence. I felt the same way now. Inside my head, I heard myself think, with weary resignation, *Of course. Botfly larvae require living flesh.*

It was impossible that he was alive, and yet he turned his head to look at me. The sound of dry skin sliding across vertebrae was like a snake moving over stone. With the eerie calm of the hurricane's eye, I saw that the black stains on his face were actually insects clustered around his nose and mouth.

Black and yellow flies. I knew them, of course. I knew their shape intimately. I had labored over paintings, using the finest brush I had to draw in every tiny, bristling hair.

Cracked lips parted. A fly clung to the corner of his mouth. His gums had receded so far that his teeth looked as long and sharp as a dog's.

". . . who . . . are . . . you . . ."

I should have been moved to pity. I should have thrown myself on the shackles and tried to break him free. But the storm's eye was moving still and the wind inside my head was picking up.

Oh god. All this time I thought the big mystery was what happened to Louisa, and really it was what was happening down here.

Underneath the mesh, the warbles began to sway.

"... who ..."

Drops of swollen white flesh began to ripple. I watched with horrible fascination as dark, blunt bodies began to struggle loose, the wolf worms birthing themselves into the world.

I staggered backward and hit the wooden table with a thud. Rough boards dug into my back.

It broke the spell and I bolted.

The candle went out when I was halfway up the stairs, the flame extinguished as I splashed wax wildly. I dropped it, clutching for the drape.

Behind me, I heard a cry. Weaker than the one that I had heard a few weeks ago, but unmistakably the same—a shrill, rasping wail like sandpaper across my eardrums.

I flung the door back and made it out of the shed before I went to my knees, retching. Acid burned my throat, roared through the back of my nasal passages. It was agonizing but all I could think was, *Please let it kill anything in there, please let them not have laid eggs in me, please God, please!*

Even when I had stopped being sick, I couldn't seem to get up. I wanted to run, I had to run, but I was shaking so hard that my teeth were chattering, and even in the midst of horror, some small part of me was annoyed by this. *I am handling this all quite badly. I expected better of me, really.*

I wanted, more than anything, to crawl into my bed and pull the blankets over my head. Then maybe the last few minutes would stop and I could push them into the past, into a thing that *had* happened, not a thing that *was* happening, right now, still.

Close the door. If I close the door, it'll be over.

I wrestled with the drape, gasping through my raw throat, and swung the door shut. I understood now. It wasn't to keep insects *out* for an experiment, it was to keep them *in*.

The lock clicked. I turned and staggered away, my stockings squelching inside my shoes.

Something touched the back of my head.

It wasn't heavy. No harder than a tap of Smiley's paw, really. It might have been a pine cone falling. I reached up a hand to the back of my head, unthinking, and felt . . . legs.

Legs and bristles and a brief, papery buzz of wings and *oh god it was huge it was on me* right now—

I slapped it away with a scream. Buzzing filled my ears but I was running like a rabbit. Wet fabric slapped against my legs with every step but I didn't care. If I lost my footing, if I stepped in a hole, I could hurt myself terribly, but at that moment, I think I would have crawled on a broken leg rather than spend an instant longer in the woods.

I hit the back door, flung it open, and slammed it closed behind me. The clock in the hall chimed a quarter to ten as I passed. I had been gone barely twenty minutes.

Twenty minutes was long enough for something to have laid eggs.

What was it that Holder had said? *Nasty fellows, botflies . . . The larva hatches out, waits for a host to walk by, latches on, and climbs inside. Mouth, nose, anus, open wound, they don't discriminate . . . Proper little monsters, they are.*

Were there wolf worms climbing across my skin right now, looking for an opening? Had the one that landed on the back of my head been laying eggs? Were they on my hands, already hatching out in response to the warmth of my skin?

Had I touched my face or wiped my nose since I'd slapped away the botfly?

I couldn't remember.

My first thought was to scrub myself raw, remove anything the flies might have left behind, even if I had to use lye to do it. I was halfway to my room before I thought of the cistern and the insect parts that swam in my basin. *Oh god, no, I can't—I couldn't—*

The cold, scientific voice in the back of my head stepped in at last. I think perhaps I had disgusted myself completely. *Think. You need clean water. How do you make sure water is clean?*

Boil it, I answered. I wobbled on the stairs, nearly falling, turned back, and went to the kitchen. I put a pan of water on the stove to boil, then collapsed into a chair. It was warm and stoking the stove made it hotter, but I was still so horribly cold.

The water boiled. It seemed fast. Had I really been sitting at the table, staring at nothing, for the entire time? It didn't seem long at all. I pulled the pan from the heat, looking at the rolling water. I had a wild urge to try and breathe it in and burn the larvae out with it, but the cold voice had taken over. *Don't be ridiculous. You must wait for it to cool. While you're waiting, take off those wet boots and skirt.*

I obeyed. My socks hung limp and sodden as I pulled them off and dropped them back into the boots. I started to shiver again. The room seemed dark or maybe it was just my vision going dark at the edges.

When the water had cooled enough that it was only somewhat painful instead of scalding, I went to the scullery and scrubbed my face, rinsed out my mouth, wiping at my nose. God only knew if it would work. Maybe they were like the deer botfly and one had already flicked larvae into my mouth when I screamed, and they would gather in clusters inside my mouth, squirming like a dozen extra tongues . . .

I gargled until I nearly drowned. Then I poured more water over the back of my skull, scrubbing violently with the harsh kitchen soap. Strands tore, but I didn't care. I had to stop it now, before I ended up like *him*, before Halder locked me away on a wire table and the flies clustered around my flesh and my fingernails grew as long as knives . . .

Mrs. Kent found me in the morning, slumped over the kitchen table. My hair was matted with soap and a pan half full of tepid water stood at my elbow.

"Miss Wilson?" she said, and then, carefully, "Sonia?"

I looked up at her blearily. I had to tell her something. I had to tell her that there was a monster in the shed and that Halder was the monster who kept it. I had to warn her. She could tell Jackson and he could bring the sheriff and they would go down where I had gone and see . . .

"Sonia, hon, what's wrong?" She took a few steps toward me.

My tongue felt thick. "Halder," I mumbled. "He's got a monster. The flies . . . the botflies . . ."

She pressed her wrist to my forehead and swore. "Sonia, you're burning up."

I shook my head. "Can't be. Too cold. You're cold."

"Hon, you're running a great big fever." She shoved her arm under my shoulders and half lifted me out of the chair. "And you sitting here barefoot? In your underclothes?"

"No. Mrs. Kent. *Rose*. The flies. There's so many flies! You have to *listen*!" I grabbed her arm, trying to make her understand, and then my vision swam sideways and Jackson was suddenly there. He swore and his wife didn't scold him for it, which was surprising.

"Sonia," said Mrs. Kent, in a no-nonsense voice, "you're delirious."

I blinked at her. "I am?"

"Yes."

"Oh." Unutterable relief swept through me. I was delirious. That meant it wasn't real. "Oh thank god," I said, and fainted.

CHAPTER 14

Of the next days, I remember little. I alternately froze and burned, wracked with shuddering that felt as if it would shake apart my bones. Those—and the bitterness of quinine sliding over my tongue—were the only things that I brought with me back to consciousness.

When I finally woke for good, I was looking up at familiar tin tiles with dragonflies on them. There was a weight on my ankles that began, almost immediately, to purr.

"Awake, are you?" asked a familiar voice. I turned my head on the pillow and saw Ma Kersey sitting by my bedside. "Going to stay awake this time, do you think?"

"I don't know," I croaked. My throat felt as dry and tattered as an autumn leaf.

"Here, here, let's get this into you." She held out a cup of tea. I took it in a hand that only shook a little. I was braced for more quinine, but it was deliciously sweet and slid kindly across my dry tongue. "My own honey," said Ma Kersey. "Well, the honey from my bees, anyway. They make it, but they're kind enough to give me some."

"How long have I been sick?" I asked.

"'Bout two days." She took the empty cup back. "Bilious fever. Nasty flare-up, it was. Rose was afraid we'd lose you. Sent Jackson to roust me at the crack of dawn and bring me back here."

I closed my eyes for a moment, fighting back unexpected tears. Gratitude, mostly. I was out of the habit of being helped.

"Sorry," I whispered. I wasn't sure if I was apologizing for having been sick or for crying.

"No need to be." Ma Kersey made a gentle clucking noise, like a contented hen. "Happens to us all sooner or later. You've had the fever before, I take it?"

I nodded.

"Thought so. Would've taken the fever a lot longer to break otherwise." She clucked again. "Though this was a mighty fine fever nonetheless. You were raving like a Baptist preacher in a whorehouse for a bit there. Wasn't sure whether to dunk you in cold water or give an Amen."

"Oh Lord." I put my hand to my head. What had I said? I could barely remember—I had been trying to warn someone, hadn't I? There was something—

The shed.

The botflies.

The corpse that wasn't a corpse.

I sat up, horrified, and the room slewed sideways. Ma Kersey grabbed my shoulder. "Here now, settle down. You haven't had a bite to eat in two days. Fever's broke, but you aren't gonna be up and around for a bit yet."

I allowed her to push me back onto the pillows. She stood up, rearranged her shawls, and said something about getting me some food. The door creaked as she left. Smiley, annoyed by all my fidgeting, stalked the length of the bed twice, then draped himself across my shins as if it was his duty to keep me in bed.

As soon as the door closed, I began running my hands over my skin, my scalp, everywhere that I could reach, feeling for . . . something.

(*wolf worms, you're feeling for wolf worms, they might be inside you* right now)

Nothing.

I collapsed back, exhausted from my brief bout of activity. Of course there wasn't. It was ridiculous. I had malaria, not parasites. Why had I thought otherwise?

(you know why)

I rubbed my forehead. I'd gone to the shed, hadn't I? And there had been a body there, and it had spoken to me . . . but it had been so dark and the flame had gone out and I had been so cold . . .

Had any of that really happened?

The memory seemed to be swathed in fog. I was almost sure that I had gone to the shed, but after that . . . had I really seen a body at all?

The mental image of skin sealed to bone like a mummy was vivid, but was I remembering something real, or constructing it out of other memories, the way you piece together a dream?

Even if you did see a body, you couldn't possibly have seen botflies on it. They don't live in dead flesh. And it couldn't have talked to you. That had *to be the fever.*

But why would Halder have a body in his shed anyway? How would he even get a body? You don't just find corpses lying around. Or . . . well, I suppose a tramp could have died in the woods, that's not impossible. Or Halder could have been out robbing graves . . . no, don't be ridiculous, he'd hire resurrection men to do it. Body snatching for scientific research wasn't as popular as it had been earlier in the century, but it certainly still happened. Would Halder pay someone to steal a dead body for him so he could use it to test a hypothesis about insects?

Of course he would. No question at all.

I pinched the bridge of my nose. Dreadful, but not impossible. My delirious vision of botfly maggots and manacles and impossibly long fingernails . . . *that* was impossible. *You didn't see any of that. You were fevered already and you've been spending too much time with botflies and your brain put together a horrible dream out of parts.*

I was grudgingly impressed with my brain. I'd had no idea that it had such a capacity for the grotesque.

The door swung open again, and Ma Kersey bustled back in, accompanied by Mrs. Kent carrying a tray. "Glad to see you up," the housekeeper said. "We were all pretty worried."

"You . . . you found me in the kitchen, didn't you?" I could just barely remember a whirl of faces.

"Sure did. You looked worse'n a drowned rat too." She set the tray down on the nightstand.

"You saved my life," I said. "Thank you."

"Bah," Mrs. Kent said gruffly. "Nothing doing. It was all Ma Kersey. I'm no kind of nurse."

I reached out and took her hand and held it as tightly as I could in my weakened state. I couldn't think of anything to say that wouldn't embarrass us both.

Her fingers were rough and callused and much stronger than mine. After a second, she squeezed back.

"Now then," she said, stepping back and shoving her hands into her apron. "You eat some of this food and you'll be back on your feet in no time."

Ma Kersey took up her station again and I turned my attention to the food. It was scrambled eggs and a sausage with gravy. Mrs. Kent apparently felt that invalids were better served with hearty fare than with thin gruel. I could find no fault with this program.

I made it through about half the meal before exhaustion caught up with me. You wouldn't think that eating would make you so tired. I drank more tea, then lay back on the pillows, half dozing, while Ma Kersey told me all the latest gossip. It was mostly names I didn't know, in situations I was unfamiliar with, but I enjoyed it all the same.

". . . and Eloise, now, she thinks she'll marry him, but everyone knows his mama's got him well and truly under her thumb. Even if she gets him to the altar, she won't get much joy of it.

But you can't tell Eloise anything, never could, not since she was a little girl..."

My mind started to drift. The only places for it to go were unpleasant though. The body in the shed—had it really been there? Had I actually seen it at all?

"...called him everything but a child of God. Well, now, Hiram wasn't going to take that from a gal young enough to be his daughter..."

Was it actually a body? I wondered vaguely. *What I saw... what I thought I saw... was practically mummified. Nothing mummifies here. It's too wet. I was standing in water. If you put a body down there, it wouldn't look like that, would it?*

Maybe I *hadn't* seen it. One of the first things you learn as a naturalist is how flawed and fallible human observation is. I've lost track of the number of flowers that I would swear looked one way, only to sit down in front of a specimen with a sketchbook and realize that it was totally different. And which was more likely, after all—that I had seen a dead body behaving in a way that bodies shouldn't behave, then began to hallucinate five minutes later, or that I was *already* hallucinating? That strange pinprick brightness around my vision, the shivering... no, I'd obviously been feverish by the time I went in.

"...so he lost it all gambling and was too afraid to tell his wife, so he made up a story about being attacked in Greensboro and whacked his own head on a post trying to make it look good. But he misjudged it and knocked hisself silly and babbled out everything to the doctor trying to patch him up..."

Halder was a strange man, and clearly he'd been violent at least once in his life, but just because somebody shoots someone else in anger doesn't mean they're likely to keep corpses in a shed. There is not what you'd call a straight line between the two behaviors. And why would he bring chickens to a room that held a dead body and nothing else? And why would Phelps be covering for him? No, none of it made any sense.

"... Martha's youngest is getting married, and good for her. Fine young man, from over Bynum way..."

On the other hand, if I'd been half out of my mind with fever and I saw something like a pile of dermestid beetles—well, I didn't know what that would look like, but a box of mealworms makes a kind of humped-up, dry brown mess as they eat and crap and shed. Suppose there had been a table with something like that on it? If the beetles had been stripping a body—a chicken, say—I could have seen bones. And in candlelight, already delirious, I saw that and my brain filled in *mummified dead body*.

(is that really what happened though?)

A knock on the door startled me out of my thoughts and Ma Kersey out of her monologue. Sally poked her head around the door, skipped in, said, "I'm glad you're feeling better, miss, I picked you these," and presented me with a handful of bedraggled flowers. I thanked her and Ma Kersey fetched the jam jar off the painting table and filled it with water and the remains of a June bug.

Sally was followed by Jackson, who gripped my hand and said, "Gave us quite a scare, Miss Wilson."

"And I hear I have you to thank for summoning my nursemaid here," I said.

"Thought he was gonna bang the house down, I did," Ma Kersey said, with a flash of gold dentistry. "Usually it's only the expectant fathers that pound on the door like that." Jackson grinned, unrepentant.

My last visitor was not nearly so welcome. Phelps appeared in the doorway like a bird of ill omen and I suppressed a guilty start. Did he know I'd been in the shed?

He can't know. He was the one who left it unlocked. Even if he suspects someone's been in there, there's no proof that it was you. In fact, you've been collapsed with malaria, so you're the last person he should suspect.

Besides, why should he care? It was just beetles, right?

(was it though?)

"Mister Phelps," I said coolly.

He didn't advance into the room. In fact, he didn't even look at me, but at the opposite wall. He was holding his hat in both hands, and I got the strange feeling that he was embarrassed. *Jesus, Mary and Joseph, is it because I'm in bed? Does visiting a woman's bedroom offend his sense of Christian morals?*

"I have prayed for your recovery," he said stiffly. "I am pleased that you are improved."

Oddly enough, I believed him. He probably *had* prayed.

"Ma Kersey here is an excellent nurse," I said, unwilling to give Phelps's God all the credit.

"She is indeed," he said, lifting a hand to touch the back of his head. I saw the edge of a bandage and raised my eyebrows.

"Pfff, that wasn't nothin'," Ma Kersey said. "Fell down and raised a goose egg, that's all. Jackson could have patched you up just as well. Just hard to work on the back of your own head, that's all."

"You hit your head, Mr. Phelps?"

He nodded gingerly and touched the bandage again. "Pride is a sin," he remarked to no one in particular, "and it hurts only my pride to tell you. A wasp flew at my face and I lost my footing. My head hit a log. Providentially, it was rotten."

"A wasp?" I asked.

He finally looked at me, if only for a moment, then rapidly away, as if my sensible cotton nightgown was an incitement to debauchery. "Doubtless you could have identified it more specifically."

I snorted. "No, no. Not while it was flying at my head—"

(black-and-yellow fly buzzing at my face)

"—I couldn't. I'm sure Dr. Halder could." I had to stop and catch my breath. "Forgive me. I'm not fully recovered, I don't think."

Ma Kersey clucked her tongue and got to her feet. "Sweet of you to visit, Mr. Phelps, but Miss Wilson needs to rest."

"Yes. Of course." He nodded sharply to me, then turned away. I got a better view of the bandage, which was large and stood out starkly against the darkness of his hair.

Ma Kersey escorted him into the studio and I heard the murmur of their voices for a minute, culminating with her raising her voice and saying, "Stop picking at it!"

She was back a moment later and dropped back into her chair. "Always the same," she muttered. "They pick and pick and then they complain it's not healing quick enough."

I smiled. Ma Kersey settled her shawls like a hen settling her feathers and sat back down.

I was tired, it was true, though mostly I had wanted to get rid of Phelps. No matter what I told myself, I was still half convinced that he must know I had been in the shed.

Which was another argument for my *not* having seen a dead body, wasn't it? Surely Phelps wouldn't just blithely accept dead bodies lying around. According to the Kents, he was even more of a zealot than he seemed in casual conversation. Surely good Christians would object to that sort of thing?

Halder had presumably asked Phelps to check on the beetles in his absence. Phelps and Halder had known each other for years, after all. What was it Jackson had said? That the two of them had been present when the supposed blood thieves were killed? That they were *in at the death*. Yes, that had been it.

Which reminded me of something that I had dismissed at first, before I had realized just how sharp Ma Kersey was.

"Ma Kersey," I broke in, interrupting a lengthy anecdote about a church service that had gone awry when birds had roosted in the organ pipes, "you told me about the three-month babies? When we were talking about the killings that happened in the woods? What *really* happened there?"

She fell silent. I was watching her face and saw her smile fade. She didn't frown, but her face went slack, as if she were no longer inhabiting the skin. I plowed ahead. "You never said *why* you thought the two people that were killed were the ones you'd delivered."

"Ah . . ." Ma Kersey shook her head grimly. "I didn't, not at first. But see, they killed 'em once and buried 'em—"

Once? I thought, but didn't interrupt.

"—but then people started thinking maybe that hadn't been enough. Lotta stories about vampires sleeping in a coffin and when you dig 'em up, they're looking all healthy, while half their kin have dropped dead. So somebody came asking me what I thought." She pursed her lips. "Me, I thought it was all a load of nonsense, but I said if they were that worried, well . . . probly some people care if you dig up their bones, but given what those two'd been up to, I didn't much care what they thought. So a group of us all went trudging off—me and the preacher and about half the men who did for 'em in the first place—and dug 'em up again. That's when I knew."

Ma Kersey was a born storyteller, same as Jackson. She didn't much like telling this one, I thought, but she still knew how to tell it. I knew my place as well. "What happened?"

"The man was dead, right enough. They'd shoved a stake through him and the worms had been at work on what was left. The woman though . . . she'd been alive at some point, under all that dirt there. They didn't get no coffins, just a deep hole, and the woman wasn't lying dead on her back like she'd been placed. Her body was almost sat up, like she'd been digging her way out. Looked like she'd *eaten* a big mess of dirt. To make room, maybe? No idea. Damndest thing I ever saw." She leaned back in the chair and studied the ceiling tiles. "Anyway, general opinion was to burn 'em, and the preacher wasn't minded to put a stop to it. Truth is, I think we were all a little scared the woman'd start moving again. So they laid 'em both out and burned 'em right then and there. Probly the man didn't need it—a shot to the head kills you no matter what you're made of, I'm thinking—but the woman . . . I dunno. I've seen some things, but that was one of the worst, her belly all stretched out full of dirt like she was gonna chew her way out of the ground."

I felt a bit ill, whether from the story or malaria or too much sausage gravy. Still, I couldn't see how she'd known that they were the same ones she delivered.

"It was the teeth, child," said Ma Kersey, rearranging her shawls again. "When we were all looking at her mouth, the way she'd been chewing through red clay like it was taffy, I saw it. Some of 'em had broken, but she had a mouthful of milk teeth like needles. So did the man. Just like a kitten. Just like the day they was born."

I stared at her. It was impossible, the whole story was impossible, but while Jackson might have been putting me on, I'd swear on a stack of Bibles that Ma Kersey believed she was telling the truth.

"Once I realized, I went out to their grandaddy's farm," Ma Kersey said, gazing out the window now, where the trees shifted their leaves against the light. "Found the old shed. Full of chains it was, and big iron cuffs like the plantation bastards used to put on slaves." Her mouth worked like she was going to spit, but she remembered that she was indoors and didn't. I thought of the manacles that I had seen—no, that I *hadn't* seen, that I *couldn't* have seen—and put a hand to my forehead.

"Full of chains," Ma Kersey repeated, "and the house empty, like nobody'd been there in a year or two. I s'pose if any of the neighbors came looking, they assumed the old preacher up and left during the war. I doubt it though." She put her head to one side, eyes bright and cold as a bird's. "But I'll tell you this—they never did find his body."

CHAPTER 15

Ma Kersey went home the next morning, informing me that I was out of the woods but to take it easy for a few days. I was both sorry to see her go and relieved to no longer be considered an invalid requiring round-the-clock nursing. I tried to give her money, but was informed that the doctor would be covering the bills as part of the household expenses. I didn't know what to think of that. I didn't like to think well of Halder, but I couldn't deny that it was a load off my mind.

My sleep was still troubled. *Troubled*, ha. Awful, frankly. My dreams no longer had the horrible immediacy of delirium, but that was the best that could be said. Nightmares about wolf worms and mummified bodies flowed into Ma Kersey's stories about the three-month babies and the possum scratching endlessly at the door. My own fault for asking, I suppose. Not that I believed for a moment that the blood thieves and the three-month babies were the same. If one family is prone to a congenital deformity like pointed teeth, then it's no surprise if it pops up elsewhere in the region. Darwin's inherited traits explained a great deal.

Even if she had been a killer, the thought of the poor woman buried alive, trying to bite through the dirt with her mouth full of malformed teeth, joined the imagery that populated my nightmares. Sometimes I was trapped underground with a body, trying to claw my way through the earth to escape. Sometimes I was trying to dig down to find someone. Often it was Louisa, even though I didn't know what she looked like, even though Ma Kersey had assured me that she'd gotten away.

Between this and the remains of the malaria, I woke up barely more rested than when I went to sleep. Still, I didn't want to complain. The Kents had had to save me once already, and I would have been embarrassed to go whining about bad dreams.

I did use the excuse of recovery to avoid painting again immediately. I rambled around the gardens instead. It was June and it was hot but not as punishing as it would be in August. The heat was part of what made the late summer malaria flare-ups so brutal. (Not that they were fun at any time of year, mind you, but it's easier to bring down a fever when the air isn't hotter than the patient.)

I wondered if I'd have another flare-up in August. It seemed desperately unfair to have two in short order. Of course, I wasn't entirely sure why I'd had this one. A doctor would probably tell me it had been "excitement of the nerves" that caused a relapse.

Between the possum and this job, I've certainly had plenty of excitement, it's true. Though I didn't think I had any nerves to speak of. Oh well, we live and learn.

When it was too warm to wander, I looked through Louisa's sketchbooks. I found myself poring over the face of the man in the last few books, the one with the lean face. Saul Gregor, the man she'd fallen in love with? It struck me as likely. There was tenderness etched into the lines, but she had never written anything beside his face. Perhaps even then, she had been too frightened of what Halder might do if he found out to commit anything to paper.

She was more right than she could have known. I sat up, rubbing my back, which ached from hunching over the wooden chest. I don't know what I was hoping to find.

Well, no, that wasn't true. I was *hoping* to find a note left by Louisa that said something like: *Hello, artist reading this, please feel free to keep working for my husband even though he killed my lover, I really don't mind and you're not a bad person.* I wasn't *expecting* to find it, but it would have been nice.

I snorted. *Idiot. Still looking for absolution, aren't you?*

The books had none to give me. The air had cooled a trifle though, and perhaps nature could give me what humans couldn't. I picked up my own sketchbook and went back outside to the gardens.

Jackson was working over by the vegetable garden. Well, I say *working*, but it mostly consisted of standing, staring at something by his feet, walking in a circle, stopping, staring up at the sky, and scratching the back of his neck. I ambled in his direction.

"Something wrong?" I asked.

"Nah, just varmints being too clever for their own good." He gave me a sheepish grin. "The doc telegrammed and told me to see if I couldn't trap another couple possums, preferably with the wolf worms."

"And?"

He nudged the object on the ground with his foot. It looked like a wooden box with a few extra attachments and a lid hanging by one leather hinge. "Caught one, sure enough, but it got out again. Since then, no luck at all. Something's springing 'em and taking the bait though."

"Raccoon?" I asked. Raccoons are as clever as the Devil and they can figure out a simple latch in no time at all.

"That's all I can think of. Got to be a pair of them together though. One couldn't do it all by itself."

I remembered the one that I had seen staring at me from the tree before the possum had showed up. Had it been infected with the same strange larva? There had been something odd about its face, but it had been too far away to tell. Somehow I couldn't regret the distance.

No, there's no lack of excitement of the nerves to go around . . .

I walked back to the garden. Fat bumblebees careened into

flowers, which swayed under their weight. Beetles rolled in the golden stamens of oakleaf hydrangea and tiny striped hoverflies hung suspended by the bottlebrushes of giant blue hyssop. I did not know the species of most of them. Normally I would have been eager to learn, but I had a gloomy feeling that if I did, I'd find out that they were parasitic on some other species. I sat down on a bench and leaned my head back, admiring the plants instead. There are parasitic plants, but not many of them, and so far as we know, beech trees don't much care if a *Monotropa uniflora* sets up among its roots.

A shadow fell over my face. I looked up, startled, and saw the unlovely face of Phelps looking down at me. I squawked and scrambled to my feet.

"Miss Wilson," he said.

"Sorry," I muttered. "You startled me."

He nodded gravely. His eyes didn't leave my face, and after a moment, it started to get uncomfortable. I looked away, telling myself that *I broke into the shed* was not actually written on my forehead.

It was something of a relief, therefore, when he slid a hand under the bandage on his head and began scratching at it.

"If you keep picking at that, Ma Kersey will yell at you," I said.

"Forgive me," he said, dropping his hand. "It itches abominably."

"That probably means it's healing."

He said nothing. He was standing too close, but the bench was already pressing against the backs of my legs. Unless I wanted to climb over the seat, I had no immediate way to retreat.

"Can I help you, Mister Phelps?" I asked, not entirely kindly.

Phelps gave this the lengthy consideration that he gave everything. "Will you walk with me, Miss Wilson?"

"Um." I cast about for a reason to refuse. "I fear I'm still recovering from my illness at the moment . . ."

"We won't go far. There's something I wish to show you."

I wanted to keep arguing, but if he suspected me of something, then it would probably only make me seem more suspicious. And from Phelps, at least, impropriety was unlikely to be an issue. "All right," I said, trying not to sound as ungracious as I felt. I shoved my pencil in my pocket.

He led me around the shaded side of the house, toward the woods. They were certainly much cooler than the rest of the grounds, so I didn't protest. Maybe he wanted my opinion on a plant? "I wish the heat would break," I said, "but I suppose that won't happen until fall."

"It is in God's hands," intoned Phelps, demonstrating his superior grasp of small talk. I stifled a sigh. Even the preacher at the church, he of the multi-hour sermons, could talk about the weather without invoking the Almighty.

"Here," said Phelps, at a spot that looked no different from any other. I glanced around, looking for whatever botanical mystery required my attention. Nothing presented itself. Sweet gum and hickory and a stand of tulip trees, a few Christmas ferns, and a willow oak with an impressive display of bracket fungus. *Lord, don't let him ask me about the fungus. I never can tell my turkey tails apart.*

"Miss Wilson," Phelps said, reaching into his pocket. "I wonder what you might think of this."

Something about the way he held his hands in that moment, one cupped over the other, was so perfectly the image of a man presenting an engagement ring that I had a brief, horrible thought that Jackson had been right. *Oh god, please tell me Phelps isn't about to propose!*

I felt a stab of relief when he opened his hands and it wasn't a ring. *No, of course not, he barely knows you, what an absurd thought.* He held the object out and I took it, unthinking.

It was a candle. White wax, half burnt, with a dribble of wax down the side and a black wick. A perfectly ordinary candle, the same kind that burned throughout the house, the same kind that I worked by in the studio at night.

The kind I'd taken down into the room below the shed.

The kind I'd dropped, half burnt, when I had fled.

Years of enduring Headmistress Silverton came to my rescue. My mind screamed, *He knows! He knows!* but not a muscle moved in my face. I looked at the candle then up at Phelps, and let a puzzled line form between my eyebrows. "A candle?"

His face was still as well. I think perhaps he was surprised. "Do you know where I found this?"

"I haven't the faintest idea. I think Mrs. Kent keeps a few dozen in the hall closet."

"I found it," he said, without acknowledging my response, "on the stairs in the shed."

I waited, projecting polite disinterest as hard as I could. "And?" I said, after this pronouncement had hung in the air for a moment.

"You're the only one who could have left it there."

I rolled my eyes with exaggerated annoyance. "In case you haven't noticed, I've been in bed for the past few days."

"You must have dropped it before that."

I briefly considered arguing that it could have been Jackson or Mrs. Kent, but throwing anyone else in the path of Phelps seemed like a cruel trick. "How do you know you didn't leave it yourself?"

"We only use lanterns."

"Fine, then maybe a rat dragged it in. They eat candles, you know." I shoved the offending candle in my pocket and folded my arms, calling on all of my experience as *schoolteacher who is getting tired of having this conversation.*

He leaned forward. He was very tall and I felt my spine trying to sway back, out of the way. I stood my ground. "Nothing goes in or out of that shed, Miss Wilson. It's built special that way. But you've been inside. You *saw*."

The lines on his face were pulling tight, his jaw clenched. Adrenaline trailed cold insect feet down my spine. I had the feeling that it no longer mattered what I said. Phelps knew what he knew. Even if he had been wrong, it would not have mattered. *Damnation. I can't bluff my way out of this, can I?*

Those washed-out blue eyes bored into mine. "God hates a liar, Miss Wilson."

"Then He must be quite angry at you for telling people that shed is full of gunpowder," I snapped.

To my astonishment, he took a half step back, as if I had struck him. His throat bobbed as he swallowed. "I have done what I must. I am . . . I *was* . . . trying to protect you." He reached up and dug his fingers into the back of his scalp.

"Why would you even care?" I asked, taking a step back of my own. I wanted to bolt and run, but if I did, like the monsters of my childhood, he was sure to chase after me. "So the doctor keeps his bugs down there. Why all the secrecy?"

Phelps's face went momentarily slack. Once again, I had the feeling I'd startled him—no, I'd *shocked* him. He looked as if I'd hit him with a board.

(*why would that shock him?*)

That was the moment when I should have bolted. I should have screamed for Jackson and run for the house. Phelps would still have caught me, most likely, but Jackson might have heard.

But I was too used to being a schoolteacher, where your control of the class depends on never showing weakness. I still thought that if I stayed calm and kept Phelps off-balance, I could get through it.

"You're a cold one," said Phelps slowly, still watching me as if I'd grown horns.

(*why would he say that?*)

And then, in a chilly little copperhead whisper under my heart, *You know why . . .*

"Take it up with the doctor," I said aloud, and turned toward the house.

I got three steps before his fingers closed over my arm. "I plan to," he said. "But you're not going anywhere, Miss Wilson."

I looked down at the hand, the knuckles as tough and brown as walnuts, then up at his face, and said, coldly, "Take your hand off me."

Phelps shook his head. "I don't think so. You're coming with me."

He hauled me forward. I tried to dig in my heels, but only succeeded in tearing long divots through the pine needles and dead leaves.

"I cannot imagine God approves of this!"

His face might as well have been carved in stone. "I do not approve of what the doctor is doing," he said coldly. "I never have."

I twisted my arm back and forth, to no avail, and drew in a breath to scream.

Phelps yanked me close, into a tight embrace, face wedged against the front of his shirt. I smelled sweat and sourness, and my shout came out as a muffled yelp. "You can't keep the Devil locked up," he said. "I *told* him."

He adjusted his grip, clamping a hand over my face. I thrashed uselessly.

"If you'd just told everyone what you saw . . ." Phelps said, almost plaintively, as he dragged me deeper into the woods. "If you'd just told everyone *then*, I would've been *glad*. It could have been *over*."

I kicked violently at his shins. I might as well have been kicking a tree for all the good it did. Phelps didn't even slow down.

When we came in sight of the shed, I thought I might be sick from sheer terror.

It was just bugs, just Halder's bugs, that was all that was in there, the rest was a hallucination, it wasn't real—

(Phelps thinks it's real)

When he stopped in front of the door, he locked one arm around my neck to hold me in place and reached for the key. I clutched at his arm, feeling half strangled. "Phelps!" I hissed. "We can still tell everyone! We'll go together—we'll tell the sheriff—"

His sigh briefly pressed his rib cage against my shoulders and the back of my neck. "It's too late now, Miss Wilson," he said. "You should have said something before. They might have hanged me, yes. I accept that. But the Devil would have finally been burned." He yanked the door open.

If he got me inside, I might never get out again. I planted my feet again, futilely. "Mister Phelps," I said, as calmly as possible, as if we were having a conversation, "I believe the Lord never sends us more than we can handle."

That was a lie, incidentally, but astonishingly, it seemed to work. He stopped, one hand on the door, one still around my neck. I could feel the side of his face against my forehead and the rake of stubble across my skin.

"We can handle this together," I said, fighting to sound as if this were normal. "Just talk to me."

It was so close. I could *see* him thinking about it. But he shuddered and said, "I'll wire the doctor," then whipped his arm off my neck and thrust me through the door. I tripped over the lip and staggered into the drape, hands out, trying to keep from falling down the stairs. The door slammed behind me.

"The doctor will know what to do," he said, his voice muffled through the metal.

I beat my hands against the door. "Phelps! Phelps, listen to me! Whatever you're afraid of—"

"There's a beekeeper bonnet on the peg," he said. "That kept them off before. I'll bring you food later." And then, almost too quietly to hear, "I'm sorry, Miss Wilson. Hanging's one thing, but I won't let the Devil take me. Not like this."

What was he talking about? What did he know that I didn't?

The beekeeper's bonnet—yes, all right, I could understand that, if there were botflies down here, that might help—but what Devil was he referring to?

I shouted the questions at him and more, pounding my fists against the door in the dark, alternately threatening and pleading, begging for him not to leave me alone, but all I heard was silence. Phelps was gone, and I was alone in the dark with the shadows of my delirium.

CHAPTER 16

I would like to tell you that I was brave and practical and resourceful, that I immediately took stock of my situation and began plotting my escape. But in truth, I slid down the wall to the floor, put my head against my knees, and began to sob.

It was all simply too much. I had been anxious and fearful and then I had been horribly ill and then I had been attacked and now I was imprisoned. Even that was far too much to bear, without even considering what lay in wait at the bottom of the steps.

You can't keep the Devil locked up.

I shoved the thought aside. *Not important right now. What's important is getting out.*

The door wasn't going to open. I wasn't going to be able to break it down without tools of some sort. My best hope would be if someone came looking for me. Someone other than Phelps, obviously.

I forced myself to think logically. Neither of the Kents were likely to wander by the shed on their own. Sally certainly wouldn't. Once they knew I was missing, they would definitely look for me though. But when would that be?

Probably not until I don't come down to dinner. Mrs. Kent will check to make sure I haven't fallen ill again. By that time, Phelps will probably be long gone.

Had Jackson seen us talking? It was possible. He'd been busy, and we'd been on the other side of the grounds. He *could* have looked up at the right moment and seen Phelps and I walking away together, but I couldn't count on it.

All Phelps had to do was claim that he hadn't seen me. *Hell, if I were Phelps, I'd pretend to be worried and join in the search, and take the woods right here so that nobody else could hear me yelling.*

Mrs. Kent would suspect Phelps of having something to do with it, but what could she do? This was still North Carolina and she'd be a Black woman accusing a white man of something, without any proof to offer the authorities.

Panic tried to rise in my throat. I studied it as dispassionately as I might a specimen I was preparing to paint. Phelps had said he was waiting for Halder. Even if no one found me, I had only to wait until the doctor's return.

Granted, he had already spent a week in Raleigh, but he must be due to return soon. He had only the one specimen, and Jackson hadn't caught any others. I just had to wait until this unexpected research angle had run its course.

The panic tried to rise again, more strongly. That could take *weeks*. Father had once become so obsessed with carnivorous sundews from the Sandhills that he spent three months there, sending occasional letters to reassure me that he was fine, and only the onset of winter had actually driven him home.

I tried to imagine spending months in the shed and felt a sob wrack my body like a blow.

No, no. Phelps is not going to keep you here for months. He said he'd wire Halder to tell him there's a problem.

When Halder gets back, surely he'll see this is ridiculous.

Surely.

I found that I wasn't as sure of that as I had been a few hours ago.

I stretched out my hand and touched the heavy drape in front of me. Somewhere, down in the dark, was something that Halder wanted to keep hidden. Something that Phelps was helping him keep hidden.

Something that he thought he'd hang for.

You know what it has to be. The body must have been real. Not a hallucination brought on by malaria, but a real thing that I had seen and then tried to convince myself I hadn't.

But . . .

No "but"s! Think!

The memory was blurry, as if I'd poured water over a painting and left only the ghosts of colors behind, but it hadn't vanished. Dreams fade, but this hadn't. On some level, I must have known that, or I wouldn't have worked so hard to convince myself that I hadn't.

Why had I been so desperate to believe that it wasn't true?

Because it was horrible. Because it was frightening.

My lips twisted. No. That hadn't been the reason, not really.

Because you would have had to do something about it.

I had talked myself into continuing to work for a man I knew was a murderer. But there was a difference between hearing gossip and discovering an actual corpse—

(if it was really just a corpse)

—being kept in a shed. So I had seized on an explanation that explained it away, that allowed me to keep doing the work I wanted so much to do. I had fallen into relief the way that some people fall into love, and let it blind me.

Of course, the malaria probably helped.

I laughed, even if it came out half a sob. Yes, the malaria had helped. I had seen things that couldn't possibly be real, which made it easier to dismiss everything else. Even now, I wasn't entirely certain of what I had seen. The body, yes, the flies . . . probably . . . but surely not *all* of it could have been real. It defied imagination.

And why would Phelps be so afraid of a corpse? Defiling a dead body was a crime, but it certainly wasn't a hanging offense, unless you were the one who had made the body dead in the first place.

Could *that* be the secret? Was Phelps killing people for the doctor to experiment on? I tried to imagine Phelps doing something so obviously sinful and couldn't. Then I tried to imagine Phelps killing people he thought were sinners, and that was much easier.

There's a way to find out, you know.

I wiped my tear-slicked face. I still had the matches that I had put in my apron days ago, and the candle that had condemned me.

Stop sniveling. Quit telling yourself stories and go look.

Light flared up under my hands as I struck a match. I found the beekeeper's veil on the peg where Phelps had said it would be. It was the one I'd seen before, that I'd thought looked like a lady's hat. That certainly argued that there were insects down below. Probably I hadn't completely hallucinated that either.

(*black-and-yellow flies buzzing against your skin*)

I set the candle down and pulled the veil on, then unbuttoned my collar and shoved the gauzy fabric down into my shirt. It probably looked ridiculous, but I was far past caring about that. Nothing should be able to crawl under it this way.

Now go down the stairs and find out what's real.

The water level had subsided somewhat, or perhaps it had never been as deep as I thought. When I stepped down onto the boards, sediment puffed up from underneath and diffused through the water like smoke. The burlap sacks that lined the walls were stained green with algae and had turned black near the bottom. Had I noticed that before? I couldn't remember.

The wooden table was as I remembered it. Enamel pan, rusted forceps. I took a deep breath and lifted the candle, looking toward the back of the room.

My throat closed up.

I had expected the body. I truly had. I had even expected the flies crawling on the dead man's face. And I had also expected that my memory of it was not perfect, that the fever had warped my perceptions.

But I had not expected reality to be so very, very different.

Memory said the corpse was a brown mummified husk, but memory had lied. This man was only recently dead, his skin ghastly blue-white. He was monstrously thin, but the hollows in his ribs were those of hunger, not of skin sealed against bone. As I watched, a black-and-yellow fly crawled across them, reaching the summit of a rib and then descending into the valley beyond.

I swept the candle flame from side to side, my horror giving way to a deeper bafflement. Could I have truly been *that* wrong?

(*you're always lying to yourself*) hissed my anxiety.

Stop that, answered the cool scientific voice. *This has nothing to do with* you. *That body is* fresh. *It cannot have been here for a week.*

I sniffed cautiously, smelling algae and clay and still air. Was there a trace of rot? I thought there was, but not nearly a week's worth. The underground room might be significantly cooler than the outside air, but it wasn't remotely cold enough to keep a body fresh.

My eyes swept down the body to his hands. I had been almost certain that the impossibly long nails were hallucinatory, but I had been wrong. They still looked more like brittle, distorted claws than fingers. And there were the manacles, which I had very much *hoped* were a dream, and the wire mesh table, and . . .

I closed my eyes for a moment, told myself that I was a naturalist and not squeamish, then leaned over and looked underneath the wire mesh.

Pale flesh hanging like grapes, stretched around the bodies of insect larvae. *Oh god, not a dream at all.* I forced myself to look, to compare it with my memory, and here it seemed that delirium had exaggerated, because my mind had screamed that there were masses of the things, dozens of bloated warbles larger than my fists, and there were not quite so many as that.

Oh good. Merely horrific instead of apocalyptic. How nice.

I straightened hastily. The room lurched a little and I looked away from the body and stared at the ordinary wooden table until it steadied again.

Well. Now I knew . . . something. But what?

Think logically. Assemble your evidence.

If the body was fresh, what did that mean?

What if this *wasn't* the corpse I had seen? Phelps must have brought it here in the last day or two. That would explain why he had been so alarmed by what I had seen, and why he believed that he would hang for it.

That would mean that he and Halder have been killing people. Possibly lots *of people.*

(oh god)

(*Halder won't let me out if he thinks that I know, I'm going to die down here, they're going to shackle me to that table and put botflies in me and—*)

The cool voice was back again, driving the sudden panic aside. *That is one possibility, yes. What is the evidence against it?*

My eyes were drawn back to the gruesome fingernails. Surely there were not two men with nails like that in Chatham County. There might not be two men like that in the Carolinas. This *must* be the same man that I had seen before.

Which could only mean . . . *he had not been dead.*

My memory of the corpse speaking, the part that I had dismissed utterly, had been *true.*

Jesus, Mary and Joseph, is that possible?

Of course it was possible. I had remembered the manacles and the nails and the wire table, hadn't I?

(*botflies don't live in dead flesh*)

The candle flame wavered as my hands shook. *Oh god. If I hadn't convinced myself otherwise, could I have saved him?*

And then, in a whisper like a drop of water falling into a cold pond, *Are you sure that he's really dead now?*

I stared at the man on the table for a long time. I had to put the candle down because my hands would not stop shaking. Part of me knew that it was reckless to burn down my only source of light, but the panic had finally broken through my defenses.

It was not the kind of animal terror that sends you fleeing into the woods or that makes you beat your hands against a door until you collapse. It was the hard savage kind that knots up under your breastbone and makes it hard to breathe and what fills your head is the knowledge that *you will have to do something about it.*

It is terrible to be helpless, but it can be equally terrible to be the one who is supposed to be able to help.

The thought came to me that Ma Kersey had probably felt this way many, many times, and somehow that was steadying.

"Right," I said. My voice sounded high-pitched and shaky, but it still sounded like me, and that was worth something. I had watched my father drown in his own bed. This was worse, but it was still only dying, and I had faced dying before.

He can't be alive. You'd smell piss and shit if he'd been down here a week. He must *be dead.*

I had to be sure.

"Can you hear me?" I asked.

There was no reply. A fly buzzed past me, shadow and gold.

"Please, if you can hear me, say something."

Silence.

"Right," I said again.

I did not want to touch that waxy flesh with my bare hands. Even if he was cold, that wouldn't prove anything. There were cases of people buried alive who had been cold when they went in the ground.

I could not see that the man was breathing, but if it was very shallow, I might not see it, particularly not by candlelight. I had no mirror to put in front of his nostrils, and the thought of laying my ear against that bony chest and listening for a heartbeat under the buzz of disturbed flies . . . I shuddered. Perhaps, if there was no other choice, but there was something else to try first.

I pulled one sleeve protectively down over my hand, steeled myself, and waved away the flies on the man's face. Most of them buzzed up angrily, bumping against the fabric of my gown. One blundered into the protective mesh in front of my face and clung there, a blurry shadow too close to bring into focus. I batted it away, heard myself moan, and thought, *Stop that. Whimpering won't help.*

Then I thought, *Oh shut up, this is the worst thing that's ever happened to you, whimper if it makes you feel better.*

One fly remained, crawling sluggishly across the man's upper lip. I lifted my arm to bat at it again, realized that it might try to escape up his nostrils, and whimpered again without guilt.

Then I set a fabric-covered finger against his eyelid and pulled it back.

For a moment, I stared into a dark hole of pupil, and then it contracted down to a pinprick in the light of the candle.

I jumped back. The candle flame went out and I knew that I had to light a match and get it going again, but even doing that much seemed, momentarily, impossible. I leaned against the wooden table in the dark, overwhelmed.

He's alive.

He's still alive.

I hadn't failed him—but now I had to get both of us out of here.

How long had the man been here?

How long does it take for someone's fingernails to grow like that?

I shook my head in the dark. No. *That* was impossible. It would take years and no human could survive for years like that.

The length of time hardly mattered though. To do this to someone for even five minutes would be monstrous.

Halder has been feeding him, *not the insects. Except that the insects are feeding* on *him, so . . .*

I blundered away, hearing the boards squelch under my feet. I had to sit down for a minute and get myself together. When I found the stairs, I climbed up and sat, still clutching the warm candle in nerveless fingers.

My great interest, Miss Wilson, is in parasitic and necrophagic species.

It is my great hope that if I can fully understand the life cycle of these species, it will unlock new ways to deal with them.

But to learn more, one must study them exhaustively.

Study them he had, in his own back garden. I had pictured cages of animals infected with botfly larvae and recoiled, but it had never occurred to me that Halder might have used a *human* model.

But why? Why *would you do that? It's so dangerous and for what? Why would anyone risk getting caught just to use a human?*

And then something that had been slowly growing on my consciousness finally intruded, and I realized that while I was sitting there, the blackness had become more of a deep, deep gray and I could make out the edges of the table in front of me.

My eyes couldn't possibly have adjusted. This was the kind of pitch blackness that you found in deep caves. And yet there was light coming from somewhere, the smallest hint of it, somewhere near the back, against one wall. I could just barely see the edge of a sheet of burlap, a square of black against the faintest edge of illumination.

My heart leapt. Could there be another way out? A door hidden behind the wall? An escape?

Something scrabbled on the far side of the room. I saw movement and heard a muffled thump, followed by a splash.

I shot to my feet, and at that moment, the man said, in a painful rasp, "Please . . . no . . . *don't let them . . .!*"

Another scrabbling sound. My brain was full of the possum trying to get through my bedroom door, the possum that had a botfly in its brain *oh mother of God, I'd almost forgotten about those*. Except that I could get away, even if only to the top of the stairs, and the man chained to the table couldn't.

Cold determination settled on me, like a glaze of winter frost. I hadn't saved the dying man when I might have, so whatever happened to him now was my fault. *So do something about it.*

My hands didn't shake as I struck one of my few remaining matches. Part of me was screaming with terror and wanted nothing more than to curl into a ball and weep, but I didn't have time for that now. I locked her away in a shed of her own and lit the candle.

Did I have anything that could be used as a weapon? My boots might serve if nothing else did. I swept my gaze over the room and spotted the enamel pan. Not heavy, but better than nothing. I picked it up, waiting.

With a scratch of claws, the intruder leapt up onto the man's prison bed. The wavering candle light revealed . . . a squirrel?

Gray fur, long brushy tail. Unmistakably a squirrel. It turned its head slightly, light glinting off one dark eye, and I saw the back of its head was strangely distorted, much too long. I didn't even need to see the dark circle of a botfly to know what had happened. It made a perverse sort of sense. *Cuterebra emasculator. Squirrel botfly.*

Relief bolstered my resolve. I was pretty sure I could fend off a squirrel, no matter what was wrong with it. I lifted the pan and took a step forward.

"No!" said the man miserably, turning his face away.

I hesitated. Was he talking to me? Was I not supposed to protect him or . . . ?

The squirrel flung itself across the man's face, belly down. For a bizarre moment, I thought that it was trying to smother him and rushed forward, splashing through the shallow water.

Then I heard the crunch.

Blood poured over the man's chin. His throat worked spasmodically. The squirrel's body seemed to collapse but it made no effort to escape. It didn't even show any signs of pain. It simply stared at me with bright black eyes while the man bit and swallowed and bit and swallowed and red crept over his cheeks and dripped through the wire mesh below.

I didn't scream. I didn't recoil. I stopped dead and simply stood, holding the candle and my makeshift weapon, and watched. My mind was a hollow silence.

At last, the squirrel pulled away. It was impossible for it to walk—it was cored to the backbone, like a watermelon eaten clear to the rind—yet walk it did. It crawled off his face and then it fell off the side and landed without a sound.

I circled the prison bed and saw, in the shadows there, a half dozen small bodies. Squirrels, mostly. A rabbit. Something on the bottom that was probably a groundhog. None of them more than a day or two old, all sporting the slack, bloody pockets of discarded warbles. Much later, I would think they were probably the source of the faint rot I had smelled, but in the moment, I have no memory of thinking anything at all.

The newest body lay draped across the others. It wasn't breathing, but then, it had nothing left to breathe with. It was dead. It *had* to be dead.

You thought that he *was dead too.*

It was the first thought to cross my mind in a full minute. It lay in isolation inside my skull, like a specimen pinned to a card.

The warble on the back of the squirrel's head began to pulse, and the thought went away again.

It did not take long for the larva to emerge. The thing was at least two inches long, so large in comparison to its host that it seemed impossible that it had been contained within the rodent's skin. I watched it thrash free of the skin cocoon and lay still for a moment, as if exhausted. It was dark brown, its slug-like body divided into fat segments, the surface stippled instead of smooth. I had labored for hours getting that stippling just right. *Ah, I thought inanely, the preservative* did *wash the color out. I will have to repaint it.*

From illustrating the life cycle of the fly, I knew that its next move would be to burrow into the leaf litter and pupate. There was no leaf litter here, nor did I intend to give it the chance to pupate. I stepped forward, slid the edge of the pan underneath it, and flipped it into the water.

Its body jackknifed, but it did not sink. I brought down my boot, crushing it against the wet boards, seeing something yellowish puff into the water, before red clay rose up and covered it.

I looked at the man on the table. Blood coated his face and throat, already starting to dry. His eyes were closed. As I watched, tears began to trickle silently over his skin, etching pale tracks into the stain.

What I wanted in that moment was not answers, not explanations, not even freedom. What I wanted was for this *not to be happening.*

I turned away. I went up the stairs, pulled the drape aside, and sat down in the corner. I pinched out the candle in an effort to save the few minutes of light that I had left. I tucked my hands into my sleeves and pulled my skirt tight so that there was no exposed skin for anything to reach. If I had had a blanket, I would have pulled it over my head to keep the monsters away.

And then, and only then, I let myself think again and stared, dry-eyed and dry-mouthed, into the dark.

I had told Phelps that I believed the Lord only sent us as much as we could handle. That was a lie, but even if I *had* believed it, I wouldn't anymore, because this was too much.

Being kidnapped and shoved into a dark hole in the ground was terrible, but I could probably have coped with it. Other people have dealt with things like that before. A dying man riddled with parasites was horrible, but by itself, I could have managed. Other people have dealt with things like that as well. The history of the world is written in dying bodies and in those who have to pick up afterwards.

Combining the two was right at my limits, but I had managed. I had been coping.

But the gutted animals—that was simply too far. A merciful god would not have piled that on top of the other two. *No one could be expected to deal with all three at once.*

And yet, horrified and nauseated and scared out of my wits, I was still a naturalist, and even as I shuddered in the corner, wrapped in a cocoon of fabric, part of me was asking, *How did he bite through the fur like that? How did he swallow the bones without choking?*

I could still hear the thin crunch of the squirrel's ribs giving way. I rested my forehead on my knees and tried to stop hearing it.

I wanted this not to be happening. I wanted the world to be different. I wanted it not to contain horrors.

Useless. "Wish in one hand, shit in the other," Esther had said once, shocking me. "See which fills up first." She'd been right though. Might as well wish for a world where your father hadn't died and left you penniless, or a world where his friends had remembered that you existed.

At last, I did what overwhelmed people have done since time immemorial, and slept.

CHAPTER 17

I don't know what time it was when I woke up. It wasn't a restful sleep, more like a fitful doze where you are thinking something and then you wake, still thinking about the same thing, and aren't certain whether you slept or not.

Certainly I had no shortage of things to occupy my mind. I kept reliving the sensation of stepping on the larvae. It had felt exactly like stepping on a grape and feeling it pop underfoot. I was never going to eat grapes again. Possibly I was never going to eat *anything* again.

When I did dream, it was an endless sensation of things crawling on my skin, jerking me awake to slap at something that wasn't there.

They can't get into your nose or mouth, I told myself. *You don't have any open wounds. You're as safe as you can be.*

I only wish that I believed it.

When the shed door opened, it took me a moment to realize that it was really happening. I scrambled to my feet as light filled the narrow space and threw a hand over my eyes, blinking back tears.

"Wha . . . ?" I said. For a moment I thought I was back at the school and expected Headmistress Silverton to scold me for oversleeping.

"Miss Wilson," said Phelps, and memory crashed back down over me.

He stood in the doorway watching me uncertainly, as if *I* was the dangerous one. I wished like hell that I was. *I should have* taken the metal pan and lain in wait and bashed him over the head with it. Granted, there was only about a three-inch clearance between the door and the drape and he would probably have been expecting it, granted he was a great deal stronger than I was and that I was coming off a malaria flare-up and had just witnessed a baffling horror . . . *fine, okay, perhaps that was an unrealistic expectation. Still.*

"Did you bring water?" I croaked. My throat was very dry, but no power on earth would have induced me to drink the water pooling in the room below.

Phelps had a lantern in one hand and . . . was that a *picnic basket* looped over his arm?

It was. There was even a gingham cloth over the top. *Dear god, this must still be a nightmare. Surely real life is never this surreal.* Phelps hung the lantern on the wall and closed the door, then pulled a flask from the basket and offered it to me. I unscrewed the top and drank greedily through the mesh, soaking it. Water hit the back of my throat like a benediction.

"Thank you," I said, lowering the bottle, then grimaced at my own reflexive courtesy. *No, it's good to stay polite. There is no point in antagonizing him.* Phelps nodded.

"Brought you food," he said, clearing his throat. He flipped the cloth back and offered me the basket, which held biscuits and cheese.

The thought of food was utterly revolting, but I was going to have to eat if I wanted to keep my strength up. It was on the tip of my tongue to say that I'd eat them later, but it occurred to me that I would have to remove the netting in order to eat, and if Phelps wasn't here, I'd have to do it in the dark. I retreated to the far corner with the basket, picked up a biscuit, thought *I will never be able to eat this*, then took a bite and realized that my body was ravenous, even if my mind wasn't.

I looked in vain for a knife to cut the food, but of course Phelps hadn't provided one. I settled for alternating bites of cheese and biscuit, washed down with sips of water, while Phelps leaned against the wall and silently watched me eat.

The biscuit was very crumbly and fell apart when I bit into it. I brushed the crumbs off the front of my dress self-consciously, annoyed with myself. If you are kidnapped by a strange religious fanatic who is holding you captive in a shed with horrors below it, it seems like you should not have to worry about your table manners, and yet . . .

When I had finished, I carefully wiped my mouth with the cloth, folded it neatly, and deliberately met my captor's eyes. "Thank you," I said again.

He looked away. "I regret the necessity, Miss Wilson."

"Ironically," I said, "there wasn't one. I had thought that all this"—I waved toward the stairs—"was part of the delirium from the malaria. It did not seem possible that it was real."

Phelps blinked at me. "Truly?"

"Truly."

He winced. "Ah," he said. He lifted a hand and scratched at the back of his head, where the bandage hung askew. "That explains it." He took a deep breath. "My apologies then, Miss Wilson. It seems I've made a mess of things."

There was genuine anguish in his voice. Could I use that? I chose my words carefully. "I don't know what is going on," I said, "or what Dr. Halder is doing down there." I *thought* I had, until the squirrel. Now I couldn't even begin to guess. "Obviously you do, Mr. Phelps."

"I don't understand all the science of it," he said cautiously.

"I'm not concerned with the science," I said, which was only partly a lie. I would probably have found the science fascinating if I had been reading about it in a journal in the sunlight a long way away. "Can you tell me what's going on?"

"The Devil," he said. "It's the Devil down there."

"I believe you," I said. Normally this would be a lie, but given that I had just seen a man eat a live rodent like an apple, all bets were off. Anyway, I wasn't planning to argue with Phelps if I could help it. "I was skeptical before, but—err—my eyes have been opened."

"Yes," he said distractedly. "I wired the doctor."

I honestly wasn't sure if Halder's presence was going to help me or not. He'd already shot one man, maybe he'd just shoot me too. Could I pretend interest in the science?

Of course there was no telling how soon Halder would return either. I'd much rather *not* spend a week down here while the doctor finished up his business in Raleigh.

I tried again. "You have always struck me as a godly man, Mr. Phelps." A pained expression crossed his face, and I hurried on. "You must have a good reason for doing this. If you explain it to me, you may find that I agree with you. It may be that none of this *is* necessary."

He stared at the wall over my head for a long moment. I picked at a loose thread on my skirt, wondering if I should push him further or not.

"Have to wait for the doctor," he said finally. "The doctor will know what to do."

"Mr. Phelps," I said desperately, "we can go back to the house together right now. I'll tell the Kents that I was lost in the woods and you found me. Then we can wait for the doctor together."

Silence welled up between us as I waited. He scratched the back of his head again, and the *scruff-scruff-scruff* of his nails against his scalp rang in that small space like words.

"Miss Wilson," he said, finally meeting my eyes. My heart sank. His tone had gone stiff and formal.

"Please," I said, cutting him off. "*Please* just think about it."

"I don't know," he muttered, half to himself. "I don't know."

"Think about it. That's all I ask."

He nodded distractedly and reached for the lantern on the wall. I jumped. "Wait! Please!" I fought back my flare of terror. "Please leave me the light. It's . . . it's very bad in the dark."

A startled look crossed his lean face. "Oh. Yes. It would be, I expect." He took down the lantern, glanced around at the shed, then handed it to me. Our fingers met briefly, and I was startled by how cold his were to the touch.

"I'll bring you more food tomorrow," he said gruffly.

"Thank you," I said. And then, as he stepped outside and I saw the door start to close, I tried one last time. "I don't believe you're a wicked man, Mr. Phelps."

He paused on the threshold. "'Behold, I was shaped in iniquity, and in sin did my mother conceive me.'"

If I had a better grasp of Bible verses, perhaps I could have offered something that would have swayed him to my side, but all I could think of was, "Jesus wept," which, while apropos, did not seem persuasive. My father's transcendentalist philosophy seemed unlikely to work. I said nothing, and after a moment he shut the door. I listened for the click of the padlock and closed my eyes briefly when it came.

My first act was to turn the lantern down as low as I could to save oil. Judging by the slosh, it was less than half full. Five, maybe six hours, if I was lucky. Certainly not enough oil to burn down the shed, which I admit, I considered. (I suspect that Phelps had thought of it too, and probably would not have handed the lantern over if he'd thought I might succeed.)

I felt a little better though. It may have been the food and the fitful sleep, but I suspect that the lantern had as much to do with it. I wondered what time it was. Late, probably. I hadn't seen any light when he opened the door, and Phelps would hardly have returned in broad daylight.

Had the Kents discovered I was missing? I hadn't heard anyone calling for me. Could I have slept through it?

If it was off in the distance, probably. But I'd have heard them if they were up close. I'm sure of it.

Surely they'd check the shed, wouldn't they? They must know it's here, even if they think it's something innocuous.

I drank another sip of water, wondering when my captor was likely to return. There was still a biscuit in the basket. I wrapped it up in the cloth, hoping that would keep anything from laying eggs on it. It didn't seem that he intended to starve me, anyway.

Too late it occurred to me that perhaps I should have worried about the food being drugged. I put a hand to my mouth, then snorted at myself. Why would he *bother* to drug me? What was I going to do? I had nowhere to run. It wasn't as if there was another way out.

And then I froze.

I'm an idiot. An absolute stone-cold dyed-in-the-wool idiot.

I'd *seen* the light coming in. Those animals had come from somewhere, which meant that there was another way into the room, and *that* meant that there was another way out.

Granted, a hole large enough for a squirrel or a groundhog might not be large enough to accommodate a human. But this was all clay held up by boards, and I would damn well dig my way out if I had to.

I made sure the net was firmly tucked around my neck, grabbed the lantern, and shoved the drape aside.

It was amazing the difference that lantern light made, compared to a single candle. Even turned down low, I could make out the slight rise and fall of the man's chest. The hollows of his ribs no longer looked like canyons. He looked unhealthy, but not like he was dying.

His eyes were closed. He might have been asleep. Perhaps eating rodents was exhausting. My mind skittered away from waking him up. *It would be cruel to wake a man who's obviously so miserable.*

(the crunch of tiny ribs under teeth)

I shuddered. No, I didn't want to wake him up.

The walls of the room were lined with burlap that had been tacked up over boards. I tugged at a panel and a broad strip tore away in my hands. I started to toss it aside, then decided I couldn't afford to waste anything that might be useful, and brought it over to the bare table instead. *Now where was that light coming from . . . ?*

I pulled down more burlap until I finally located it. There was a gap between the boards and one of the support pillars, perhaps six inches wide, and in this gap, something had bored a hole. I peered into it, angling the lantern as best I could, and saw that it ran generally upward. An animal burrow, by the looks of it. *Or a hole dug by animals, anyway.*

I carefully avoided looking at the dead animals. If a parasite could drive a possum to try to break through a door, presumably it could also drive one to dig.

And even to climb onto a table and offer itself up as a meal . . . ?

I remembered the wasp and the cockroach. Yes. Apparently even that. Whatever was going on here, it seemed that it was a horror spawned as much by nature as by . . . whatever Halder had done.

Enough. It doesn't matter right now. What matters is getting out.

The burrow was large enough to fit my arm into, no more. (Not that I had any intention of sticking my arm into a dark hole that was currently being used by infected rodents.) Could I widen it? Possibly. It would take a great deal of work digging through the clay, but it wasn't as if I had anything else going on.

The gap between board and upright was too small for me to fit through though. I examined the board and my heart sank. A foot wide and two inches thick, and reeking of creosote. The smell made my nose wrinkle, but it drowned out the slowly increasing rot from the pile of gutted animals, so I was forced to be grateful.

The board had been nailed into the ceiling beam from the other side, so that the weight of the earth pushed it more firmly against the support. I put my shoulder against it and shoved. I might as well have been trying to move a brick wall.

All right. Look at this logically. If I could break through a two-inch plank, I'd simply have broken down the door, but maybe I didn't need to break it. If I could dig out the space behind it, maybe I could loosen the nails and get the board turned slightly. I only needed a few more inches of clearance to fit my head through, and then it was just shoulders and contortion, right?

. . . sure, yes, of course. A walk in the park, definitely.

I tested the edges of the burrow. Hard orange clay, gritty and mixed with small pebbles. I'd heard Jackson curse it often enough. Shovel-breaking stuff. "Good thing I don't have a shovel to worry about," I said out loud, and barked a laugh.

Ah, we're moving on to that stage of the breakdown, I see.

Well, if a groundhog could do it, so could I. I had smaller claws but a bigger brain. And an enamel pan.

It took hours. The clay did not want to yield. I scooped up water and poured it over the edges, trying to soften them, which didn't help much. Clay takes up water slowly and gives it up even more slowly, which is why I was standing in an inch of water right now. I chopped at the edges of the hole with the pan, scraping off fractions of an inch at a time, until it felt like I was trying to shave my way out.

Still, the hole got bigger. When I finally allowed myself to take a break, the opening was twice as large, and I'd dragged several pounds of earth out from behind the board. I gazed at it, feeling a flush of triumph.

Granted, a hole ten inches wide was not notably more useful than one five inches wide, but at least I'd accomplished *something*. Maybe I'd get lucky and it would rain. Then I could stand in a foot of water and haul mud out until it collapsed or I did.

Don't think of the woman, the blood thief, buried alive. Don't think of her trying to chew her way through the clay. I gritted my teeth. Perhaps I too was buried alive, but at least I had plenty of air.

My shoulders and forearms ached. So did my neck, from

wedging myself against the board and digging blind behind it. Nature was also calling, which presented its own set of challenges.

I did not want to use my sleeping area as a latrine, but I had no intention of hitching up my skirts in a room full of botflies. I settled for using my trusty enamel pan as a crude chamberpot and carrying it downstairs to dump out. I had not previously considered the many, many uses of an enamel pan in adversity, but I was about to declare my undying love for this one.

How long had it been since Phelps came? How much more light did I have? Had it been hours? It *felt* like hours.

I had just started digging again when the man on the table said, "What are you doing?"

I was so startled that I dropped the pan. I picked it up hastily and looked over to see that he had turned his head to face me. The dried blood lay in a flaking brown mask over the lower half of his face and his teeth seemed very white against it.

"Trying to dig my way out."

He considered this while I scraped more clay loose. "Why?"

"A distinct lack of social engagements," I snapped. What the hell kind of question was that?

"So you're trapped here too?"

Oh. Perhaps he hadn't realized. No, why should he? He must have thought that I was working with Halder and Phelps. *And you were, weren't you? Halder, anyway.*

Shut up.

"Yes. Phelps locked me down here."

"I see." His voice sounded stronger, no longer so dry and raspy. Squirrel guts must make a serviceable lubricant. I scraped more clay out of the hole, wondering what to say next. I had so many questions that I hardly knew where to begin.

Are you sure you even want the answers?
Really sure?
(the crunching sound of tiny ribs)

. . . yes. I do.

Stupid question. Of course I wanted answers. I always did, didn't I?

"I thought you were with them," the man said.

My laugh could have etched glass. "I'm not." I tested the board again. It continued not to yield in the slightest.

It occurred to me that I was being extremely short with a man who had, let's face it, been manacled to a wire table for at least a week, probably more. I was not in the best emotional state myself, but compared to what he'd been through, the last few days had been a pleasant stroll through the woods.

"Sorry," I said, stepping back from the hole. "I . . . um." I glanced over at him, at his limp hands hanging down like rain-blown peonies, and the long, dreadful nails. "You've been down here awhile," I said finally.

He made a rough clicking sound in his throat. It took me a moment to recognize it as a laugh. "Yes," he said. "Awhile."

He turned his head a little when he said it, and perhaps it was because of the better light or just the angle or something about the way he held his mouth, but suddenly I *recognized* that face. I knew him. I had seen him just recently, not as a living man but as a watercolor sketch, the planes of the face sketched out by someone who thought he was handsome, even though there was nothing handsome about him now.

"My god," I said. "You're Saul Gregor."

CHAPTER 18

"I am," said the man chained to the table, "though I fear you have the advantage of me." Another hoarse, clicking chuckle.

"Sonia Wilson," I said automatically, and my brain was so far gone from normal matters that I actually thrust out my hand to shake. We both stared at it, and then I said, "Oh hell, I'm bad at this," and pinched the bridge of my nose, feeling tears start to threaten again.

(You'd think being in mortal peril would eliminate any sense of social awkwardness, but apparently it just means that you get to spend the last moments of your life embarrassed.)

"It's not something you get good at," Saul said.

A fly buzzed somewhere in the room and I hastily shook my sleeve back down over my hand. "I looked at your manacles," I said. "I don't know if I can break them." They were great heavy things, the locks welded shut with rust. I doubted that my faithful enamel pan would be able to smash through them.

"That wouldn't be a good idea right now," he said, somewhat cryptically, and closed his eyes again.

"It can't be very comfortable."

"It's not."

I swallowed. My mouth felt dry, but it was probably nothing compared to his. "Are you thirsty? I have a little water left."

"Keep it."

"I have most of a biscuit—"

"No."

This was beginning to remind me of when my father was

dying. I would ask if he needed anything—tea or fresh pillows or more blankets, *anything*—because dying was too large and I couldn't fix it but at least I could make tea. Toward the end, he had wanted less and less, and eventually I realized that I was just trying to make myself feel as if I was helping him.

Except that my father had pneumonia, and Saul Gregor was chained to a table, and the two weren't similar at all, were they?

I started digging again. Digging I understood.

"Are you real?" asked Saul abruptly.

I had a mad urge to deny it, but that would have been cruel. "I'm pretty sure I am," I said, and didn't add: *not as sure as I was a few hours ago*. It would have been much easier not to be real. If I wasn't real, none of this was real either, and that made a lot more sense than a world where it was.

Another scoop of clay hit the ground. The hole was definitely real though. My shoulders wouldn't ache so badly if it wasn't.

"Sorry," said Saul quietly. "One gets these ideas . . ."

"Yes, of course." Lying down here in the dark, one had to imagine all sorts of things. "I don't blame you."

He lapsed into silence again. I tried to think of something else to say, and settled on, "Everybody thinks you're dead."

"Do they?" Saul sounded only mildly interested.

"The story is that Dr. Halder shot you while you were running away with Louisa."

That got his attention. Wires rattled, jerking my gaze back to him. He actually lifted his upper body a little way up, maybe half an inch, before collapsing back. "Louisa. Is she . . . ?" He swallowed, tried again. "Does Halder mistreat her still?"

"What?" I asked blankly.

"*What is he doing to her?*" Saul shouted, and the flies all took flight from his face, buzzing around in a panicky cloud of black and gold.

"He doesn't do anything," I said. "She got away. Ma Kersey and the rest, they got her away."

An idea was starting to form in my brain. It explained everything quite neatly. It just happened to be impossible, which was a definite strike against it.

"Away?" Saul stared at me, his eyes flat and oddly reflective in the lantern light, like coins. "Away where?"

"I don't know. Ma Kersey wouldn't tell me. She didn't want Halder to find out and go looking, since I guess they're still legally married. I've never met her."

I heard an odd, jagged little snap, and looked down to see that Saul had clenched his hand into a fist. Two fingernails had broken off and a third had torn partway free.

The idea poked me again. I shoved it back down. A hypothesis is no good if it requires the impossible as a condition. If you don't know how an orchid is pollinated, there's no point in suggesting that fairies do it, even if that would explain everything neatly.

(how long does it take fingernails to grow like that?)

"You're sure?" Saul said. "You're sure he's not keeping her prisoner somewhere?"

I considered this. It's impossible to prove a negative, of course, but this didn't seem like a good time for that particular discussion. "I'm pretty sure. Mrs. Kent would never allow that to go on."

"Rose Kent . . ." Saul breathed. "No, she wouldn't." He sagged, his fingers falling slack once more. The two broken nails were floating on the surface of the water like chitinous leaves. *Raw sienna mixed with white, a wash of Payne's gray for the shadows . . .* I looked away.

"He lied," Saul said, and began to laugh again, louder this time, an awful throat-tearing sound that was too much like his scream, the same dreadful sawing violin note. "The bastard *lied* to me. Oh god, Louisa!"

"Please stop," I whispered, my hands clamped over my ears. In another room, that laugh would have echoed, but here it sank into the muffling burlap and that was somehow worse, as if the laugh was still there, burrowed into the walls, waiting to pupate into something worse. "Please, *please* stop."

To my surprise, he did. It took longer for the laugh to die away inside my head. I slowly lowered my hands, feeling foolish. *It's just a laugh, what's wrong with you?*

"I'm sorry," Saul said. "It's just that I've spent so long thinking he still had her. He said he did. That he kept her locked up, painting pictures. I kept picturing it . . . and now . . . now I find out it was lies all along . . ."

The idea needled me again, more insistently. "How long?" I asked. "How long have you been down here?"

"I don't know," he said. His smile was ghastly. "How long has it been since he shot me?"

There, you see? It does *explain everything!*

It's still impossible. No one could live this way for that long. He'd have rickets and bedsores and . . . and . . . it's just not possible.

"Over a year," I said.

"About that, then," said Saul Gregor.

"That's not possible," I said in a shaky voice. "You can't have—no one could survive—"

"Believe me, I didn't want to." He gave me a wry look. "I'd beg you to kill me, if I thought it would take."

I stared at him, not understanding the words, wondering if his mind had slipped. That happens to prisoners sometimes, doesn't it? Who could blame him? Maybe it only *seemed* like a year. Maybe . . .

The long nails floated by on the surface of the water, like little boats.

"Look, you can't have been down here that long," I said, hearing myself use the schoolteacher voice, as if I had caught one of the girls in an obvious lie. "You would have rickets."

(I don't know why my mind settled on rickets as the problem. In my defense, I was not at my best.)

Saul stared at me. I swept my eyes down his body, looking

for signs of brittle bones, realized how ridiculous that was, and looked away. I'd forgotten he was nude. It hadn't bothered me when he was an anonymous body, but now that he had a name, it seemed indecent.

"I probably do," he said finally. "I've had everything else by now."

Oh god, the man was lying on a bed of wires with botfly larvae dangling from his back, and I was lecturing him that he hadn't suffered correctly. "I'm sorry," I said, mortified. "I didn't mean it like that."

"The screwworms were the worst," he said, almost dreamily. "The botflies come out so easily, but the screwworms don't. He practiced digging them out over and over, trying to get the trick of it."

Halder had bragged about his monograph on the best way to remove screwworms. I pressed my hand over my mouth. It must have seemed like a *century*. "I'm sorry," I whispered.

Saul was quiet for so long that a fly landed on the side of his face. I picked up the pan and flung myself at the hole again, trying to drive out the mental image of the jar on Halder's desk, the hundreds of screwworms packed together. Surely they could not all have come from Saul's flesh. That wasn't possible either.

Surely.

I hit a stone and began prying at it with my fingers, trying to tug it loose.

"How did you end up in Halder's ill graces?" Saul asked abruptly.

"Too much curiosity." Briefly I outlined how I'd come down and gotten caught.

"Ah. I am sorry to hear that . . . Miss . . . Wilson, was it?"

"Yes. Halder's supposed to be coming back," I added. "I suppose when he does, he'll shoot me too." I did not want to think about the alternative, that I might wind up on a wire rack of my own, my flesh colonized by maggots to appease a dreadful curiosity.

"Perhaps," Saul said. "He stopped being interested in me a while ago, I think. I don't know how long. I was hoping he might let me die."

There was nothing I could say to that. A just god would not allow anyone to be trapped like this, but even an unjust one ought to strike me down if I uttered some platitude like *where there's life, there's hope* to a man in Saul Gregor's position.

I was spared the necessity of an answer when we both heard it. A scrabbling sound in the hole, coming down toward the room.

I stepped back quickly, skirt dragging through the water. Saul shuddered. "Whatever that is, Miss Wilson, I'd take it as a favor if you didn't let it near me."

It was a rabbit, and not a very large one at that. The Chatham rabbits would be embarrassed to claim kinship. It fell clumsily out of the hole, hit the water, splashed helplessly for a moment, then finally heaved itself up on the pile of bodies. With its fur plastered down, it looked smaller than the squirrel had. There was a single large warble under its left ear.

It made a jump for the table, couldn't reach, and fell back. It lay as if stunned for a moment, then slowly dragged itself back to its feet.

"Please," said Saul.

I will not be afraid of such a wretched creature. I will not.

I grabbed a piece of burlap, wrapped it around my hand, and reached down to pick it up by the scruff of the neck. It weighed almost nothing.

The rabbit kicked feebly once, then dangled from my hand, panting. White showed all around its eye, though it didn't seem to be focusing on me at all. I fancied I saw a ripple through the skin of the warble.

Now what?

I had never even killed a chicken for dinner. I steeled myself, waded to the far corner where the water was deepest, and held it under the surface of the water. It struggled briefly—very briefly—then went limp.

It must be a better death than having your guts bitten out. I knew that was true. It made no sense that my vision was going blurry.

I held it down long after I was sure that it was dead, because I wasn't sure if I could do this twice. The warble began to pulse more frantically, squirming as it too drowned, and I gritted my teeth and kept holding the poor limp body underwater until nothing was moving at all.

"I'm sorry," said Saul, as I laid the sodden rabbit on top of the others.

"Yeah," I said. I scrubbed at my eyes with my sleeve. I was being foolish. "It's fine. It's not fine, but . . . it's fine." I took a deep breath. "They're trying to feed you, aren't they? The flies."

Saul nodded.

"How? *Why?*"

"I believe they figured out that I was starving to death."

I shook my head. "No . . . I mean, *how?* They're insects. Some of them feed their own young, but feeding you? *Why* would they do that?"

"Because they don't want me to die, I assume. Much as I might wish to."

I paused. "Oh. That's why you want them to stop, then." Silly me, thinking that it might be because it was horrible to bite into a live squirrel.

"Yes. They feed *on* me and now they *feed* me, but I don't . . ." He trailed off and began coughing, a dry hack as if something was trapped in his throat.

"Can't you just . . . not eat what they bring?" I asked, when he had finally quieted.

Saul sighed. "If you were dying of thirst and someone poured water in your mouth, could you keep from swallowing?"

It seemed to me like there was a significant difference between swallowing a mouthful of water and eating a rodent down to the backbone, but what do I know? All I could do was offer him my extra biscuit, and he'd already turned that down.

"It's just that what they're doing makes no *sense*." I started hacking at the hole again. "Wasps lay their eggs in caterpillars so that the larvae have something to eat, but they don't start feeding the caterpillar."

"And I'm the caterpillar?" Saul gave another clicking chuckle. "These are . . . special, I think."

I paused for a moment. Certainly they were enormous, and I hadn't looked too closely at one. Were they a different species than the ones I'd drawn? Something that showed unusual behaviors?

It wasn't hard to imagine Halder hearing of a strange new species and deciding to test it out on someone he despised. Someone that had been in his power. If he'd shot Saul and Saul hadn't died outright . . . yes, I could see that.

"Did he ever say anything about them? About the species?"

Saul's lips twisted. "He might have. I can't say that I was always in the most receptive mood to listen. I know he kept bringing new ones down. Most of them died, until finally some didn't. But even if they weren't special before, they are now."

I started digging again. I was becoming very fond of this hole. When I got out of here, perhaps I would give up being a naturalist and just dig holes for a living.

No, I probably wouldn't, because even now I couldn't stop myself from asking, "Special how?"

Saul was silent for a few minutes. I thought maybe he'd fallen asleep. I hit another rock and started prying at it, but only succeeded in bending the edge of the pan.

"They've fed on me," he said at last, clear reluctance in his voice. "I don't know what that would do. It doesn't usually happen that way."

It was my turn for silence. The rock was at least the size of my head. I excavated around the edges, turning those words over in my mind, trying to make them fit, and eventually gave up. "I don't understand what you mean."

"It changes things. They're different now, I think. They grow faster, anyway." He said something I didn't quite catch, that might have been "same as us," or "shame on us." One of the two, anyway.

"That smacks of Lamarckism," I told him primly, getting my hands around the rock at last. I braced my foot on the wooden board and threw my weight against it. The rock popped loose unexpectedly and I dropped it, because the alternative was to have my fingers smashed, and fell back into the water with a splash.

"Jesus, Mary and Joseph!" Cold water spread through my skirt and my drawers. I stood up, slapping futilely at my dress. Saul snorted with laughter.

"Thank you," he said, as I attempted to wring out the soggy folds. "This is the best entertainment I've had since Phelps lost hold of a chicken a few months ago."

"So glad I could amuse," I said coldly. I was starting to think that Saul Gregor wasn't the nicest person. On the other hand, being wired to a table for a length of time that was almost certainly *not* a year couldn't be good for one's personality. "So the chickens *were* for you." I had been pretty sure, but it was nice to have confirmation.

"Yes." His amusement faded. "Halder figured out that birds were better than animals for his purposes."

I had a pedantic urge to lecture him that birds were also animals and the word he wanted was *mammal*, but I squelched it. "What purposes?"

"Keeping me alive. Barely."

I had no idea how either one was keeping him alive. I pictured him biting into a chicken instead of a squirrel. *No, the feathers would get in the way, wouldn't they? Although the fur should have as well* . . . "What's the difference?"

My skirts were as wrung out as they could get, which arguably gave us something in common. My drawers stuck clammily to my skin. I felt unpleasantly as if I had wet myself.

"Oh no," Saul said softly. "Halder won't win that easily."

"Huh?" I looked up, but he had pressed his lips together and turned his eyes to the ceiling.

Fine. Be that way. I tested the board again with my shoulder, and thought I felt a very slight give, but now the damn rock was in the way, and it was too large to fit through the gap. I cursed under my breath. Saul continued to say nothing.

I was not going to get angry. I wasn't. You don't get angry at people who have been imprisoned and tortured. You just don't. Even if they are being weirdly cagey about things that might be important. They are obviously not responsible for acting oddly under the circumstances, and getting angry is counterproductive and . . . oh. Hmm. I had apparently just knocked a chip out of the pan by bashing it against the rock. Hard.

"You may be exactly what you say you are," said Saul abruptly. "But Halder has been trying to pry things from me for a long time, and I haven't . . . I think I haven't . . . told him anything. If putting you in here with me is his way of trying to trick me, I'm not falling for it."

It was the hesitating "I *think* I haven't" that made my anger fall back and slink away in shame. God only knew what Halder had done to him, and if I thought *my* delirium had made me an unreliable observer, how must Saul feel?

Besides, what would knowing do to help me? It certainly wouldn't get us out of this shed any more easily.

"You don't have to tell me anything," I said. "Unless you know a better way to dig."

"Sorry."

I scraped out more dirt and dumped it atop the dead animals. It occurred to me that this had to be quite recent, because Phelps would surely have noticed the growing pile of corpses. "So they haven't been feeding you long," I said. "The flies, I mean."

"No. Not long."

I scrubbed at my face and only barely stopped myself from tearing a hole in the netting trying to scratch. "Maybe it's more like ants and aphids than caterpillars."

Saul turned his head to look at me. The flies had settled again, but he didn't seem to notice and I pretended not to. "Ants?"

"Some ants keep aphids. Ant cows. They feed the ant cows and then the ant cows excrete a substance that the ants eat."

"I don't know if being an aphid is much better than being a caterpillar."

"I'd much rather be an aphid. The aphids aren't being devoured from the inside out."

Saul stared at me. His eyes were pale green in the lamplight, and their expression was suddenly so cold and empty that I realized just how supremely tactless my statement had been. I began to stammer out an apology when the door to the shed slammed overhead.

Both our heads jerked up. I thought, *No, wait, it's too soon, the lantern hasn't burned down, it's still daylight*—and then Phelps came down the stairs, saw us both, and shouted, "Get away from him!"

CHAPTER 19

My captor had a much larger lantern in one hand and another basket over his arm. He set the basket down on the step with exaggerated care, reached into his vest, and pulled out a gun.

The barrel winked in the orange light. I stared at it blankly. My brain said *Prussian blue and burnt umber for the metal, antimony orange for the reflections.* This was not helpful under the circumstances.

"Move away from him, Miss Wilson," Phelps said, leveling the gun at Saul. "He's dangerous."

"He's chained to a table."

"I feel she makes a valid point," said Saul, sounding as if he were standing in someone's parlor, not naked and tied to a table. "Don't you, Phelps?"

The gun trembled. This didn't make me feel any more confident. A scared man with a gun is much more dangerous than a confident one. What if he shot Saul? What if, after everything, the man bled out in front of me? *And it will be your responsibility if he does, because you didn't get help that first night.*

I would like to say that I thought about what I was doing, that it was an act of considered courage, but it wasn't. I didn't really think about what I was doing. I just clutched the pan in front of me with both hands and walked slowly forward, until I planted myself between Saul and the cold eye of the gun.

Phelps bit his lip. He looked awful. His skin looked looser and he seemed to have aged a decade since the night before. His hair stuck out from his skull in ragged clots and his eyes showed white all around the iris.

"Miss Wilson, you *need* to get away from him." His voice was pleading now. "I brought you more food and more lamp oil. Knew this one wouldn't last all day and I hated to think of you down here in the dark. Just . . . just come over here. Please."

My nails scraped on the enameled pan as I gripped it more tightly. Would it stop a bullet? Probably not. I didn't *think* Phelps would shoot me, but I didn't want to find out. I took a deep breath.

"What Halder has done to this man is monstrous," I said. "But we can still make this right. Just help me—"

"He ain't a man," snapped Phelps. "Don't you understand? He's one of *them*."

"One of what?"

"*Devils.*" Phelps's hand twitched and the gun jittered sideways. My flinch must have been visible, because he set the lantern down and took a two-handed grip on the pistol.

Devils? Oh god, was this the shape of his delusion? My tongue stuck to the roof of my mouth as I tried to figure out how to navigate these waters.

"They look like us," said Phelps, "but they ain't human. I've seen it, Miss Wilson. I know. They're *blood thieves*."

I swallowed. "Mr. Phelps," I said carefully, "I know that there was a frightening incident a few years back. I know that there were a lot of stories around the . . . the two people . . . doing those awful things. But you have to understand that people were whipping themselves into a frenzy. Like a sort of lynch mob. The stories that people made up afterward, they weren't *real*."

Phelps closed his eyes briefly. If I had been closer, perhaps I would have gone for the gun. Then again, maybe I wouldn't have. When he opened them again, he was looking at me almost pityingly.

"Miss Wilson, they weren't just stories. I know you're educated and think you know better, but I was *there*. That girl we buried was a devil and I *know* that for God's own truth."

My knuckles were beginning to ache from clutching the pan so tightly, but I couldn't make them relax. "How do you know, Mr. Phelps? Did Halder tell you? Because—"

"I know," Phelps interrupted me, "because I killed her twice."

I am not always the quickest thinker. My response to this dramatic statement was to say, "Err . . . what?"

Saul made a sound behind me, the faintest huff, as if he wanted to say something but didn't quite dare.

"There were two of 'em," said Phelps. He sat down on the step, lowering the gun barrel just a fraction. I didn't fool myself that he couldn't snap it back up in a hurry. "Never saw the boy until the end, but I recognized that girl right enough."

"Oh?" I said. *Every minute he's talking is a minute he isn't shooting. And it's daylight, so maybe someone will have seen him.*

He nodded. "About six months earlier. Had a couple of shoats penned up. Heard squealing one night and grabbed my gun. Thought maybe a bear decided he wanted a taste of pork. Only it wasn't a bear."

"What was it, then?"

"It was that girl. Three pigs dead, with bites taken out of 'em. Lotta bites. Couldn't quite get through the hide, but she'd kept trying 'til she hit a spot on the throat she could get through. And the fourth one . . ." He stopped and swiped a hand at his hair, which turned into pawing at the back of his head, a terrible grimace on his face. It reminded me of how a dog will sometimes scratch its ear until it begins to yelp in pain, but doesn't stop scratching. The gun lurched back and forth and my stomach lurched with it.

"Mr. Phelps—"

He shook himself. "Sorry, Miss Wilson."

"You should have Ma Kersey look at that again," I said. "It might be infected."

Phelps tilted his head, still doglike. "You really don't know," he said almost wonderingly.

"As wise as a serpent and as innocent as a dove," Saul said, speaking up for the first time. "You should let her go, Phelps. She's got no part of this."

"The Devil quotes Scripture," Phelps said, his eyes narrowing.

"*Shut up*," I hissed to Saul. And to Phelps, more loudly, "You were telling me about the pigs, Mr. Phelps?"

"Oh, aye." He shook himself. "That fourth pig wasn't dead. It was sat half in her lap and she was tearing chunks out of its face and *it let her do it*."

I was suddenly horribly conscious of the pile of dead animals who had let themselves be gutted. *Keep him talking*. "That must have been very . . . ah . . . unsettling."

"Yes, Miss Wilson, it was." With anyone else, I might have suspected sarcasm, but Phelps sounded earnest. "I didn't know about the devils then. I shot her."

My eyes dropped down to the gun again. I had been hoping that Phelps had a philosophical objection to shooting women, but apparently I was being thwarted at every turn today.

He gestured with the gun. "Would have been a lot of questions. People would have seen a dead girl and not what she was doing. I was a different person then. I'm not proud of what I did, but I dumped the body in the woods, as far away as I could take her, and hoped nobody'd come looking. And nobody did."

I had one unbroken nail left after digging. I felt it break against the metal pan and looked down, bemused, at my own white fingers, as if they belonged to someone else. "Ah," I said.

Phelps's gaze was unfocused. I don't think he was even seeing me anymore, though he'd probably focus quick enough if I moved. "When word came down they'd cornered the devils who did for all those people, I grabbed my gun and went out. And there she was. Exactly the same."

Things were slotting into place in my head that I didn't like, all of them just as impossible as Saul having been locked down here for more than a year. Nevertheless, I wasn't ready to completely abandon reason yet. "It may have simply been a family resemblance or—"

"She recognized me too. Asked if I was gonna shoot her again."

"You must have been mistaken about—"

"She left half her guts on the floor of my hogpen."

I stopped talking.

"Hope you didn't let any of the hogs eat *that*," said Saul, with a clicking chuckle.

Phelps had hunched over as he spoke, but now he stood up straight, unfolding himself like a praying mantis. I took a hasty step back and felt my back bang into Saul's table. Something landed on the back of my neck and I had a horrible feeling that it was a botfly.

"I told 'em," Phelps said. "I told 'em that a bullet wasn't enough. I told 'em those two were devils. They didn't want to listen, but the preacher finally did. And I was right, wasn't I?"

Ma Kersey's description of the dead girl eating clay beat against my brain like a fly trapped in a cup. I lifted my hand, trying not to make any movements that might startle Phelps, and slapped at the back of my neck. Wings brushed my hand and I shuddered.

"Mr. Phelps," I said, desperate to keep him talking, "perhaps you're right. Perhaps that girl had . . . had a condition unknown to science. But it does not follow—"

(thin bones crunching under Saul's teeth)

"—that Mr. Gregor has it as well."

"Miss Wilson," Phelps said wearily, as if I were a particularly slow pupil, "I watched the doctor put two bullets in him. One in the knee and one in the back. Both of 'em came out the other side. Look at him now. Do you see any scars?"

I blinked foolishly then turned around, my eyes sweeping over Saul's prone body. His knees both looked like perfectly ordinary knees. I hastily averted my eyes from his groin, but his belly and ribs were smooth and unmarked by anything but the dark bodies of resting flies.

He must have been mistaken. There'd be enormous scars. He'd never walk again.

Halder missed. Or this isn't the same man. Or . . .

My gaze continued, inexorably, up to Saul Gregor's face. He met my eyes and his lips twisted in a small, rueful smile. Then he nodded.

"Really?" I said weakly.

"I could have gotten away if it wasn't for the knee," Saul said. "We heal very fast, but even our kind can't run on a shattered joint."

Oh.

Say that you were a scientist who studied parasites. There is only so much that you can observe from dead specimens. You need to watch their process through living flesh. But host animals are small and often hard to keep alive, particularly if you wish them to be infested over and over. How often can you pull a screwworm out of a rabbit before it dies of massive infection?

Say that you learned about another kind of human. One who heals at an astonishing rate. One that feeds on blood and viscera and who can endure astonishing hardships.

Say that your wife was about to run away with someone, and you caught them. You shot him and crammed his body into the shed you had once kept animals in, expecting him to die, but instead he healed, and you realized that he was one of these others.

Say that you realized this was the solution to your problem. A subject that would not die, no matter how many holes you put in him, digging screwworms out of his flesh. No matter how many botflies lived beneath his skin. An endless source of material for your studies . . . assuming that you were willing to commit atrocities that no one should inflict on another living being.

Say that you hated him enough to do it anyway.

"It *has* been a year then, hasn't it?" It sounded like my voice, but it must not have been me talking, because whoever it was sounded very calm. I was certainly not calm.

"Yes," said Saul.

"And no rickets," said that calm voice, somewhere off in the distance.

"And no rickets," Saul said, as if rickets mattered at all, but if I focused on something very small, perhaps I would be able to survive the next few minutes after all.

"Did Louisa know?" It was suddenly very important to me that she had known. If she had, and had loved him anyway . . . well, I would trust the judgment of a woman who could paint beetles more beautifully than anyone I had ever known.

If she hadn't—if Saul had lied to her—then I did not know what I was going to do next.

"She knew," Saul said. I met his eyes and there was no trace of a lie in them.

"He's a devil!" Phelps shouted, and I jumped. Strange as it sounds, I had, for an instant, forgotten that there was a man with a gun in the room. "He's a tempter! Don't listen to him!"

I glanced back at Saul, filthy and gaunt, chained down on his bed of pain. A tempter? Only if pity was a temptation.

"Mr. Phelps . . ." I began, with no idea how to finish that sentence.

Phelps opened his mouth. At first I thought he was about to

speak, but then I saw that he was panting. He scratched at his scalp and winced, pulling his hand away. I thought there might be blood on it, but the light wasn't good enough to be sure. "Lord have mercy, it hurts," he said, almost to himself.

"Let me help you," I said.

He shook his head miserably. "No one can help me," he said, taking another step forward. "'Ye serpents, ye generation of vipers, how can ye escape the damnation of hell?'"

"It's driving you now, isn't it?" asked Saul, almost conversationally. "It wants you to come closer, doesn't it?"

Phelps nodded his head up and down, quick and jerky. He grabbed for the timbers beside the stairs and clung, one-handed, half turning. I caught a glimpse of the back of his head.

His scalp was raw and bloody, scored with scratches, and the lump in the middle was crowned with a dark larval circle.

Not a goose egg after all.

I felt no surprise. Either I was numb, or, far more likely, I'd suspected all along but hadn't let myself think of it. I wondered how far the larva had dug into his brain. It was low on his skull, close to the brain stem. Perhaps it was a miracle he wasn't paralyzed.

No, no. The wolf worm needs them to be able to walk. It wouldn't chew through anything vital. Like the wasp larvae in the caterpillar, it keeps its host alive as long as possible so that it can continue to feed.

"Phelps," I said. "Phelps, it's just an insect. I watched Halder dissect a possum that had one. I saw what he did. I can get yours out." (This was a staggering lie, of course, but if I could just get the gun away from him and get him out of the shed, I could get him to Ma Kersey and maybe we could do *something*.)

His fingers jerked, releasing the timber, and he stumbled forward.

"I think it's too late, Miss Wilson," said Saul.

"It takes two weeks for them to reach maturity," I argued,

as Phelps blundered across the floor. "It's only been a couple of days for him."

"The ordinary ones, perhaps. But things like us can grow very quickly indeed."

If a creature like Saul could gestate in human flesh in three months, why should a botfly be any different? What changes had been wrought on the evolution of these insects, down in this dark hollow in the clay?

"Devils," wept Phelps. He hit the wooden table and fell heavily against it, gasping for breath. "Samson," he added nonsensically. "*Samson.*"

If I were braver, perhaps I might have tried to snatch the gun away from him. I didn't. God knows where the bullet would have ended up, in these close quarters. "Let me help you," I said again.

He ignored me, sliding along the table as if being dragged forward by an invisible hand. "O Lord, have mercy," he prayed, taking a jittery step toward Saul, then another. "As you had mercy on Samson, have mercy on me."

"The Lord has nothing to do with this," said Saul. There was a new note in his voice, something dark and gloating. I took a step back, then another, as Phelps stumbled in my direction. His pupils were huge and seemed to fill his whole face.

"No," Phelps said, half begging, his hands stretched out toward me. "No, please, stop it, *stop it!*"

"I can't stop it," I told him, retreating. "I can't, I can't, I would if I could!"

It was only the truth. I hated Phelps and I was afraid of him and I still would not have wished this on him.

"Not long now," said Saul pleasantly.

Phelps paused, swaying on his feet. "No," he said, sounding momentarily lucid. "No, it isn't."

"Come on, then," Saul said, his voice deepening and darkening. "Come a little closer. You know you want to. I didn't want to feed again, but for you, Phelps, I'll make an exception."

The muscles in Phelps's face twitched and spasmed, but his next words were clear enough. "You think I'll go alone?"

"You're alone now," purred Saul.

"Samson brought . . . Samson brought the temple . . ."

I had already retreated until my back hit the wall, but at his words, I started forward. "No!"

"*Samson brought the temple down!*" Phelps cried, pitching up against Saul's bed. His arm came up again with the gun pointed at Saul.

Saul screamed in his face.

That horrible sawing-violin shriek would have startled anyone. My heart stuttered in my chest. It drove Phelps back a step and that was enough, that was all I needed. I lunged forward and swung the faithful enameled pan and the angle was bad and I *knew* it wasn't heavy enough to knock him unconscious, but maybe he'd drop the gun and I could grab it or maybe there'd be a miracle or maybe the world would end but I had to do *something.*

It slammed against the back of Phelps's head and something gave under the blow. Something that felt almost exactly like a grape popping.

Phelps's back arched and he screamed and pitched forward. He dropped the gun and I dove for it, past his legs, and it vanished into the muddy water. I had a moment of panic that I'd grab it wrong and hit the trigger and shoot myself in the face, but then I felt the cold metal under my hands. I came up with it and scrambled out of the way, just as Phelps's scream was cut off and replaced by a horribly wet *crunch.*

I turned.

Phelps's feet drummed against the floor as he spasmed. He had fallen across Saul, and I did not need to see the red tide pouring across Saul's chest to know what had happened next.

It occurred to me, very distantly, that the merciful thing to do would be to shoot Phelps now. I looked down at the gun in my hands. I was shaking so hard that my teeth began to chatter and I had to clench my jaw to stop them. If I tried to aim like this, I would probably hit Saul. Saul, who had his face buried in the hollow between the other man's neck and shoulder.

Would it matter if I shot them both? End it here?

To really end it, you'll have to burn Saul's body. Possibly while he's still alive.

The crunching had changed to something softer and wetter. Phelps had stopped thrashing and lay limp across the table where Saul had been chained for twelve long months or more.

(he's not human)

(he's something else)

(a devil)

Some things were too monstrous to inflict, even on devils. I lowered the gun.

Phelps's last breath came out in a long gurgled sigh and was still.

I hit the wall and slid down it, hands over my ears, trying desperately to block out the sounds of Saul Gregor feeding.

CHAPTER 20

A long time went by, or perhaps it only seemed like a long time. I was cold and wet and the water was full of blood. Flies buzzed through the air, settled, buzzed again. The soft, obscene sounds went on and on, until at last they stopped.

Eventually, Saul released his prey, and Phelps slid off the table and fell facedown into the water. I winced a little at the wet thudding noise the body made when it hit the boards, though I knew he was long past caring.

"I think," said Saul, stretching as luxuriously as a man who was pinned to a table could, "that it is probably safe to release me now."

He looked better. A *lot* better. The hollows in his ribs had filled out completely and there was muscle along his arms now. No one seeing him now would assume that he was dead or dying, and certainly not that he had been down here for an unspeakable length of time.

"Why aren't you mad?" I asked, thinking about how long that year must have been.

"Who says I'm not?"

The gun was still in my lap. I picked it up. Saul sighed. "Madness, for most people, is something that happens inside your brain. Something being damaged. But those parts heal like everything else. I would go a little mad for a time, I think, and then they'd toss me some food and the madness would heal."

I tried to picture what that must have been like and couldn't.

Red fanned lazily through the water at my feet, a brilliant

color that you only get with cadmium and other heavy metals. And blood, of course. Most of Phelps's blood had gone into Saul, but there was still enough to dye the water crimson. "This is why you didn't want me to set you free, isn't it? You thought you might do . . . that. To me."

"Yes."

I nodded. "You could have explained that to me."

Saul gave me an ironic look. "Strangely enough, when you feed primarily on blood and entrails, you don't go around telling everyone."

Well, that was fair enough. "You told Louisa though."

The cords of his neck stood out briefly as he lifted his head, then let it drop. "We could never have children, you see, and she deserved to know why. But I would have told her anyway."

"Good." I pushed myself to my feet.

"I would have dealt with those children too, if I'd been here. Poor doomed souls. I heard rumors about them and came as quickly as I could, but of course it was much too late by then. I might have been able to save them, if I'd heard about them sooner."

"*Save* them?"

"It wasn't their fault. They were like ducklings raised by hens, with no one to teach them how to swim. It is not easy to be what we are, but there are . . . ways . . . to mitigate it. To do as little harm as possible. Not the sort of things a child could work out for themselves. They would have only known that they were not like others, and prey to a monstrous hunger they could not possibly explain."

I thought of Jackson's grandmother, telling him tales of blood and hunger, and wondered how many of those tales came from Saul's people, or from their abandoned children. I would have liked to feel sorry for those doomed three-month babies. Perhaps someday I would.

"Ma Kersey said they were born with sharp teeth," I said.

"Yes."

His teeth looked perfectly normal at the moment. I wondered whether the sharper teeth folded back against the roof of his mouth, like a snake's fangs? No, surely that would affect his speech, give him some kind of lisp, wouldn't it? Unless the upper palate was significantly deeper or perhaps had a slot for the teeth to fit into . . .

"They're in my throat," said Saul, rolling his eyes. "I'd offer to show you, but I don't want you to run away screaming before you unlock these things. After that, you can run away screaming whenever you like. I may too, actually."

I rubbed my forehead. "Are you a vampire, then?"

He made a scoffing sound. "Is a manatee a mermaid?"

"Only if you're desperate to see mermaids, I suppose."

"There you go, then." He pursed his lips. "Incidentally, while this is a fascinating conversation, I suspect I'd enjoy it even more if I wasn't chained to a table."

"Right," I said, setting the gun down on the table and examining the manacles. They were still as unyielding as ever. "I could go out and get a file. No, what am I thinking? I'll go get Jackson—"

"No!"

I blinked at him. "But the door is open now."

"I would rather not have anyone see me like this," said Saul, returning to his former dryness. "Specifically, covered with blood alongside Phelps's corpse."

Ah. Quite. "I take it the Kents *don't* know, then."

"Rose knows that there is something odd about me, but not the exact shape of it. I prefer that as few . . . err . . . of your people know as possible. It is safer for everyone that way. If you can get me free now, that would be best."

(It occurred to me much later that what Saul actually feared was that I would leave and not come back. But that was later, and my capacity for clearheaded thought was not high at the moment.)

Saul looked down at the manacles. "I can probably rip them out, if you remove the nails."

"Nails?" I looked blankly at his overgrown fingernails.

"There are nails in my forearms," he said patiently. "Also my shoulders and both shins. They prevent me from pulling my hands and feet out of the manacles."

I had to brace my forearms against the table for a minute to hold myself up. "Oh."

Completely logical, of course. You'd need something like that if you were imprisoning someone who knew they'd heal up even if they managed to pulp their own hand yanking it free. Halder had clearly thought things through with monstrous thoroughness.

The nails were placed just behind the wrist bones. Skin had actually grown over the top of the left one, which was probably why I had missed seeing it before. They had been hammered into the wooden cross beams on the table in a horrible parody of crucifixion.

Calm Me took over again, because otherwise I was going to begin screaming and not stop until my lungs gave out. "Right," I said again. I set my fingers on the right nail, pulled, got exactly nowhere. Saul's skin was still too cool. Squirrel botflies disliked human hosts because we were too cold. I wondered if these had adapted to a wider range of hosts.

"I can't get it out," I said. "Give me a minute." I prowled the room, trying to find something that I could use as pliers. My eyes fell on the rusted forceps. If they didn't fall apart when I tried to use them, perhaps that would work.

"I hope I don't give you tetanus," I muttered.

"I don't believe I can get it."

"Lucky you." The forceps didn't want to open at first, but eventually yielded, though not before leaving red handleprints in my fingers. I hooked them under the head of the nail, pulled, got nowhere, started to wiggle them back and forth, then stopped. "Oh god, I'm sorry. That must hurt."

"Yes, but having you cut my arm off will hurt a lot more." I froze. Saul's smile was ghastly. "You don't want to know what I'll do to be free of this place."

I set back to work. After a few seconds, the nail actually slid a little way out of the board and I redoubled my efforts. "Thank god this was here," I muttered.

"That's what Halder used to dig the screwworms out," Saul said pleasantly. And then, "If you keep stopping every time you're horrified, we'll never get out of here. My people *can* die of old age."

"How . . . fascinating . . ." I said through gritted teeth as I worked. A moment later, it came loose from the wood. I could actually feel the—texture? viscosity?—of the flesh change as the nail slid out through gristle and flesh. It was incredibly nauseating, but I told myself that *I* wasn't the one with a nail in my arm so *I* wasn't allowed to be sick. I leaned on the table and breathed heavily through my nose, then gave a final tug and pulled it free.

Clear fluid seeped through the hole. Saul lifted his forearm as far as he could, flexed it, and nodded. "If we both pull on the manacle now . . ."

I wrapped more burlap over my hands, grabbed the rusted metal, and pulled with all my strength, while Saul shoved upward.

The metal bolts held. The wood did not. Months of damp took their toll with a splintery crunch. Saul's arm jerked up, the manacle and a chunk of wood clinging to his wrist like a bracelet.

"Oh god," he said, with a moan that might have been pleasure or pain or both. "You have no idea how it feels to bend your elbow for the first time in a year."

I shook my head, moving to the other manacle, but Saul waved me off, reached over, and plucked the nail out of his left wrist as if it were a splinter. The second manacle yielded immediately to his two-handed assault.

It began to occur to me that, manatee or mermaid, Saul was substantially stronger than an ordinary human being.

He flexed both arms, then began calmly snapping the overgrown nails off each hand. I didn't want to watch, but I did anyway.

Saul had barely finished when he suddenly slapped a hand down against his chest, once, twice, then again. At first I couldn't tell what he was doing, then I saw the dark smears left behind.

"You little *bastards*," Saul said, his voice thick with feeling, and began swatting at the flies on his face. Some buzzed out of range, then began to settle again, and were immediately crushed.

I slid my hands into my sleeves and simply waited. If any man on earth had ever deserved to swat a fly, it was Saul Gregor.

With the flies dead, he lay quiet for a moment. I assumed that he was recovering from the pain. The underside of both arms was a ragged mass of torn skin, and I couldn't imagine how his joints felt, moving after so long.

"Best done quickly," Saul said finally—and sat up.

All the flesh that had grown through the wires and hung beneath, filled with the dangling bodies of the botflies, was suddenly yanked back against the mesh. Much of his back simply tore away. In other places, mostly around the edges, pale rags of skin came up, still attached, to dangle in long skeins from his ribs. Warbles swung like grotesque beads, or were forced open and their contents disgorged onto the floor.

The sound was indescribable.

Saul did not scream, but he made a hard, awful sound and sat forward, his breath hissing through his teeth.

The room tilted and darkened around me. I dug my fingers into the wooden tabletop and told myself that *I* wasn't the one who had just flayed my own back and *I* didn't get to faint. It was a much harder sell this time, but after a moment it worked.

"Jesus, Mary and Joseph," I croaked, pulling my apron off to staunch the bleeding.

Except there wasn't any. Or not much, anyhow. Saul's back was a landscape of pink and yellow meat shot with red, oozing more clear fluid but little else. I could see the white islands of his spine protruding from a skinless sea.

I draped my apron over his back. I can't swear that it wasn't just so that I wouldn't see it any longer.

"Thank you," Saul rasped, plucking the nails from his legs and tossing them aside. The manacles sheared away from the wood. I looked away before he pulled his thighs loose from the rest of the mesh, but the sound followed me anyway.

Saul stood up, took a staggering step forward, and leaned against the wall. His chest heaved like a bellows. "That was much worse than I expected," he said, to no one in particular.

I rushed to him, trying to figure out how to support him before he fell over, without touching the horrific ruin of his back. I ended up pulling his arm over my shoulders, trying to take as much of his weight as I could. "I'm sorry," I said. "Oh god, I'm so sorry."

He nodded. Violent tremors wracked through him. How long did it take for something like this to heal? Would it be five minutes or five days or five months?

"Come on," I said. "Let's get out of here."

"Yes." Leaning against me, he managed to take a heavy, leaden step toward the stairs.

(This was, incidentally, the first time I'd ever been in a naked man's embrace. As far as I was concerned, you could keep it.) I cast around desperately for something to distract us both. "Tell me about how you met Louisa."

"Louisa," he muttered. "Yes." Another dragging step. Something lightweight was knocking against my ribs, and I was pretty sure that it was a botfly warble. I deliberately didn't look, because if I saw it, I would have to scream and Saul needed me to be calm right now.

(wolf worm wolf worm wolf worm)

"You met Louisa," I prompted him.

"Yes. I'd come here . . . come here . . . I was looking for the children. Rumor. I said that, didn't I? A man told me about 'blood thieves in the woods,' but he was drunk. Wasn't sure if it was one of us or not. When I got here, people told me Halder had been there when they were killed." I steered him past the wooden table. Water sloshed around his bare feet. My own feet had been cold and wet for so long that I had stopped feeling them at all.

"So you met with Halder?" I asked.

"Yes." He put out his other hand and touched the wall, leaning against it. "Sorry. Need a minute."

"Yes, of course." I made certain that he was stable, slid out from under his arm, and picked the lantern up off the stairs. A botfly finished its struggle to emerge from one of the rags of skin and fell into the water with a *plop!*

"Met her in the house. She came into the room." He swallowed, and a little of the strain on his face eased. "Like she brought all the light with her. She was alive and she made you feel more alive just by being there." He shook his head. "Halder . . . stupid bastard . . . didn't see it. Such a goddamn waste."

I relocated the lantern and straightened, rubbing my aching shoulder. "Can you handle the stairs?"

"I think so." He leaned down and broke off a few toenails. "Phelps did me that much good, at least."

I decided not to comment on that.

Half carrying Saul up the stairs wasn't easy. They were broad, thankfully, but I slipped at least once and would have gone to my knees if Saul hadn't been there to pull me back.

"We're almost there," I told him. "You're doing good."

"So are you," said Saul dryly. "Am I helping you up the stairs or are you helping me?"

"Let's not get hung up on the details." I pulled the door open. Judging by the color of the sky, it was early evening, but it seemed extraordinarily bright after my day spent underground. The sound of cicadas droning in the trees made me want to weep with relief. I stepped outside and turned back to make certain that Saul didn't trip over the lip on the threshold.

That's when I heard the gun cocking behind me.

"I suggest you keep your hands where I can see them, Miss Wilson," said Dr. Halder. His gun was smaller than the one Phelps had carried, which I had foolishly left on the table below, but his hand was also a great deal steadier. "Step away from my test subject, if you please."

"Test subject?"

"He's a parasite, Miss Wilson." Halder's lip curled. "No different than any of the others that I study. Step away, please. I don't want to tell you again."

Unlike Phelps, I was pretty sure that Halder wouldn't hesitate to shoot me. I stepped away. Saul stood framed in the doorway, swaying slightly on his feet. "Halder," he said.

"You're looking better, Saul. Been feeding, then? Perhaps on Miss Wilson, here?"

"I haven't touched Miss Wilson."

"Doctor," I said, thinking that it was just my luck that I would have to negotiate with two men with guns in the same day, and that I hadn't learned nearly enough the first time. "Doctor, we don't have to do any of this. Just let us walk away, and we won't tell anyone. No one would believe us anyway."

And, God willing, we'll be out of range when you discover Phelps's body.

"Don't be fooled, Miss Wilson," Halder said. "He may look human, but that's simply mimicry at work."

"Mimicry?" I said. Comprehension worked slowly through my brain. "Like those caterpillars that look like bird droppings?"

"Caterpillars again?" murmured Saul. I shot him a sharp look.

Was he not taking this seriously? Of course, if he gets shot, he'll heal up fine. Some of us aren't so lucky.

"More like the fireflies that pretend to be females of a different species. Then they devour the males who respond to their flashes. Saul, don't even think about it. You know that I'll shoot your knees out if I must."

Whatever Saul had been thinking, he must have stopped. I tried again. "Doctor, Phelps believed in devils, but I know you're a man of science. Surely you can't believe—"

"It is because I am a man of science that I believe, Miss Wilson. I have observed, I have tested, and I know that my logic is sound. This is not a human being. He—it—is a member of a species that evolved to prey upon ours. Darwin himself could not deny it."

"It doesn't follow that—"

"Do you know how they reproduce?" asked Halder pleasantly, as if I hadn't spoken. "Just like wasps, as it happens. They deposit their children inside a woman, and those children devour their host. Just like the wasp, they save the vital organs for last, so that they can grow as large as possible. I suspect the females have ovipositors for just that purpose, but sadly those fools burned the single female specimen we encountered before I could dissect it."

"I tracked their father down, if that makes you feel any better," said Saul, never taking his eyes off the gun. "He won't do it again. Or anything else either."

"Which hardly changes the fact that your species requires us as hosts," said Halder. "You are parasites upon us, in every sense. Without us, you would die out in a single generation." He gestured with the gun, and both Saul and I twitched. "With the information that I have gathered, I think it likely that they can be eradicated." He paused, eyes flicking briefly to my face. "You could help me, Miss Wilson."

"What?"

Saul's hand pressed briefly against my back. A message of

some sort, I thought, though I wasn't sure what. "Help you?" I asked.

"Indeed. Phelps assumed that you'd go to the authorities. I think he was wrong. You understand the importance of my work, don't you?"

I took another half step away from Saul, moving slowly. "It's very important, yes. Just as you said, if we know enough about screwworms, we can find a way to stop them."

"Exactly!" The lantern light flashed off his spectacles. "And this, Miss Wilson, is far worse than screwworms. Imagine how many of them there may be, living among us, devouring us . . ."

"There aren't *that* many," said Saul.

Halder's gaze swung back to him. "So you say. But I can hardly trust you, can I?"

I took another step forward and tried to compose my face. It wasn't easy. Dealing with Mistress Silverton had been one thing, but she had never held a gun on me. Fortunately, Halder expected me to look horrified. "Are you saying that there are more of them out there? Killing women to . . . to reproduce?"

"That's exactly what I'm saying, Miss Wilson. Did you see him feed on Phelps?"

So he suspected Phelps was dead. I didn't have to fake my shudder. "I did. It was horrible."

"That bastard deserved it," growled Saul.

Jesus, Mary and Joseph, let this be what he wanted me to do. "Would you have done that to me too, if you were hungry enough?"

Saul's laugh was an ugly thing. "I *did* tell you not to get too close to me, sweetheart."

"There," said Halder. "You see? We can only ever be prey to a thing like him."

I licked dry lips. "Have you found a reliable way to recognize them yet?"

"I have had some promising results with blood tests, though

of course, none of them would be foolish enough to allow themselves to be tested willingly." He gestured with the gun, which was now pointing more toward Saul than to me. "I am somewhat hampered by having only one specimen. Still, I am confident that we can find a way."

I lowered my hands, waiting to see if Halder would protest. He didn't. "If Phelps had just explained things to me, instead of shouting about devils . . ."

Halder sighed. "Phelps was a useful tool that outlived his usefulness, I am afraid. He never understood the importance of what we were doing."

I nodded. "It *is* important, isn't it?"

"You fickle little bitch," growled Saul, and made an abortive lunge in my direction.

I dodged out of the way easily, ducking toward Halder, and heard the gun go off. A bullet whined past me and something stung my shoulder. *Oh God, have I been shot?* I staggered forward with a cry, tripped, and sprawled full-length on the ground.

For one crucial second, Halder took his eyes off Saul to look at me.

Saul moved in a blur. He grabbed the hand with the gun, yanked it upward. Halder pulled the trigger, but the shot went into the air. Saul dropped his head and Halder began to swing the lantern toward the other man's face, then slowed. The lantern's handle fell from his fingers and oil splashed over the dry pine straw, lighting immediately. More hit my skirts, which were fortunately too wet to go up. I yelped and rolled, scrambling to my feet with speed, if not grace, and began slapping at my skirts.

When I finally looked over, neither Saul nor Halder were moving, and I realized belatedly that Saul's teeth were sunk to the gums into Halder's wrist.

"Oh," said Halder, his voice remarkably calm. "It would appear that your saliva possesses anesthetic qualities."

Saul opened his mouth. I caught a flash of sharp teeth vanishing.

"Yes," he said, clamping a hand on the back of the doctor's neck. "Useful for a parasite, don't you think? Miss Wilson, get his gun, please."

"Let me put this fire out first," I said, stomping out the last flames on the pine straw.

"Time is something of a factor, Miss Wilson."

"So is not burning alive," I snapped, but hurried to take the gun from Halder's fingers. He tried to hold on to it, but his fingers were rapidly going limp. A moment later he crashed down to his knees. Saul moved his grip to the fringe of hair at the back of the doctor's head and held him up.

"Miss Wilson," Halder said, still very calm, "you can still help me. You have the gun."

I took a deep breath. "Why the botflies, Doctor? Why did you do that?"

"For science." His words were beginning to slur a little.

"And did you tell other scientists what you were doing? Invite them to read your notes and see your experimental setup?"

"Of course not."

I shook my head. "Then it wasn't science, Dr. Halder. It was just you torturing some poor bastard in a hole in the ground." I stepped back, lowered the gun, and nodded to Saul.

"Hmm," said Saul thoughtfully. "Now what shall I do with you? I have so many ideas . . ."

Halder said nothing. I don't know if Saul's saliva had paralyzed him completely, or if he simply didn't have anything to say.

"I could put you down in that hole, Halder. Down with those wolf worms you fed on my flesh. I could even find some screwworms, I expect. You made cuts on my thighs so that the screwworms would burrow in exactly where you wanted. Do you remember?" He shook Halder, just a little. "Answer me. You're not *that* numb."

"I remember," said Halder. His pupils were huge behind the

lenses of his spectacles, as if he'd been eating opium. Phelps had said that his pig let the blood thief bite off its face, and now I understood why. Like the cockroach paralyzed by the wasp, Halder had no more will of his own.

"Even if I can't find some screwworms, the flies will have you soon enough," Saul said. "These move fast. One was eating through Phelps's skull, did you know that?"

"Really?" Halder took a deep breath and seemed to rally a little. "Did it take control of his motor functions, then? I theorized . . ." His mouth slackened, and his theory was lost. His very last theory.

Saul ignored him. "Well, Miss Wilson? What should I do?"

My mouth was dry. The long shadows had fallen over Saul's cheekbones and down onto Halder's slack face. Neither of them looked human, or holy.

If I were a good person, perhaps I would have argued for Halder's life. I probably wasn't a good person, so I decided to be an honest one. "Saul," I said, "if you want to kill him, do it. I'm too tired to sit in moral judgment right now. I won't stop you. I don't think I *can* stop you. I just want this to be over."

Saul huffed something that might, under better circumstances, have been a laugh. "For me—for what Louisa went through—I should probably make you die slow. But we're all very tired."

He moved again, very fast, and Halder fell over on his side with a red ruin where his throat had been. I looked away as soon as I realized what I was seeing. My shoulder still hurt. I looked down and saw a splinter of wood sticking out of it. The bullet must have knocked a sliver loose from the wall and hit me. I pulled it out and it hurt and it was very important to focus on the pain, because the alternative was to focus on the sound bubbling out of Halder's lungs.

And then Halder's gurgling breath stopped, and there was only silence, broken, very faintly, by a whippoorwill.

"It's over," I said, in a high voice. "It's finally over."

Saul said nothing. He said it for long enough that I turned and met those pale, pale eyes. The whippoorwill called again.

It occurred to me, like a splash of cold water, that I was the only person left who knew *what* Saul was, or even that he was still alive. The only one who knew that he'd killed both Phelps and Halder. The last loose end.

It would be incredibly easy for him to tidy me away. No one would think it odd that I had been killed alongside the other two, and no one would suspect a man who had been dead for a year.

He took a step forward, and I took a shuffling step back.

"Miss Wilson," he said, and I wondered what he read in my face, and whether it would make him more or less likely to leave me alive.

I was sure that Saul was grateful for my part in his rescue, but was he grateful *enough*?

"It's all right," I said. "I'm all right. I'm fine. So are you. We can just go home."

The whippoorwill called for a third time.

His eyes narrowed.

And then I heard the familiar sound of a shotgun being cocked and Mrs. Kent said, "Turn around slowly—" and we turned and Saul said, "Rose?" and Mrs. Kent said, "*Saul!?*" and I thought, *Surely he won't kill me in front of her?* but then Saul was rushing toward me and I closed my eyes so that I wouldn't see the blow coming.

At least I died in the woods.

A long, long moment crept by, and Mrs. Kent said, "Dear god, what's *happened* to you?" and it occurred to me that I wasn't dead. I opened my eyes and saw that the world was at an unexpected angle, and then I realized that my knees had given out, but that Saul Gregor was holding me upright.

Jackson was carrying the lantern. He reached out and took

the gun away from me before I could drop it. *Of course he has the lantern and Rose would be the one with the shotgun. It only makes sense.*

"Halder's dead," Saul said. "Phelps too."

I looked up into Mrs. Kent's face.

"Well," said my friend Rose, swinging the shotgun away, "about damn time."

CHAPTER 21

There were four of us around the kitchen table that night—or more accurately, three of us at the table and Rose cooking fiendishly as if she could unmake what had happened to us by sheer force of biscuits.

Saul ate them too. *Does he digest them normally, or does he have to cast them up again, like owl pellets? I should ask. Later.*

After two changes of bathwater, Saul looked infinitely better. His back was probably still a horror show, but if you couldn't see that, he just looked like a very tired human. Rose brought him one of Halder's dressing gowns, which barely reached his knees, but was probably an improvement over my apron. I took my own bath, heated with water from the big boiler in the scullery, and scrubbed with soap so harsh that it stung. My skin did not quite stop crawling afterward, but I was able to tell myself that it was only my nerves.

"Knew we shouldn't trust Phelps," Jackson said, for the third or fourth time. "He talked a good game, pretending to search for you, but I knew something was off . . . Love, sit down, for god's sake, you've made enough food for an army."

Rose muttered something uncomplimentary, but finally pulled the pan off the stoves. "All right, all right . . ." She dropped into her chair and folded her arms. "How long were you down there?"

"About three months, I think," Saul said. I lifted my head at that. His expression didn't change by so much as a fraction, but he met my eyes for a long, long moment. I took a slug of coffee and looked away.

"Three *months*?" Rose clamped a hand over her mouth. Jackson swore, hard and heartfelt, and put a hand on Saul's shoulder.

"After I got shot, I was out of commission for . . . well, quite a long time," Saul said. "I was half out of my mind with fever and I just knew I had to get away. Wound up in a jail out in Tennessee, after I knocked somebody down that I shouldn't. They dug the bullet out of me and I pulled through, but it was a pretty miserable time. When I finally got out, I came back here, thinking Louisa must still be here, but that bastard Phelps caught sight of me, and . . ." He spread his hands. "You can guess the rest."

Rose reached out and took Saul's hand, while Jackson tightened his grip, their heads bowed as if in prayer. "I'm sorry," Jackson said finally. "Shit, Saul. I'm so sorry."

"Miss Wilson here saved my life," Saul said. "If she hadn't found me down there, I don't know how much longer I would have lasted."

I looked away, recognizing the meaning of those words. Much, much longer. Years, perhaps.

"The hero of the hour," said Jackson, beaming, and Rose reached out her other hand and took mine.

We sat like that for a little while, and of course it was Rose who was the practical one. She stirred and said, "What are we going to tell the sheriff?"

"Can we just hide the bodies?" asked Saul.

"Not smart," said Jackson. "Halder may be a recluse but they'll notice Phelps isn't at church. And Phelps has animals on his farm that somebody's gotta tend to, and they'll wonder why I knew to go feed 'em."

"Then we'd best get all our stories straight," said Rose, and got up to put on another pot of coffee.

Jackson went for the sheriff late that night, and I went up to bed to snatch what sleep I could before I had to lie to the authorities. Saul went with me, stopping just inside the studio door.

"Are you going to tell them the truth?" he asked.

"The truth?" I looked at him blearily. "We just got done rehearsing that story three times over."

"Not the sheriff. The Kents."

I was so tired that it actually took me a moment to realize what truth he meant. "Oh, that you didn't spend the last year in a Tennessee jail?"

One corner of his mouth lifted, showing perfectly ordinary blunt teeth. "I did spend some time in one once, you know. Just not that recently."

I snorted. "No one would believe me. I don't even know that *I* believe it, and I saw all of it happen."

He nodded. At the doorway, he added, "Thank you. You saved my life once, and this . . . this saves it again."

"You saved mine, so I suppose we're even." I didn't want to ask the next question, but I knew that I needed to. "Was it true, what Halder said? About how your people reproduce?"

The shadows through the windows were blue-black, the color of bruises, the color of the shadows under Saul's eyes. "It's true enough." He gripped the doorframe and I heard the wood creak slightly. "But even a parasite may come to understand its own nature, and choose to live another way."

There didn't seem to be anything to say to that. We nodded to each other, and he turned to go.

"Hey, Saul?"

He stuck his head back through the doorway. "Yes?"

I dredged up a smile. "I promise not to treat you like a bizarre specimen or an experiment, but if you don't eventually show me how your teeth work, I'm going to go out of my head wondering."

He laughed, for once without that awful clicking sound. "Remind me, and I'll show you."

He let himself out of the studio, and I fell down on the bed and into a dark and dreamless sleep.

The story we cooked up about Halder and Phelps was a simple one in the end. Jackson went for the sheriff, saying that there was some kind of big animal in the woods and it had killed Halder but he'd shot at it and run it off. A couple of deputies came out and we let them discover Phelps and the dead animals. I said that something had chased me and I'd spent the night up a tree, hoping not to be eaten. No, I hadn't gotten a good look at it, just that it was big. I'd finally come down and was trying to find the house when I heard the gunshots and shouted for help, and Jackson found me.

The sheriff asked a bunch of questions about the shed and I told them that Phelps had been awfully eager to keep people away from it. With the record of the telegram at the station calling Halder urgently to come deal with a problem in the shed, the sheriff concluded, logically enough, that Halder had been keeping some kind of dangerous animal and that it had gotten out and savaged him. They scoured the woods for a week and told people to be on their guard, but when nobody else showed up with their throat torn out, people started to relax.

(I'm pretty sure Saul and Jackson went down into the shed first and cleaned up a few things that might have led to awkward questions, but I didn't ask. I did ask what they did about the botflies down there, and Jackson showed me a bag of Paris Green insecticide. There wasn't much we could do about the ones that had gotten out, but at least the sheriff didn't get infected when he went down to check it.)

A couple reporters did turn up to ask questions, but it was so difficult to find the house at all that most of them just lay in wait for Jackson when he went into town. The one who showed up on the property got a very chilly send-off. The Kents' hound had a remarkably bloodcurdling bay that did not betray his desperate desire to be loved by everyone and everything.

None of us mentioned Saul at all, and no one asked. Sally

went home to her family so it was just the four of us, and the sheriff never even searched the house.

It was a strange time. None of us knew what was going to happen next. Halder died without a will, so everything would have gone to his next of kin, namely Louisa, wherever she had vanished to. The lawyer, with much hemming and hawing, allowed us to draw our last month's wages from the bank, but made it clear that no more would be forthcoming.

I should probably have been looking for another job, but it felt as if I would be abandoning Jackson and Rose to their fate. And for some things, at least, it was useful to be a white woman with a large vocabulary. The lawyer had not unbent until I spoke to him sternly about the terms of our employment and the estate's duty to pay outstanding debts. It shouldn't have mattered that I knew the right words to say, but it did, and it shouldn't have mattered that I was white, but the lawyer was that sort of man, so that did too.

Saul also needed my help. His back was healing at a frightening rate, but the way that the skin had torn meant that there were long stringy bits hanging down that had to be dealt with. I was a poor choice compared to Rose or Ma Kersey, but I was also the one who wouldn't be surprised by how fast he healed. So I gritted my teeth and cut the ragged ends free, feeling like a torturer's apprentice. In time, that too healed.

There was also the matter of the botflies. New warbles appeared on Saul's skin for almost a week after he was freed, and I removed the ones he couldn't reach himself. "Farmers do this for cattle," he told me, on the third or fourth day. "I never quite appreciated how the cattle must feel about it."

"I hope they feel grateful," I grumbled.

"Rest assured, Miss Wilson, I am far more grateful than any cow has ever been." He swept me a bow that might have been more charming if he weren't shirtless and if I weren't holding a jar with half-grown larvae wriggling at the bottom.

"Hmmph!" I said, handing him the jar.

Truth was, we joked about it because otherwise neither of us would ever stop screaming. There was a stretch where the new skin on his back was so fragile that it was transparent, and I could actually see the wolf worms moving under it. I learned how to skewer each one and pull it out with as little damage to Saul as possible, and then I'd joke and he'd joke and then I would go sit somewhere with my head between my knees until I was sure I wouldn't be sick.

But I got off lightly, all told. I spent five days checking my skin obsessively for new lumps. My own collarbone sent me into a panic at least twice. I boiled endless amounts of water and took baths so hot that I shrieked when I lowered myself in, but I had to be *sure*.

"Oh honey," said Rose, when she found me with the scissors, cutting my hair down to a ragged fringe so that I could better feel my scalp.

"Sorry," I said, feeling wretched and pathetic and more than a little mad. "I'm sorry. I just can't handle all this *stuff* in the way."

Rose sighed and set down the bundle of towels she had been carrying. "Come here. Let's see what I can do."

I hung my head while she worked, hearing the *snick-snick-snick* of the blades. More hair fell away. "Shame you're a white girl," she said absently. "When I did this, my mama managed to braid it so you couldn't hardly tell."

I raised my eyebrows. The back of my neck felt prickly and exposed. "You did this once?"

"Sure . . . back when I was eight."

I hung my head. Rose snorted. "And once again when I was about twenty. Found my man cheating on me and just knew I needed to cut my hair off. Mama said it was easier to fix when I was eight though."

"I can't imagine you cutting your hair off over a man," I admitted.

"Yeah, well. He did me a favor in the end. Met Jackson not too long after that." She finished and set the scissors down. "There. Can't say it's fashionable, but it looks more like you've been sick than like somebody took a knife to it."

"You keep saving me," I said, running my hands through the shorn ends. "I'm sorry you keep needing to. I swear, I'm not normally so . . ." I trailed off, not sure what word I wanted. *Helpless. Useless. Lost.*

Rose snorted again. "You got that lawyer to hand over the money. That's worth a lot more than a haircut, hon."

"Yes, but . . ."

"The rest was Halder, not you. Don't be too eager to take up the blame." She handed me a dustpan and we swept up the cuttings together. She left me running my fingers over my skull, waiting for the wolf worms to rise.

My dreams, after that first night, were endless and vivid and terrible. The doctor from Siler City came out and diagnosed me with disordered nerves, and told Jackson (for lack of anyone else, I suppose) that it wasn't to be wondered at, given what had happened to Halder. He gave me laudanum. I took it for a week, found myself craving it too much, and dumped the rest of it out. I could not afford a laudanum habit. The dreams returned. I endured them, because there was no other choice.

Once or twice, I even thought about asking Saul to bite me, the way that he had Halder. Then I thought about getting addicted to someone's saliva and how much more inconvenient that would be than laudanum, and I didn't.

After a week, it seemed like I had gotten away uninfected. I cried a little in my room, then washed my face and went to help Rose in the kitchen.

And so we waited, all four of us, like an indrawn breath. Waited for healing or for something to happen. I finally wrote a letter to Headmistress Silverton, asking if my old position was still open. It cost me a great deal of pride to write it, and when I received an answer in the post, the envelope sat, unopened, on the studio table.

We might have waited until the house fell down, or at least until the contents of the larder ran out, but then, nearly three weeks after Halder died, Louisa arrived.

I recognized her immediately when I walked into the studio and saw an unfamiliar woman standing there. She fit into the place as I never had. You only had to take one look at her face to recognize that she had come home.

She wasn't beautiful. That surprised me. It shouldn't have, I suppose. Halder had married her for her money and her skill with watercolors. It was just that Saul loved her, and so some part of me assumed that she must have been beautiful as well. But Louisa had broad hips and a broad face, her skin dusted with old measles scars, and her teeth were crooked when she smiled.

Then the force of that smile hit me, and I had an inkling what Saul must have seen when he said that she made you feel alive just by being in the same room.

"Miss Wilson?" she asked, taking a step forward. "It *is* Miss Wilson, isn't it?"

"You're Louisa," I said, my mind blank with astonishment. "You came back."

"Of course I did." She took both my hands in hers. "Saul and Rose have told me so much about you. I can't ever thank you enough for what you've done."

(She *meant* it too. That was part of what was so astonishing. It wasn't just words. You couldn't doubt that she meant every word that she said.)

"It was nothing. I mean—no, I don't mean it was *nothing*, but—" I floundered a bit and tried again. "Anyone in my position would have done the same."

"I doubt that highly." She squeezed both my hands and released me and I took a step back.

It was easier to look around the room than at the naked gratitude on Louisa's face. "I . . . err." I swallowed. "This is your room. I should move my things out."

Louisa started to protest, but I waved my hands, trying not to show the pang that I felt. *Things are changing again. You had a little time, but now that's over. On to the next thing, whatever that is.* "I should have gone before now. I just . . . err . . . hadn't." I went to the table and began hastily picking up my brushes. Some of which were *her* brushes. *Oh damn . . .*

"Do you have somewhere to go?"

She asked it softly and kindly and certainly did not mean for it to feel like a knife of uncertainty sliding between my ribs. I picked up the unopened envelope from Headmistress Silverton. "No need to worry," I said. "I'll be fine."

Louisa was silent for a moment, then said, carefully, "Do you mean that you'll actually be fine, or do you mean that you don't want to impose?"

I met her eyes, startled. They were a muddy hazel color, nothing to incite a poet's fancy, but in them, I saw a terrible understanding.

Of course. She fled with nothing and had to make her own way for the last few years. She's been there too.

"I . . ." I licked dry lips. "I don't actually have anything lined up," I admitted. "If I could stay for a few days, just long enough to send some letters, and see . . ."

"Miss Wilson, you can have a few *years*, if you want it. And the estate certainly owes you for the work you've done. I can never repay you for saving Saul's life."

I shook my head. "You don't need to repay me for that."

"He says that you know about him."

"I do, but . . ." I spread my hands helplessly. "You don't have to buy my silence about that. I won't tell anyone." A laugh crackled out of me. "Hell, no one would believe me anyway."

She snorted. "I know. I felt the same way when I found out. It's all completely mad, isn't it?" She rubbed her forehead.

"Completely. Utterly." I felt a sudden rush of fellow-feeling for the only other human who knew about Saul's people.

"Did he show you the teeth?"

"*Yes!*" I shoved my hands into the remains of my hair. "I didn't know whether to scream or have him do it again in better light!"

(Saul's teeth were indeed in his throat, after a fashion. They lay far back until he flexed some muscle or other, then they swung forward and fitted behind the front set. It was shocking to see and I still wasn't sure how he didn't slice his tongue to ribbons.)

"It's called a 'pharyngeal jaw,' I think," said Louisa, reminding me that she too had spent a long time as a naturalist. "At least, that's what they call it in moray eels. I don't think most mammals have them."

"Let me guess," I said. "You told him that and he said, 'Oh, so now I'm an eel?'"

"Oh, so you *have* met him!"

Our eyes met and we both began to laugh. I won't swear that it wasn't a trifle hysterical on my part, but maybe it was for her too.

"I'll stay," I said, when I had wiped the tears from my eyes. "At least for a little while."

"Oh, good." Louisa hooked her arm through mine. "Because as it happens, there's a project I need help with, and I think you're the only other person who will understand."

It was Ma Kersey who sent for Louisa, I eventually learned. She hitched a ride into town and sent a telegram to her family back in Robeson County, where she had sent Louisa a year prior. The telegram then passed through a few dozen sets of hands, and was finally delivered to Louisa, nearly three hundred miles away. Such was the power of Ma Kersey's family connections.

Seeing Louisa and Saul together eased a fear I hadn't known I had. There was nothing predatory in Saul's eyes when he looked at her. He looked more like a worshipper gazing on the face of his god. Even his acidic tongue softened a little, though Louisa was more likely to go off into fits of laughter than to take offense to anything he said.

The one thing he asked of me was not to tell Louisa how long he had been trapped in the shed. "It would only hurt her," he said, "and what good would it do any of us now?"

I agreed, and not because I was afraid. Saul had a strange, perhaps even twisted moral code, but it seemed that I was firmly on the safe side of it.

(Besides if he killed me and dumped my body in a hole, it would have upset Louisa, and I'm pretty sure that Saul would have gnawed his own arm off rather than upset Louisa.)

I moved back into the room I'd stayed in the first night. I missed the light of the studio, but as it happened, I had plenty of other work to occupy me, and most of it involved Halder's papers.

"I can't read them," said Louisa bluntly. "I hated him. I still hate him. I'll end up burning it all in a fit of rage."

"I don't think anyone will care if you do."

She sighed, running her hands through her hair. "No. That's the thing. I can't decide what to do about his book."

We stood in Halder's office—or more accurately, I sat behind the desk while Louisa paced back and forth like a caged beast. Smiley tried to twine around her ankles a few times, realized that she was not going to oblige by tripping over him, and had settled down on my lap to sulk.

"He put in years of research on his book," Louisa said. "I don't want him to get credit for it. I don't want anyone to read his name and think he was a great scientist." She paused in front of the table where I had stacked all the dozens of illustrations liberated from the cabinet. "But *I* worked on it for years, too, dammit."

"Ahhh." Suddenly everything came clear. Of course she had. All those magnificent beetle shells and delicate fly wings, all those tiny, elegant antennae . . . those represented more than a decade of Louisa's life.

"Saul thinks I should leave it all in the past," she said. "But I can't let all those paintings go. For years, they were practically my reason for living." She flashed me a quick smile. "I don't know if you feel the same way about yours."

"I'd hate to see them wasted," I admitted. "I already got paid for them, so maybe it shouldn't matter to me what happens to them now, but it does."

"Exactly." Louisa tapped the tabletop. "What I'd *like* to do is find some other entomologist who can take his notes and the completed plates and produce something useful from them. And that doctor can have his name front and center, and we can have our names on the frontispiece and my late husband can be a footnote somewhere in the back."

I thought of Halder's near-apoplectic rage at the thought of other people stealing his work, and felt a smile begin to spread over my face. It wasn't a nice smile, but it was deeply genuine.

"*You* understand," said Louisa, with an echo of that same malicious smile.

"Oh, I *do*."

"However . . ." Louisa spread her hands. "I don't *know* anyone. But if you're willing to go through his correspondence, maybe you can find someone. Someone who isn't as detestable a human being as my late husband was."

I nodded. "Between that and the naturalists my father knew, I suspect I can come up with something."

"That would be worth a great deal to me, Miss Wilson."

"Please," I said, picking up the first letter. "Call me Sonia."

EPILOGUE

As I write this, it has been eleven months since Halder's death, and I am still living in the house that Louisa's money built. *Observations on the Habits and Developmental Stages of Parasitic Insects* will be published tomorrow, written by an enterprising young doctor named Ainsley. It includes plates credited to Sonia Wilson and Louisa Gregor, and while it is unlikely to be in most drawing rooms, I am told that it will be invaluable to academics in the field. Halder's name appears only in the author's note, where Ainsley notes that his widow very graciously bequeathed his notes and his collection to the author, which "went a fair way to making this work possible."

(I still don't believe in Phelps's devil, but if He exists, I imagine He read that author's note aloud to Halder. Eternal flame would not even begin to compare.)

Louisa and I sat around drinking Jackson's moonshine the day that the acceptance letter arrived from the publisher, toasting each insect more and more extravagantly. By the time we reached Rex the *C. hominivorax*, we were both sitting on the floor giggling helplessly, and Rose took our drinks away and told us that we were setting a terrible example for Sally, then finished both cups off herself.

Now that it's done, Louisa has been urging me to write the book about medicinal herbs that I kept imagining. I've been working on it off and on. Hopefully with my name out there as a scientific illustrator, another publisher will be willing to take a chance. (Ma Kersey says that I should call it *Ma Kersey's Wit and Wisdom* and include a section on remedies to enhance male virility. I still can't quite tell if she's serious, but if I do write it, she'll get half the money. It's her knowledge, after all.)

I live in Halder's rooms now. They don't hold the memories for me that they do for Louisa, and the light is almost as good. I offered to move out again, but Louisa said that while she'd be damned if she was moving out of the house that her money built, it was too big a house for just her and Saul and the Kents. I allowed her to persuade me. Louisa is still a better painter than I am, but I am a better naturalist, probably because Halder rarely bothered to teach her anything. Between the two of us, I truly believe that we'll make some fine books.

Saul and Louisa were married last spring, once enough time had passed that no one could connect him to the deaths. The story was that he had seen the notice of the doctor's death in the papers and come back to propose to his lost love. The people who might have been surprised about Saul's reappearance would have had to admit that they thought Saul had been murdered and hadn't done anything about it, so the matter was allowed, somewhat gracelessly, to drop.

Ma Kersey, I suspect, knows more than she lets on. But she keeps her own counsel, and in return, Saul keeps her table liberally supplied with venison and the world-famous Chatham rabbit. And if the deer has been drained and gutted before being delivered . . . well, that's simply how one field dresses a carcass, after all, and there's nothing unusual about it.

The wedding was held at Rose Kent's church, because Louisa insisted that Rose be the matron of honor and even this long after the war, some people who call themselves Christians have opinions about Black folk in white church ceremonies. The preacher was happy to do it, and his sermon was only about fifteen minutes long, which for him was a great sacrifice.

Not long after the wedding, Rose informed us that she and Jackson were leaving. Louisa offered her anything she wanted if she'd stay, but she refused. "It isn't you," she said. "I stayed here too long, hating myself for it, and now I'm leaving all that behind. Finally."

They didn't go all that far. We see her Sunday at church. She laughs more than she did and she looks younger, and sometimes we all look at one another and remember that there's a secret between us, but it doesn't last long. Sally's cousin came to be the housekeeper, and she's good at it, but not half the cook that Rose Kent is.

The shed in the woods was demolished not long after Louisa returned. Saul and Jackson pulled down the support timbers below and the next heavy rain brought the whole structure down, leaving only a deep, water-filled hole. In spring, the chorus frogs sang from the edges and the green-lipped bronze frogs laid gelatinous masses of eggs. It may fill in over the years, but until then, it serves the frogs well. I am glad that they get some use of it, but I avoid it myself. So does Saul.

As for the other residents of that miserable hole . . . well. Saul has stalked the woods for months, looking for animals infested with the strange parasites that had grown in his flesh. He found plenty in the early days, but none since winter. Possibly that means that they have all been wiped out.

Possibly it simply means that they learned not to try to feed him.

I still don't know what to make of the wolf worms. Ainsley—who I chose because he was the only person who was not a condescending ass when I wrote to Halder's many correspondents—and who knows only that there was an unusual mutation among the *Cuterebra* population—suggested that the speed at which they reproduced may have made them vulnerable to a fluctuation in the host population. If too many squirrels were already weakened by botflies, then having the next wave of flies show up in a week would not give them time to recover.

It's as good a theory as any. Mr. Darwin tells us that it does not matter if something is extremely well-adapted to survive, if it is not also well-adapted to reproduce. And perhaps the flies themselves, deprived of their part of their life cycle bathed in the strange fluids in Saul's flesh, reverted back to their normal behavior, and now are no different from any others that one might find, except perhaps capable of surviving in a wider range of hosts.

Every now and then, I will see a black-and-gold fly in the garden. Even now, my throat closes up. It took some time before I stopped panicking at the sight of bumblebees, but I managed eventually. It is hard to be afraid of creatures who fly headlong at flowers and miss more often than not. But I still cannot abide the flies.

I have never quite shed the vision of Phelps clawing at his scalp as he was dragged forward by his own traitorous limbs. I suspect that I never will. There are nights when I feel something touch me and my skin crawls so fiercely that I have to light the lamps and change the sheets before I can lie down again. There are dreams where I feel lumps moving in my flesh, and when I touch them, I realize that there is something living inside.

Once or twice, I've caught a glimpse of an animal watching me from the woods. They never get close enough for me to see if there is a wolf worm riding them. I know that it is unlikely, I know that multiple generations have come and gone and it is unlikely that they have survived. I know that a mere insect can't possibly recognize my face or think of me as the person that took their prey away.

I know all this, and yet I do not walk in the woods the way that I used to. Not alone, at any rate.

And yet, despite this, I stay here. Because the wolf worms are not the only thing I fear. I have had too many dreams where I am devoured alive by some creature inside me, a three-month babe waiting for its chance to be born.

It is very hard for me to look at strangers now without

wondering if they're truly human. I force myself to travel, to go out among people I do not know, but even knowing that I am far more likely to run afoul of my own species, I cannot quite put aside that fear. Even among humans, not everyone is as strong as Saul, to choose another way. I sit on the train and people smile at me, and even as I smile back, I wonder if there is another set of teeth behind it.

Some thoughts burrow into your mind as thoroughly as a wasp larva burrows into an unsuspecting caterpillar.

The trick, which I am still learning, is how to live without being devoured by them.

ACKNOWLEDGMENTS

It's rare that you can trace the exact origins of a book, but in this case, I think I can put my finger on it. When I moved to North Carolina in 2004, I lived in a little duplex that backed onto a greenway. It had far more birds than anyone would expect, which began my great love of bird-watching, but it also had squirrels . . . and the squirrels had giant freaky lumps on them.

It was squirrel botflies, and dear god, the population behind the house must have been the unluckiest squirrels in the state, because they were infested. Sometimes you'd see squirrels with three, four bots on them. Sometimes you'd see a squirrel with a sort of loose, bloody pocket where the bot had been. I was fascinated and horrified.

I was also not yet a novelist, so I merely filed this away in my brain. Over a decade later, when I was thinking about horror plots, I remembered the visceral squick of the botflies and thought, "Huh. What would happen if one of those latched onto a vampire?"

I ran this plot idea through my usual test, which was to tell my friend Shepherd my idea. If he made The Face, it was probably gold. (The Face is a kind of tight-lipped grimace while he tries to figure out what the hell is wrong with me.) He made The Face. Then I added screwworms and The Face intensified. (This method is also where the underground children in *A House With Good Bones* came from—I was singing the Potato Song, which includes a line about coming from underground. I tried to explain it was a metaphor for having children, and Shep said,

"Children do not come from underground!" and I said instantly, "The underground children do," and Shep made The Face. It took me a while to figure out what the children actually were, but that was the genesis. Thanks, Shep.)

The rest of the story came together quickly, thanks to another friend. A few years ago, Ainsley Seago, entomologist extraordinaire, took me on a behind-the-scenes tour of the Carnegie Museum of Natural History, which included a whirlwind tour of bugs on cards, butterflies in paper sleeves, gorgeously illustrated books from previous centuries, and—perhaps most importantly—involved the phrase "patented caterpillar inflator."

"Shit," I said. "I gotta put that in a book."

I'd wanted to do a historical novel about a scientific illustrator for ages, because I used to be an illustrator myself and it's always nice to be able to vent about the difficulties of watercolor. So all those factors just kind of came together into *Wolf Worm*.

Ironically, I was most of the way through writing it when I was diagnosed with breast cancer. I'm fine, they got it all, but in my blazing need to finish the book before I started chemo, let me tell you, I had a lot of thoughts about alien invaders inside your flesh. Thanks to the whole crew at UNC, particularly Dr. Saladayga, for making sure that I was around to write this author's note a few years later. (Seriously, that woman is a goddamn surgeon. I mean, literally, yes, she is a surgeon, but also the scar is tiny and hidden and other doctors go, "Wow, that was an amazing job.")

The Lumbee tribe of North Carolina, the People of the Dark Water, of which Ma Kersey is a fictional member, would have been listed as Croatan on the census records of the time, and did not adopt the name Lumbee until the mid-1900s. Kersey is one of the most common Lumbee surnames. (It also happens to be my grandfather's surname. Small world.) The history of the Lumbee and their struggle for official recognition is a long and difficult one, but it is not my story to tell, so I suggest you visit the tribe's official website and learn about it from them.

Screwworms are real, and the fact that this is not common knowledge is because of a truly extraordinary combination of science and international cooperation dating back to the 1950s. Sterile male screwflies are released every year, and as the females only mate once, this keeps the population in check. Over many years, the species was pushed south through Mexico to Panama, where the line was held for decades, with sterile males being released at the sight of outbreaks. Unfortunately, COVID-19 meant that scientists were unable to go out and meet with local people to hear reports of outbreaks, with the result that the screwflies have jumped north again, with outbreaks throughout Mexico and probably soon into Texas. This is very, very bad, and I hope like hell that when the book comes out, it's not a "ripped from the headlines!" moment. All I can say is that when I wrote it, they hadn't come north yet. I am Cassandra, not an ambulance chaser.

The Devil's Tramping Ground exists, and in fact I used to live just off Devil's Tramping Ground Road, which has been renamed Scenic Byway 902 for reasons that presumably involve property values. Many of the entomologists mentioned in the book do exist—Asa Fitch was a particularly famous one, and Halder was probably right to be jealous. The Megatherium Club also existed and many of the members lived in suites in the Smithsonian Castle, until they were evicted for holding sack races in the halls.

The Chatham rabbit is real and was, at one time, extremely gastronomically famous.

We may all write books alone, but we sure don't publish them that way, so huge thanks to Lindsey Hall and the whole crew at Tor; my agent, Helen Breitwieser; to Ainsley again for reading it over and correcting my entomological sins; and to the really impressive copyeditor, Lauren Hougen, who caught that

I had shamefully misremembered the date of the extinction of the Carolina parakeet, which is the sort of thing that will haunt an author for years to come.

Penultimate thanks go as always to my husband Kevin, who had to read this book at random intervals to assure me that it was not terrible, who held everything together while I endured many months of chemo, and who is the great love of my life.

And finally, to my readers, thank you for reading another one. Until next time—

T. Kingfisher
Edgewood, NM
June 2025

ABOUT THE AUTHOR

T. Kingfisher (she/her) writes fantasy, horror and occasional oddities, including *Nettle & Bone*, *What Moves the Dead*, *A Sorceress Comes to Call*, *Hemlock & Silver* and *Wolf Worm*. Under a pen name, she also writes bestselling children's books. She lives in North Carolina with her husband, dogs and cats, in an area with absolutely no botflies.

ALSO BY T. KINGFISHER

Hemlock & Silver

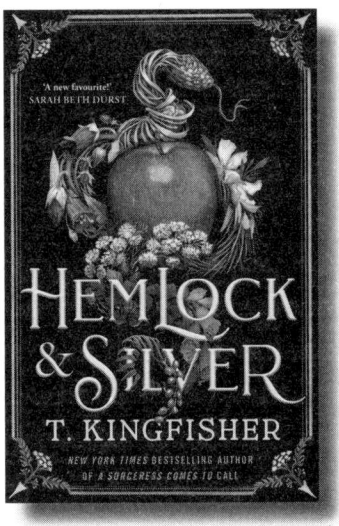

A dark reimagining of Snow White steeped in poison, intrigue and treason of the most magical kind.

Healer Anja regularly drinks poison.

Not to die, but to save – seeking cures for those everyone else has given up on.

But a summons from the King interrupts her quiet, herb-obsessed life. His daughter, Snow, is dying, and he hopes Anja's unorthodox methods can save her.

Aided by a taciturn guard, a narcissistic cat and a passion for the scientific method, Anja rushes to treat Snow – but nothing seems to work. Nothing, that is, until she finds a secret world hidden inside a magic mirror. This dark realm may hold the key to what is making Snow sick.

Or it might be the thing that kills them all . . .